Deceiving Jane

Author's Note

This is a DARK ROMANCE. It contains some dark content and sensitive situations that may be triggering to some readers. Only for readers 18 years and over.

This book is dedicated to anyone out there struggling internally. You are never alone.

Deceiving Jane

Billionaire CEO of Waldorf Enterprise.
My best friend's much older brother.
My boss.
He wants to break me and holds the stigma of my father's tainted
reputation against me.
Desperately, he's tried to scratch the surface of my fortified exterior.
His plan backfired.
All he's done is make himself dependent on me.
In doing so, I've discovered his secrets.
I saw the man beneath the calloused veneer.
And he's cracked through my wall.
I allowed myself to believe he was a man incapable of deceit.
But the man behind the veneer was the illusion.
The lies.
The secrets.
The deceptions.

Donavon Waldorf...is a snake.

ONE

Jane

The car service drops me off in front of the towering building in a part of the city I didn't think I would see much of anymore. It's corporate-based. As in walking distance to the majority of every corporate building in Manhattan. Including the one in which I hope to score an internship. A *paid* internship I might add.

I gaze up at the tall, swanky building then double check the address on my phone to make sure I'm at the right place. I know the city well, so I know I'm not lost, but this cannot be right. A doorman opens the door for me, and I hesitantly walk inside the lavish lobby. The wheels of my suitcase click over the travertine tiles as I precariously balance under the weight of my duffle bag and backpack while adjusting the potted plant against my hip. It's hardly half of my belongings, but it was time to flee the confines of my parents' home. I packed what I could as soon as I got the green light to move in. I look around and know this has to be some kind of mistake. I must be in the wrong building. I have to be. I know Kenna is doing well for herself these days and that her brother is probably the richest man on the east coast, but no way.

I turn to leave the way I came when the man behind a desk calls out to me. "Ms. Donahue?"

I spin around with wide eyes. "Yes?"

He gives me an amiable smile. "Ms. Waldorf said we should be expecting you here soon." He picks up a phone, and murmurs something into the receiver as I stand there awkwardly. He gives me his full attention again as he puts the phone down. "Someone will be by to help you with your luggage in just a moment."

"Oh, no. It's—"

"Ms. Waldorf insists," he presses.

I reluctantly nod with a tight smile. Kenna probably thought I would be pulling up with a moving van or something. I can certainly manage my three bags, not to mention the fact that I don't have any money to spare for a tip.

A man in a service uniform comes from somewhere down the hall and instantly approaches me to take possession of my bags. "Thank you," I reply, though my voice is hardly more than a whisper. "Of course, Ms. Donahue," he says and leads us both to the elevators.

"Please don't hesitant if you need anything, Ms. Donahue," the man behind the desk calls out and I don't have the chance to thank him as the elevator doors close on us.

The bellhop already pressed the button to the eighteenth floor, and we ride it up in silence as I'm caught inside a daze. Maybe Kenna forgot to mention a third roommate or something. Or maybe she accidentally forgot another zero in the cost of rent. *Shit.* This will be a very uncomfortable conversation to have if the rent is much more than I thought I agreed to.

The lift stops on the eighteenth, and I pray the elevators never go out of order. The man holds the door for me to exit first. Everything looks newly renovated and pristine. From the shiny tiled floors to the freshly painted walls, it's all just too much. I meekly follow behind since he obviously knows where we're going and it's only five doors down until we stop.

1812.

The man takes it upon himself to knock on the door three solid times. Hardly a few seconds pass when the door swings open and we're met with a beautiful grinning woman. "Jane!" Kenna squeals and yanks me in for a crushing hug.

I'm not one for physical affection, so I do my best to hug her back with a giggle. "Hi, Kenna."

She pulls back still flashing her sparkling smile, then turns it to the man carrying my bags. "Thank you, Brian." She lets him step inside. "Just leave them here."

"Sure, miss." He looks to me. "Anything else for you, Ms. Donahue?"

"Um, no. Thank you." I go to grab my wallet attached to the back of my phone when he spins around and walks out before I can pull any cash out.

Kenna notices my intentions. "Oh, you don't have to worry about that." She closes the door. "They get paid more than enough to accept tips." I open my mouth to argue, but she cuts me off. "They're not even allowed to take them." She eyes the three bags I have. "Do you have more downstairs?"

"No. The rest is still at my parents'. I'll go back in the next few days for it."

She squeals again enthusiastically bouncing on her toes, her elation contagious. "I really am so excited to have you as my roommate." She takes my suitcase and begins rolling it further into the apartment. "I'll take you to your room first so we can drop your stuff off and then I can give you the full tour."

I stiffly follow her as I gawk at the sheer size of the place. This is Manhattan. I prepared myself to be sharing a studio with someone for this price. "Uh, Kenna?"

"Hm?" She glances at me over her shoulder as we walk down the hall.

"When we were messaging, you said it would be $700 a month..."

"Yes." She stops and turns to face me. "Is that going to be a problem?"

My chin drops as I shake my head at her with wide eyes. "A problem? No! I just don't see how it could only be $700."

She grins. "Including utilities."

My eyes somehow grow wider in shock. "I don't understand. There's no way my share of the rent is only that much."

She laughs and I walk with her once again. "Okay, so here's the thing. I don't *need* a roommate. My brother actually bought me this place and I happen to have a great job. I wanted a roommate because I hate living alone and I travel so much for my job, it'd be nice not have to always cart Luna to and from my parents' house when I'm gone."

"Luna?"

"My cat." She stops and cringes. "Shit, I forgot to mention her, didn't I? I hope you aren't allergic to cats."

"No, I'm not allergic."

She gives me her gorgeous smile. "Great! Now, let me show you your room."

We turn into the doorway on our right and I nearly drop my plant in awe. I cannot believe I'll get to live here. I was more than prepared to share a tiny space with at least one or two strangers for a few years. Not have my own *fully furnished* room in a newly renovated apartment building at the heart of the city.

"Oh my God," I rasp.

"Now, you don't have your own bathroom. I mean, we're not sharing one, but there isn't an ensuite."

I scoff and shake my head. "That's perfectly fine with me."

I continue studying the room. It's practically the size of a studio apartment and with a queen size bed with a gold frame in the center with two matching nightstands on either side. The décor is beautiful and feminine. The curtains are a cream color matching the plush carpet.

"I stripped the bed for you. I figured you'd want your own sheets and stuff on it." She shrugs. "Some people are weird about that."

I laugh. "I did not expect the room to be at all furnished. I was planning to sleep on the floor till I could afford a bed."

Afford...still such a contrast to the life I grew up in. Never did I ever have to worry about being able to afford anything. My parents were rich, now...not so much.

"Well, good thing you have a cool ass roommate."

I grin over at her. "Seriously."

"Okay, let me show you around then I can help you unpack."

I officially won the roommate lottery. Not only is this place absolutely amazing and lavish, but Kenna helped me unpack everything and now she's cooking me dinner while I watch her from the comfy couch with a glass of red wine in hand. It's all almost too good to be true.

"So, tell me about your job."

"Oh my God, I love it. I get to travel everywhere while doing what I love. Couldn't ask for anything better." Kenna works for a well-known designer in the city. She's always had a passion for fashion and it's amazing that she gets to do what she loves.

"Do you ever model for them?"

She glances up from the stove top with a dry look. "No way."

"You act like that's a crazy question!" Kenna is gorgeous. She's almost six feet tall, with long golden hair, and striking features.

Pink touches her cheeks as she shakes her head. "I'm no model."

Kenna and I went to the same high school. She was two classes older than me, but we both played soccer and were very close at that time. After she graduated and left for college, we kept in touch through social media, but haven't seen each other since.

When I saw her post about needing a roommate in the city, I jumped on it. She immediately said yes, and here I am. It's a little awkward I'll be interviewing for a paid internship with her brother's company, especially if I don't get it. I'll have to find two jobs to make as much as I would've there.

"Are you sure I can't help you with anything?"

"No way, girl. I can't remember the last time I got to do this. Feeling like I'm entertaining. When I *am* home, I'm either crashing or preparing for my next trip."

"Do you not have many days off?"

Her golden locks sway when she shakes her head. "Not really. I mean, I do get most evenings off, so we'll definitely get to do girls' nights like these."

I get up to assist when she begins pulling plates out and we head over to the dining table to sit.

"I can't wait to have more nights like this," she says as if she's been feeling just as lonely as I have.

Most friendships didn't survive all the drama surrounding my family in the past few years. Very few stuck around; those that did were only there for the media coverage even though all the attention was negative. The one that mattered the most stayed strong, and that was Bonnie. My best friend since we were kids.

"Oh my God," I mumble around a bite of delicious chicken. "This is so good, Kenna."

She smiles. "Thanks. I enjoy cooking."

"I'm more of a takeout girl, but I happen to know the best places, so you better let me do dinner for you soon."

"As long as you feed me, I'm happy." She shoves a bite into her mouth. "So, when is your interview?"

"First thing Monday morning." She nods her head and avoids eye contact as if in deep thought. "You're not going to say anything, are you? Like to make sure I get the job?"

She peeks out through her lashes, guilt ridden. "Do you want me to?" she asks me innocently.

"No. Definitely not. I do not want any special treatment. I want to know that I fairly earned it," I say sternly.

She nods her head. "Okay, then I won't say anything. But I'm sure you'll get it."

After dinner, we work together to do the dishes then head over to the couch to drink the rest of the bottle of wine and put on a movie. We end up talking throughout the whole thing and both pass out before it's over.

I can't explain the sense of security that washes over me, it's as if I can sleep without one eye open for the first time in years.

Two

Donavon

"**D**onavon!" my sister sings out after letting herself in. She called ahead, but I still feel that instant urge to shut her out. Feeling like things are already disheveled and tampered with.

"In my office!" I shout as I continue going through emails.

She appears in the doorway and leans a shoulder against it while rolling her eyes. "Of course, you are. Where else would you be?" she snarks.

"I'll be just a minute."

"Yeah, yeah. Famous last words. I brought lunch, so hurry up before it gets cold."

I slap my laptop shut and rise to my feet. "Done."

We head into my kitchen, and I grab us some drinks as she sets out the food. "I got pad thai," she announces.

I round the island to join her. "Sounds good," I murmur. Not a fan of it, but it's not something she would know. "So, to what do I owe the pleasure of this impromptu visit?"

She opens her mouth in faux shock. "Can't I want to visit my big brother because I miss him?" I cock an eyebrow at her. "Okay, so..." *Here we go.* She wants something. "You know how you said I could get a roommate?" I nod. "Well, I did. She just moved in yesterday."

I drop my fork, the imminent protectiveness surging to the fore. "You what? You let a complete stranger move in without consulting with me first?"

"Would you please let me finish before you go accusing me of doing something stupid?" I take a calming breath and gesture for her to continue as I pick my fork back up. "As I was saying..." she drawls out dramatically. "She moved in yesterday, and I didn't *consult* you because I already know her. We played soccer together in high school. She's my friend, so I didn't need you." She pauses. "She actually has an interview at your company for the internship on Monday."

I feel her staring at me. "Okay...?"

"Do you think you could make sure she gets it?"

I frown at her. "Did she ask you to do this?"

She starts shaking her head vigorously. "No. It was actually one of the first things she said to me when I brought up her interview. She made me promise not to interfere in any way. She wants to earn it."

Good. Even though I hardly ever say no to Kenna, I would never hire someone that tried to manipulate their way through the process. No matter their capability. "I'll call John and—"

"No need." She whips out some papers with a grin. "I already talked to John and had him send me her resume." She places it down on the table between us making me glance at them. "You can look it over and see for yourself that she's qualified for the job."

"Internship," I correct.

She rolls her eyes again. "Whatever."

"She still has to interview."

"Well, duh," she sasses. "I don't want her to know I'm at all ensuring her position there."

"Why do you want her to get it so badly?"

"Because she's my friend." She shrugs. "She's been through a lot recently, and everyone deserves some help when they need it."

I don't bother digging into the girl's problems. It's none of my business. "Fine. I'll take a look at her resume and if she is in fact qualified, I'll make sure she gets the internship."

Her face lights up in victory. "Yes! Thanks, Don."

We fall into comfortable silence and eat. After a few minutes, she says, "Oh, and one more thing." I eye her over my plate. "Don't fuck her."

I choke on my food and have to swallow it down with my water. "I'm sorry…" I cough and wipe my mouth. "What?"

"I said don't fuck her." She's completely serious.

"Kenna." I lean back in my chair. "First of all, you said you went to high school together, so that puts her at what? Twenty-four?"

"Twenty-two actually. She was younger than me."

I scoff and shake my head. "So, she's way too young for me, and I don't even look twice at anyone who works, let alone *interns*, at my company."

"She's like, stupid gorgeous," she presses.

"I don't have any difficulty finding beautiful women." I move forward and pick my fork back up.

"Okay, ew." She scrunches her nose up. I ignore her, hoping this conversation will be over soon. "But, seriously, please don't fuck her. She doesn't need a broken heart on top of everything else."

"Ouch," I say halfheartedly.

"You know damn well what I'm talking about. You don't do relationships, so please just don't."

Easy enough. "I promise not to go anywhere near her." It's completely unnecessary for me to say, but I'll say it to end this conversation already.

I let her tell me about her recent trip to Italy and how much she still loves her job. She doesn't ask much about me, and I don't give her anything. There isn't much to tell other than talk about work anyway.

Kenna reminds me to look over her roommate's resume again before leaving. Her absence gives me some serenity. The silence blankets me, easing the anxiety within. I dispose of the carryout containers and wipe down the table and any other surfaces touched by my sister.

It's nothing personal and has nothing to do with germs. It's habitual, erasing any remnants of someone being in my home.

I've preferred total and complete seclusion for years now. It's difficult hiding my compulsiveness and uncontrollable rituals for long periods of time. So, in my own home, I can relax and not feel like I'm being watched or judged.

I grab the papers from the table and head back into my home office. I place the papers on the surface of my desk as I sit down. Sighing, I lean forward to straighten everything. Nothing is out of place, but it's one of those compulsions I cannot ignore. It gives me that extra sense of discipline and perfection.

Exhaustion begins to seep in. I've barely slept all week, which isn't unusual, but it always catches up with me. Times like these where I know how many emails I still have to sort through and that I still need to make an appearance at the club tonight, makes me wish I could give more responsibility away to my siblings. But in doing so, I'd be giving up some control. It's not something I'm capable of doing.

The thought of that unwelcome sense of chaos that I detest, gives me that second wind I need.

Picking up the resume, I begin going over it. From the looks of it, she seems to have the proper education for the internship in the marketing department. I'll have John double check her degree and credentials and as long as they are legitimate, she can have the position.

I go back up to the top to review her name and when I read Jane Donahue, I abruptly lean forward to make sure I'm seeing it correctly.

I dial Kenna. "Hey," she says after the first ring.

"Jane Donahue…" I leave a pregnant pause. "As in Alfred Donahue's daughter?"

Alfred Donahue was once an esteemed businessman. A family man that came from practically nothing and built an empire from the ground up. Then the skeletons began to surface, and once the first one came to the light, they didn't stop coming out.

Thousands of people lost their jobs and any promise of lifesavings. Thousands were scammed and lost everything. Woman after woman came forward to claim sexual assault and inequality in the workplace. He's ignoble. Despicable. Vile and revolting.

Kenna sighs. "She is Alfred Donahue's daughter, yes. But she has nothing to do with what her father did. She's not too fond of him either. Please do not hold that against her, Don."

I stare down at her credentials, mentally preparing myself to be able to overlook this major defect in her DNA. If I even possess the capacity to do so. I send employees home for having a stain on their shirt, how will I ignore the fact that there is a Donahue in my building?

"Please, Don?" she begs again. "You don't even see the interns, right? You can pretend she's not even there."

"Fine," I agree regretfully. The things I do for family...

"Yes! Thank you, Don! You're the best."

"Yeah, yeah. I'll talk to you later."

"I love you!"

"Love you too."

I hang up and remain fixated on the paper in my hand. Tossing it in the trash, I call John to tell him we're hiring Jane Donahue.

THREE

Jane

Professional. Secure. Independent.

Those are the words I think of when I hear the clacking of my heels on the tiled floors as I walk through the lobby at Waldorf Enterprise for the second time.

Similar to the first visit, I'm nervous. But instead of being nervous for my interview, I'm nervous for my first day of work. The interview ended up going great. They called back the very next day to give me the good news, and one week later, here I am again. Only weeks out of college and I have my first job in the big city.

Internship. But it's paid, so I'm ecstatic.

There was a sense of urgency to get out of my parents' home. I was so tired of losing sleep at night and never knowing what I'd wake up to each morning. The guilt for leaving my mom comes in waves, but I can't protect her forever.

My father has always been a tyrant, not only in business but at home he was just as harsh. When he ran his company into the ground and all of his dirty little secrets were discovered by the media, things only got worse. He turned to alcohol and projected his animosity on my mother and me.

Stepping into the elevator, I try not to blatantly stare at the handsome man who enters first, keeping his head down on his phone screen. But he's a man that you cannot help but to gawk at. Even with his head bent and his body slouched against the wall, he's definitely over six feet tall and fills out his bespoke suit with broad shoulders and what must be solid muscle. Even in his face, everything is tense and well-defined with sharp angles and smooth skin. His dark brown hair is neatly styled and perfectly set in place. Something he takes time to do and uses hair products to achieve the sexy look. Soft and full looking. The length is a little longer on top than on the sides that fades into the sideburns that connect to his perfectly groomed facial hair that makes my fingers itch to run my nails through the coarseness.

His whole face is flawless. Just as I wonder what color his eyes are, they snap up to meet mine. I give myself only half a second to look at them before averting my gaze, ignoring the scorching heat in my cheeks.

Blue. Dark blue. Not like the ocean, but like the sky as soon as the sun sets. Midnight blue. And they belong to Donavon Waldorf. Kenna's brother—and my new boss. The freaking owner of the building and the company. And I was boldly staring at him.

Awesome, Jane.

I keep my eyes glued to the elevator doors and a cold sweat breaks out on my back, trickling down my neck and tingling my spine all the way down. I can feel the dark gaze burning into the side of my face, and I know he's still looking at me. Never have I felt so insecure in all my life, even more so than when my last name was slandered. I suddenly feel like I'm under a microscope, being assessed and dissected.

After my father's demise, I've experienced being under a spotlight, but I've never felt so undeserving to breathe the same air as someone.

When the elevator finally stops on my floor, I'm ready to tuck tail and run. I pray his office isn't on the same floor as mine. I cannot fathom the thought of running into him from time to time.

Of course, with my luck, I go to step off the lift and so does he. And to further my humiliation, my shoulder bumps into his firm upper arm.

"Oh, I'm so sorry, Mr. Waldorf. Excuse me." I go to step back without looking at his face.

"After you," his voice rumbles lowly and his arm lifts to hold the doors open.

I give him a tight smile, avoiding his eyes. "Thank you," I murmur and quickly move past him.

Speed walking to the reception desk, I put a little more effort in the sway of my hips. Thankfully, Kenna, the fashion expert, helped me pick out my outfit for my first day, so I know my ass looks good in these high-waisted dress slacks. They hug my butt and upper highs, then fall straight into a wide leg. The nude-colored heels with a few modest inches on them compliment the cream-colored blouse tucked into the waist of my black slacks.

Approaching the front desk, the woman behind it smiles at me and I can feel him continue past us. "Hi, I'm here for my first day, I'm an intern. Could you point me in the right direction?"

"Yes, take this hall and look for Sam Scott's office. Four doors down and on your left."

I return her friendly smile. "Thank you."

"Good luck!"

I thank her and turn to head down the hall she directed me in when someone appears at my side. "I'll walk with you," the handsome young man says. Handsome, but not comparable to Mr. Waldorf. *Damnit, Jane. Stop thinking about him.* "It's my first day too." He flashes me a nice smile and holds his hand out in greeting. "I'm Nick."

I smile and accept the handshake. "Jane."

"Nice to meet you."

"You, too." We drop our hands and continue to walk.

"So, where are you from?"

"Here," I reply.

"Oh, so you pretty much know your way around the city then, huh?"

I nod. "I do. How about you? Where are you from?"

"Girard, Kansas."

"Girard, Kansas?" I look over at him. "I've never heard of that before."

He chuckles. "Not surprised."

"Well," I say as we both stop at the door with a plaque that says Sam Scott. "Here we are." I sigh and take it upon myself to knock on the door.

Mr. Scott invites us inside of his office and we all make our introductions. Then he shows us to the conference room further down the hall where the rest of the interns are meeting. There's only a handful of us at first and I sit down next to a girl who looks to be around my age.

"Hi, I'm Jane," I say to her and reach a hand out.

"Hi, Jane. I'm Madison."

Nick and Madison both introduce themselves then we make small talk while others trickle into the room to finally fill it to capacity around the large conference table.

All of us are fresh out of college and certainly blessed to have this opportunity. Jobs are difficult to come by these days, and paid internships are practically nonexistent. With the bearish reputation of Mr. Waldorf, it's certainly surprising that he is generous enough to pay the interns here. Putting this on your resume is invaluable as it is.

It isn't long before Mr. Scott enters the room and gives us the rundown of the company's policies and what we'll be expecting from our time here and what is to be expected from us in return.

"Excuse me, Mr. Scott. Will Mr. Waldorf be joining us at all today?" a girl asks and others join her in soft murmurs with stars in their eyes. I squirm in my seat shamelessly wondering the same thing.

Mr. Scott gives a knowing grin. "Unfortunately, no. You won't be seeing much of him other than in passing or at company events during your internship. Now, if there aren't any further questions, I'll be sending you all off to your designated workspaces."

Luckily, I get hooked up with the other marketing major named Madison, but Nick heads off into a different department.

"I guess we'll just wait for Ms. Shaw," Madison says.

"And that is…"

"The head of the marketing department. Didn't you meet her at your second interview?" she asks.

I frown at her. "Uh, I didn't have a second interview."

Her eyebrows raise. "You didn't?" I shake my head. "Then good for you! Must've killed the first one."

That better be the reason… No, Kenna promised not to say anything. She wouldn't.

"Well, she's super nice."

"Good to know."

"Good morning, ladies," a pretty woman says as she saunters up to us and we all stand. "I'm Miranda Shaw," she says to me after greeting the others.

I shake her hand firmly. "Hi, Ms. Shaw. I'm Ja—."

"Jane *Donahue*," she adds and gives me a perusal which I find odd.

"Yes." I clear my throat and wipe my clammy palms on my slacks. The way she said Donahue, it's clear she knows who my father is. *Great.*

She finishes giving me her thorough once over then faces the other girls with her forced smile. "Well, you'll be stuck with me for the next several months. Let's get started, shall we?"

After a few hours of orientation, we're released for our lunch break. There's a nice cafeteria some floors down that Madison and I head down to, and we meet up with Nick sitting at a table with some other interns.

I sit down with my lunch and overhear a couple of girls gushing over Mr. Waldorf. "Okay, I have to see what all the fuss is about," I murmur to Madison, pretending not to know and pull out my phone. Madison and I hover over the screen as I look him up, and damn. He is just as fine as I keep picturing in my head. I've only seen a few pictures of him with Kenna on her social media, but they were from years ago. He's aged well.

"I'll admit he's a pretty good-looking dude," Nick says leaning over to eavesdrop.

"He's hot as shit," Madison says.

"Yeah, and supposedly a man-whore," Nick says causing me to scoff.

"Of course, he is. He's hot and rich. They're all the same," I say putting my phone down.

"Not all of them," Nick disagrees.

The day flies by and I'm in high spirits leaving work. It doesn't seem like the job will be very high paced, but to have a good paying job is what I worked hard for. As long as I can support myself independently, it'll all be worth it.

My new colleagues are heading out to happy-hour, but I'm ready to be off my feet and alone with a glass of wine. Plus, there is money to be saved. I've learned the hard way; the rug can be pulled out from under you at any moment.

When my father's trial came around, he miraculously avoided jail-time, but we lost practically everything. Vacation homes were seized, cars were repossessed, and so were most of our assets. Including my trust-fund. We were able to keep our home in the city, and the clothing on our backs.

I get home and I'm greeted by Luna, Kenna's black cat. She rubs against my legs and I crouch to pet her. "Hey, pretty girl."

I notice a beautiful plant on the dining table with an envelope sticking out of it. Approaching it, I see that it has my name on it and pluck it out to read it.

Congrats on your first day! I'm sure you did great!

-Kenna

I smile and finger the silky leaves of the plant and admire the gorgeous pot it's in. I love that she remembered me talking about how much I love plants and afraid the ones left behind will die before I get to go get them.

I send Kenna a quick text thanking her for the thoughtful gift and that my first day went well. She immediately responded by telling me that she's bringing home sushi and a bottle of champagne to celebrate.

I know Kenna means well, but I hope she doesn't see me as some charity case.

FOUR

Donavon

Draining the rest of my iced latte, I envision the young woman from a couple of weeks ago. The one with the flawless skin and hair the same color as my coffee.

I seem to use coffee as a marker of time and several of them cross my desk on a daily basis, and every time I pick one up, I think of her and the loose curls that hung down her back. She stood there tall and poised. Even when I caught her so brazenly staring at me. She refused to back down so quickly, holding her ground for a moment then insouciantly turned her head and kept her eyes forward as if unaware I remained watching her.

When we stopped at our floor, I purposely tried to squeeze through the doors with her, just to touch her. To catch her scent and see if I could make her squirm. Her voice was sweet and mellifluous as she almost stumbled over her words, slightly flustered. Her fresh and floral scent crept into my senses, warm and inviting. It was adorable the way she refused to meet my eye and scurried off the elevator, swaying her hips up to reception.

I continued to my office with a smirk and a small burst of energy for the day. But now it's vexing how many times I have thought about her in the past two weeks. Her bluish eyes, latte-colored hair, and long legs. One minuscule encounter.

There's a soft knock on the door and I yell out for whoever it is to enter as I get myself to focus back on my work. I don't bother to check who it is as they quietly approach my desk and set down a small stack of papers on the edge. I eye the documents, instantly imbued with agitation from the abrupt invasion.

"These are from Mr. Scott, sir," the familiar and melodic voice has my full attention, yet my eyes remain on the forms now cluttering my desk. I'm no longer annoyed with the items being out of place, but I need to focus on them instead of getting distracted with her presence.

I nod my head and snap my gaze back to the screen on my laptop, my hands needing to move. She takes it as her cue to leave and as soon as she spins around, my eyes snap up to her backside. Before I can abstain, I say, "Who are you?" My voice is as harsh as it typically is when I'm irritated.

She stops in her tracks, and when she spins back around, I'm entranced. "I'm an intern, sir." My cock slightly twitches from the word 'sir' leaving her full lips. "Also your sister's roommate, Jane."

"Jane *Donahue*," I spit her name like a curse as my teeth grind.

Her cheeks are now tinted pink as she tilts her face downwards to the floor. "Yes, sir." *Fuck, why do I like hearing her call me 'sir' so much?* She peeks up at me through her thick lashes. "Can I get anything for you, Mr. Waldorf?" I don't answer and just stare blankly back, purposely trying to bring her discomfort. "Okay, well it was nice to finally meet you." I have a feeling she doesn't mean just as her boss, but also as her friend's brother. She waits a couple seconds hoping I'll respond, then finally gives up and turns to awkwardly leave.

The woman that has been stuck on my mind turns out to be an intern here, and not any intern. My sister's friend and Alfred Donahue's daughter. What a fucking joke the universe has played on me.

She's close to the door now and something inside possesses me to stop her again. "I need you to get me an iced latte."

I go back to my work, ignoring her body pivoting around. "Sir?"

Why the fuck does she have to keep calling me that?

"I said I'd like an iced latte."

She stands there in silence for a long moment before responding with a polite, "Okay." I don't dare look up until she leaves, and then I can finally take a breath.

I don't want this girl anywhere near me, so why? Why the fuck did I have her do something to come back?

I'm hardly able to keep my mind on the work ahead of me knowing she'll be back. Because I asked her to, goddamnit. And all too soon, she comes knocking on the door in the same courteous manner. I give her permission to enter and keep my eyes trained on the screen.

She comes in and sets the drink down on my desk causing my eyes to snap to it. I can already see the ring it'll leave on the surface.

"Can I get you anything else, sir?"

Fucking Hell. Eyes back on the screen. Tell her no and let her leave.

I don't say anything, and she gets the hint to leave, but something is terribly wrong with me today because I stop her. *Again.* "Actually, Ms. *Donahue.* I'm ready for my lunch."

"Your lunch?"

I give in and look up at her, and fuck if she isn't beautiful. "Yes. My lunch." She stands there as if bemused by my simple request. "Is there a problem, Ms. Donahue?"

"Uh, no. Not at all, Mr. Waldorf." Her lips move and I fixate on them. "What would you like?"

"Go ask Maggie." I avert my gaze, and she makes a quick getaway.

Two weeks.

For *two weeks* I've had her run around for me with these mundane tasks, all so that she can come back. I hate anyone in my office, I hate speaking to anyone more than necessary, I hate the Donahues. But every time she goes to leave, I make another request for her return.

I can't seem to send her away with any permanence. It's always the plan, then she waltzes in looking more radiant than she did the time before. And somehow, I feel less anxious after each encounter. Less anxious to have her in my space, and less anxious to have to converse with another human being. She's becoming more competent each day as well. Hastily learning my needs.

Fetching my lattes and lunches when an easy phone call to Maggie, my receptionist, would do. Having her go and inform Sam of meetings in the conference room when it'd be easier to pick the phone up and tell him myself. Everything that would take less time to do myself than having to ask her and explain anything to her. But I continue to ask. Continue to rely on her.

"I have your dry cleaning, Mr. Waldorf," she says as soon as she enters my office without knocking. She stopped after about a week of running around for me. She also dropped the polite smile and sweet tone. She hangs it up on the hook next to the door. "Can I get you anything else?" she asks with a tight smile lingering near the door, hoping that today will be the day I release her.

Today, she wears a beige pencil skirt with a black blouse tucked in. It hugs her plump ass and I wish I could get a better sight of her long legs that I would love to spread...*fuck*.

"Yes, I have a business meeting this afternoon at one, and I would like to meet them—"

"Sir," she snaps, earning my absolute attention. "I am not here to be your personal assistant. I was hired as an intern, and I'm supposed to be working under Ms. Shaw in the marketing—"

"You are here as a paid intern, and I am your boss." I admire her bravado, but she needs to remember who is in charge here. In or outside of the office.

"You're my boss's boss," she makes the lame attempt at an argument.

"Do you want this internship, Ms. *Donahue*?" I rest my elbows on the desk.

"Yes, sir," she says tightly and my cock jumps.

"Then I suggest you do as I say and make me a reservation at my usual spot for four at one o'clock."

The heat from her fervent gaze matches mine as we have a standoff. She wants to say something, but she's prudent to think better of it and hold her pretty tongue. "As you wish, *Mr. Waldorf*." Her voice and cloying smile both seem to satisfy that sweet tooth of mine.

I don't allow myself to smile until she officially leaves, giving me a good shot of her ass. Now, I have no choice but to sit here, pretending to work until she comes back.

Before my lunch meeting, I have to make a short appearance in the conference room. Some of the interns will be in attendance, including Jane. My fingers flex tensely at my sides as I head to the room, knowing I'll be forced to be in a small space with so many people. But knowing Jane's familiar face will be one among the rest—it's like an anchor for my repression and control.

Entering the room, everyone falls quiet as I take my seat at the head of the table, unbuttoning my jacket on the way. I begin speaking without taking a single face in from the crowd, but I don't need to look to know that Jane isn't here, and I'm instantly enraged. I need her here. I need her calming presence. Sitting in a room full of people, speaking to them, their eyes all on me, it makes my skin crawl and the back of my neck tingle.

The door suddenly opens, and a flustered Jane comes in with her head down to try and inconspicuously make her way to an open seat. I'm internally relieved, but the enmity has already grown and outweighs everything.

"You may leave the same way you came, Ms. Donahue." Her wide eyes snap up, but I ignore her and continue what I was saying before she came in.

"Excuse me?" she practically screeches.

My nostrils flare. There's something about riling her up that's pleasing, but no one, including her, will get away with any contest. Let this be a lesson for her and everyone else in this room. "I don't have the habit of repeating myself, but if you're too daft to understand the first time, then I will say it a different way." I face her. "I do not tolerate tardiness, so you may leave in the same manner in which you arrived."

She's breathing fire as she glares back at me. Her tardiness is my fault, but I won't give her the satisfaction of admitting it. I look away and dismiss her by going back to my speech, and she storms out of the room with clenched fists and smoke billowing in her wake.

Knowing she'll certainly be confronting me for my boorish act has me speeding through the meeting and swiftly heading back to my office. Eager to receive the wrath of Jane.

"What the hell is wrong with you?" she starts as soon as I open the door to my office. "You are purposely singling me out." The words leave those pretty lips of hers before I even have the door shut. She stands in the middle of my office fuming, and I have to shove my fists in my pockets to walk by her.

"Get out," I say heading for my desk as she follows close behind.

"Mr. Waldorf, if you would just—" she says more calmly, but I need her out of my sight.

"If you insist on me repeating myself, yet again, I'll have security remove you and have you out on your ass. From your apartment as well." It's a low blow and completely uncalled for, but it should get the job done.

It doesn't extinguish her fire, though; it only fuels it. She shakes in front of my desk, then abruptly grabs the two pens meticulously placed on the edge and slams them back down a few inches away. Knowing damn well it will bother me to have them out of place.

I almost want to laugh. If anyone else were to do that, I would feign indifference but be burning inside. I don't feel the boiling rage, but there most certainly is heat coursing through me.

Not saying another word, she spins and leaves the room.

She has yet to rat me out to my sister about my total abuse of power over her, but I think she's finally had it with me. Any minute now I will be getting a call from Kenna. Or worse. Our mother.

If I'm lucky, she'll quit, and I won't have to deal with my family or with Jane any longer. I can go back to the life I am used to.

FIVE

Jane

It's a pleasant surprise to find Kenna home Saturday morning when I enter the apartment carrying a couple grocery bags. She wasn't kidding when she said she worked a lot.

"Hey! What are you doing home?"

"It's the first Saturday of the month. Family dinner."

"Oh, right." I put the bags on the counter, and she helps me unpack them.

Kenna had told me about the monthly mandatory family dinners and I couldn't help but be jealous of the family dynamic, asshole brother notwithstanding.

Their parents married after being high school sweethearts and accidentally getting pregnant with Donavon at only nineteen. They waited seven years before having Benjamin, then Allison less than two years later. They thought they were done, but when Allison was going on six, they decided to have one more, and that was Kenna, putting Kenna and Donavon fifteen years apart.

Not only did I not have any siblings, but I've never had that close relationship with my parents. I remember being close with my mom when I was little. But with how our relationship is now? I'm thinking it was all in my head. My mind conjuring up fond memories as a way of self-comfort.

"Come with me!" she blurts out.

"What?" I spin around from the cabinets.

"Yeah, seriously. Come home with me for dinner," she beams.

"Oh, no. I could never intrude on your family like that. I actually might go out with some people from work later." Not a total lie. Nick invited me out, but once again I declined.

I know I could go out, but between spending uncertain cash and dealing with a social setting, I'm not ready to yet. I used to love being out and socializing and making new friends, but when my father's face was plastered on every screen, and they began going after my mother and me, I wanted to hide.

"Please? My mom keeps asking when she'll get to see you."

"Really?"

"Yeah, considering I talk about you all the time with her. I think she's under the impression you and I are together."

We both laugh. We might as well be a couple at this point. Her and I don't bother with a life outside of work and opt for coming home and hanging out together when we can. It's been over a month now of living together and it was only natural to pick our friendship back up where we left it in high school.

"Won't your brother be there?"

"Donavon will be, yes. Benjamin is out of town on business. But, so what?" She pops the cork on a bottle of red wine and pours us each a glass without asking.

"It might be weird though. Being in Mr.—I mean Donavon's family home when he's my boss."

I haven't said a word about how he mistreats me at the office. How I run around as his little errand girl and ordered around like a servant. The man never even says please or thank you. Ever! Kenna has been nothing but great to me, so I would never want to cause her any family drama. Plus, I am no snitch. I can handle her asshole brother myself.

"You don't even see him at work though, right?"

Too much of him actually. "I am an intern." I shrug and sip my wine.

"Exactly. My brother is nothing if not professional." She rolls her eyes and I want to roll mine as well but for a completely different reason. "He'll be fine with it. Believe me."

I don't know what to say. I feel like she will take offense if I refuse her invitation and go out with friends I hardly know instead. "Okay, if you're sure."

She grins. "Yay! My mom and sister will be so excited."

I'm instantly a nervous wreck inside. I have no idea what to wear to this. Kenna's family wasn't always rich like they are now thanks to their successful despot of a son. In high school, their dad worked in construction and from what I remember their mom stayed at home, all living a more modest life. It was Donavon's success that made them wealthy. *Is there such a thing as modest wealthy people?*

Kenna said to dress casually, but the fact that I'm seeing Donavon has me overthinking everything. Which is crazy because I don't do this every morning getting ready for work. This is different though. I'm encroaching personal territory where I'll be in a nonprofessional setting.

Hours and several outfits later, Kenna pokes her head inside my room. "You look pretty. You ready?"

I guess it's too late to change my outfit again. "Yup." I grab my mini backpack and follow her out of my room.

"The car should be here soon."

"Car?"

"Yeah, how else would we get there?"

"I thought we'd get a cab or something."

She laughs as we exit our apartment. "Donavon would never allow that."

"Allow it?"

"Donavon thinks he's the head of the family. Haven't you heard he's a control freak yet?" she jokes.

Don't I know it. The man looks like he might combust if someone moves something slightly out of place on his desk. He doesn't even like it when anyone places something down on it. I've come to realize he prefers to be handed things so he can decide where they go. One of his many idiosyncrasies.

"I may have heard that. But it is nice that he sends a car." Her parents live outside of the city, so it takes almost an hour to get there.

"Nice, maybe, but it's his way of making sure we all go." We step inside the elevator. "So, how's it working for him?"

I stiffen a little from her question. I absolutely hate lying. Especially to Kenna. *He's horrible to me!* "He's fine, I guess," I say without looking at her.

"I mean working there in general."

"Good!" I say with a little too much enthusiasm. "Good." I clear my throat. "So far, I really like working at his company," I flat out lie. It's been one hellish nightmare after another. When I'm able to make it back to Miranda, she loads a bunch of work on me as if she's trying to punish me for Donavon having me jump through hoops, like I'm asking for his hazing.

"And my brother? When you do see him occasionally, is he nice to you?"

The elevator comes to the ground floor. "He's polite, yes."

Lies. Lies. Lies.

"I'm bummed Benjamin won't be there tonight." Apparently, he works at the company too, but I have yet to meet him.

"He must be traveling more than usual this month or something." We head out to a black sedan. "Hi, Ron," she says cheerfully to the older man holding the back door open for us.

"Good evening, Ms. Waldorf." He then looks to me with a warm smile. "And you are..."

"Oh, this is Jane Donahue."

"Nice to meet you, Ms. Donahue."

I smile. "You too."

The car door shuts and we're off as soon as Ron climbs in behind the wheel and my stomach begins to turn.

"Benjamin will totally hit on you by the way."

I snort. "Is he a—"

"Manwhore? Yes. He's harmless though. A huge flirt really. But who knows? Maybe you too will hit it off." She grins over at me.

"So, every first Saturday of the month, huh?" I overtly change the subject. Dating someone whose brother I constantly fantasize about? It's not a likely relationship.

"Yup, I complain like it's such a hassle sometimes, but really, I look forward to it."

"So, what is your brother like outside of work?"

"Donavon?" I nod and she snorts. "I'm sure much of the same. Hardly cracks a smile and has to dominate everything. You should see him making his plate." She laughs.

"Why?"

"He is such a freak sometimes," she says jokingly, but for some reason it makes me feel bad. I've noticed his OCD tendencies, and for someone as superior as him, it must take a toll on his mental state. Being out of control of your own urges. "You'll see."

I chuckle and shake my head. "Maybe it's an oldest sibling thing. Especially with the age gap between you. He is practically old enough to be your father."

We both laugh. "True. I mean, he wasn't always a saint, but he really is an amazing brother. He would drop everything for any one of us. Everything he's worked for was for our family." The way she words it makes it seem like there's another story there, but I focus on the sentiment behind it.

It's hard to grasp the thought of Donavon being such a family man when he seems like he is hellbent on making a grown man cry each morning he walks into his office. Or anyone for that matter. He does not discriminate. He definitely does not tiptoe around *my* feelings at all.

Sooner rather than later, we're pulling up to a nice home in a suburban neighborhood. The closest I've ever been to the suburbs was the Hamptons.

I hop out of the car first then let Kenna take the lead. She goes right up to the door and opens it shouting, "Helllooooooo!!!"

There's already chatter coming from somewhere further into the house that only grows louder with Kenna's arrival. I continue following her as we walk through the warm home until it opens into a large kitchen full of people.

Right away, we're bombarded. An older woman with the most genuine smile comes for me with open arms. "Jane!" I'm a little hesitant when she embraces me in a firm hug.

"Hi, Mrs. Waldorf."

She pulls back still smiling and holds me by my shoulders to get a thorough look at me. "Oh, call me Annie. And wow. You have grown into such a beautiful woman."

I smile back at her hazel eyes. "Thank you. And thank you so much for having me over for dinner."

"Or course! We're so happy to have you. Dan! Come see Jane!"

A handsome older man approaches me and offers me a handshake with a warm smile. "Hi, Jane. Nice to see you again."

"Nice to see you too, Mr. Waldorf." He's as tall as Donavon with dark blue eyes, yet not as dark as his.

"You can call him Dan, hon," Annie says then wraps an arm around my shoulders. "Allison! Come say hi!"

When the attractive young woman comes walking in my direction, I think to myself, *are they all models?* She's as tall as Kenna and just as stunning. This family could take over the world with their looks alone.

"Hi, Jane," Allison says and takes me in for a light hug. "It's nice to finally meet you. Or meet you again, I should say." I smile and look over at the handsome man that comes up to her side. "And this is my fiancé, Josh."

Once the introductions are over we're handed drinks, and all the while I can feel Donavon's intense gaze on me.

Six

Donavon

I'm enraged.

Not a single person gave me a heads up that Jane was coming tonight. Invading yet another space of mine. Sure, it's my fault she invades the safe space of my office, but this is crossing the line.

"Beer?" My dad appears in front of me with a cold bottle.

I gladly accept, tearing my eyes away from the intruder. "Thank you." I take a large gulp.

"Well, you're in a mood," he grumbles and stands next to me with his own beer.

"When aren't I?" I respond dryly.

He chuckles, shaking his head. "True, but it got worse when Kenna came in with her friend. Jane works for you, doesn't she?"

"She's an intern," I say too defensive.

"Is she causing you any problems?"

"No, she's fine." If my father knew how I've been treating her, he'd be more than disappointed. He'd be furious.

"Then why are you looking at her like you want to kill her?" he mutters making me realize that I am once again glowering her way.

I avert my glare. "I don't find it appropriate to have an employee here in our home."

"Oh, lighten up, son." He gives my shoulder a good squeeze. "She's Kenna's best friend and roommate. I'm sure she can be professional."

I *know* she can be professional. She's proven that with the last few weeks working for me. My fixation with her isn't her fault, it's mine and the way my brain functions. I get obsessed. In my youth, it was partying, fighting, and sex. It wasn't until I almost cost my father his life that I turned my addictive personality towards something worth obsessing over. My education and success. Now, it's Jane.

Her father has nothing to do with the umbrage I carry for her. I tried deluding myself into thinking that was the sole reason, but truth is, she's taken over my every waking thought. My newest and greatest obsession.

I'm not sure if my obsession with her is because of the way her presence and the thoughts of her thwarts my habitual tendencies and incessant thoughts I haven't ever been able to control, or it's because of my obsession with Jane, I've felt less out of control and compulsive. Subconsciously reliant on her, and I have never felt so helpless without someone before.

I join Josh and my father out back while the ladies finish up making dinner. "So, where's Benjamin?" Josh asks as we sit around the fire pit.

"He's on a business trip in L.A. We tried to schedule around it, but it didn't work out."

My brother works for me, doing most of the traveling for any out of state or country meetings with potential and preexisting clients.

It's always been uncomfortable for me to stay the night anywhere but my own bed. Even as a child I couldn't do sleepovers with friends, and when I was older, I could never get myself to stay the night in a female's bed the entire night, nor have them sleep in mine. Having my own territory where I feel secure enough not to have to hide anything is paramount to my sanity.

Mandatory family dinners were my idea. I could see how it was breaking my mother's heart when we began to drift apart as a family as we were all getting older. It started when I went off to college. Not only was I a typical college student busy with their studies, but

I was always pushing myself to get perfect grades. Simply passing was never good enough. And I've always loved my parents and my siblings, but I wasn't always the greatest at showing it. Going weeks without speaking to them felt normal to me, but I've known since I was a young child that I don't think like most normal people do. It's supposedly natural for humans to miss each other and need that connection through some form of communication.

Then out of college I was working my ass off to build up my company, consuming all of my time and eventually the others were going off to college. Family dinners were very far and few in between for years. We've always been close, and I could see how the distance was only growing. So, I declared family dinners every first Saturday of the month was a nonnegotiable gathering.

As soon as my company turned into Waldorf Enterprise and I was making profit, I made it so my father could retire. But being a blue-collared guy, he couldn't completely retire from work. Instead, he let me loan him the money it would take to start his own construction company flipping homes. I've offered for him to work at my company, but he said he would never be an office guy. He loves hard work with his hands. Something I've always admired about him as a man.

"I'm still surprised you allowed him to miss out on family dinner, even for work," Josh teases. He and Allison have been engaged for a few months now. They met in college and he's an alright guy that treats her right as well as making a good living for them both. All I can ask for.

After some more light conversation, Kenna pokes her head outside to obnoxiously announce that dinner is ready. I can hear Jane inside laughing and I clench my fists, reminded that she's here. That laugh that I have only heard from a distance, yet to witness for myself.

Dinner is always set out in a family style fashion. Large platters of food filling up the center island in the kitchen. There are never any regulations on how we all get our food or what order we go in. So,

I'm going one way, and Jane is going another. Our paths eventually crossing.

"Hi, Mr. Waldorf," she says softly, the usual menace absent from her tone.

"Jane," I say flatly and avoid looking into her icy gaze. It's the first time addressing her as Jane. I only ever do it in my head.

"Ew, call him Donavon when you're outside of work," Kenna asserts herself. "When you call him Mr. Waldorf, it sounds all sexual for some reason."

"Yeah, like a sexy rich boss and hot assistant romance," Allison adds and they both giggle like little schoolgirls as Jane's cheeks heat up and she scurries away.

"I'd prefer it if she weren't to call me Donavon. Ever."

"You will not be a jerk to her, Don. For tonight, she can call you by your first name. So suck it up, punk." She spins around, stalking off as puerile as her rant.

I'm the last to head out back, so there are only two open seats left for me to choose from; both of which are next to Jane. Being the asshole that I am, I sit down in the one that'll leave an open seat next to her.

I place my utensils down over my folded napkin and straighten them. "We need to have a discussion about how family dinner is for family," I mutter low enough for only my mother next to me to hear.

She swats at my arm. "Donavon, you be polite."

"I'm serious. This is for family, not an open invitation to a BBQ."

"Josh isn't family," Allison chimes in from the seat across me. Keeping her voice low so that Jane doesn't overhear.

"Significant others are an exception," I retort.

Allison leans forward with a sly grin. "Do you have some kind of beef with Jane?" she utters lowly, hoping for some gossip.

I shake my head. "No." I shovel some food on my fork. "It's about this being intimate family time spent together."

She scoffs leaning back in her chair. "Says the guy who grunts more than actually speaks."

One side of my mouth tilts up. "I may not speak much, but I listen well."

"Alright, you two," my mother interjects, most likely to shut down what might become an argument between us siblings. "Donavon." She leans over to me to speak softly. "Jane isn't just any friend. Her and Kenna are close friends and live together. Plus, she could use some family time like this."

"We are not her family," I all but growl.

"Would you stop it?" my mother scolds me in a high whisper, making quick glances over to Jane. "Kenna said she doesn't have any siblings and she isn't very close with her parents. She thought she needed this, so please ease up some."

Nothing like your mother still being able to put you in your place as a grown man nearing forty. I sneak a glance over at Jane and let my mother's words sink in. I was so preoccupied with all the wrongs her father has done; I had never stopped to think about how it affected her. She was only going into college when it all started, practically still a child. Her father deserved far worse than what he got ordered by the court, but her and her mother were also pulled through the wringer when they had nothing to do with his crimes or his business he mutilated.

We wrap up dinner and I head inside to help with the dishes. I dismissed my father and Josh once there weren't many left to do. When I turn the water off, the noise from the outside filters in as I dry my hands. Through the window over the kitchen sink, I can see Jane sitting next to Kenna around the fire. They look like they've had a little too much wine as they whisper and giggle together. Her smile that reaches her eyes has me fidgety and on edge. I know I need to divert my gaze before someone catches me, but I'm unable to.

She gets up and heads for the back door of the kitchen and I don't say anything as she comes inside, heading towards the bathroom on the first floor. I fold the hand towel back up and follow in her direction.

I wait patiently outside of the bathroom, and when she opens the door, she gasps. "Oh, God. You scared me." She gives a nervous chuckle.

I push away from the wall to stand toe-to-toe with her, but my feet do not stop advancing. Her eyes widen and she backpedals us right into the bathroom. I close and lock the door behind me making sure we have full privacy.

"Donavon, what are you doing?" She glances between me and her only exit.

The bathroom is small as it is, but I crowd her space even more. Her back flattens to the wall, and I place a palm on it above her head. I've never been this close to her, which is a complete mistake. This close, I can see how light her eyes really are. And how there's some green in them. Her unblemished skin and thick eyelashes...

"Mr. Waldorf," I correct her.

Her cheeks turn that beautiful rosy shade that has my cock thumping against my pants. "Right. Sorry," she murmurs and looks away.

"I don't want you here." I lean in closer, and her eyes grow wider as she averts them.

She sighs, her shoulders sagging. "I told Kenna it wasn't a good idea. I did try to get out of it."

I bring my head down slightly to invade her space even more. Because that's all she does with me. Physically and mentally. "Next time, try harder."

Her eyes snap up to mine with newfound defiance. "We're not at work, *Mr. Waldorf.*"

"No. We're in my family home. Somewhere you have no business being."

"Your sister invited me, and I couldn't think of way to decline without being rude," she snaps. "But for your own peace of mind, I will make myself scarce whenever the first Saturday of the month rolls around."

"Be sure that you do."

She gives me a sardonic smile. "Yes, sir. Anything else, Mr. Waldorf?" she sasses.

I glance down at her lips and when I lift my eyes back to hers, I find her staring at my mouth. Her breath comes in quicker and shorter, on the verge of panting. I'm instinctively drawn closer to her, and I can feel her breath on my neck and smell the sweet wine of her mouth.

Her eyes flutter, and my heart begins to palpitate. It's not racing, but it pounds in my chest, trying to jump right out of me to get to her.

She sharply sucks in air and her eyes shut when I lift a finger to trail the seam of her lightly parted lips to discover once and for all if they're as soft as they look, and I'm not at all disappointed. Silk. Plush. So pink.

I lean in closer, hovering my lips over hers and I find her breath labored, her chest rising and falling in short winds. Grasping some fortitude, I bypass her mouth and press my lips to the shell of her ear, and she shivers. I fist my hand against the wall and my other one at my side. All I want to do is touch her.

"You can go now," I rasp.

Her breath stills and her eyes snap open. She purses her lips and her nostrils flare as she breathes fire up at me. Aggressively shouldering past me, she storms out and I'm left with a stiff cock and very dirty thoughts of Jane Donahue.

SEVEN

Donavon

The door to my office flies open, and I don't need to look up and see who it is. There's only one other person aside from Jane that comes into my office without knocking. Jane confidently breezes into the room while my brother swarms in like a hurricane.

"You weren't at the club last night," he says first thing, taking a seat in front of my desk. Not without moving the pens around on my desk first, just to fuck with me. I don't give him the satisfaction with any kind of reaction.

"Hello to you too, Benjamin," I say without looking.

"Why weren't you at the club?" he presses.

I sigh and pinch at the tension between my brows. "Wanted to get some sleep for once." Not a complete lie. I do suffer from insomnia, so every once in a while, I come to my breaking point and crash.

He raises both eyebrows. "Were you with someone?"

"No." He shouldn't even have to ask. He knows that the only place I am with other women is at the club. I do not do dates, and I definitely do not have women over at my place.

My office door opens again and instinctively I focus back on my work. I'm sure Benjamin will be hypnotized by the sway of Jane's hips as soon as he gets a good look at her. "Here's your latte," she says holding the cup out for me to take from her rather than putting it anywhere on my desk. I obtain it and place it on the coaster to my right, and I see her absentmindedly moving my two pens back in their place.

I'm sure it didn't go unnoticed with my brother. I can only wonder what he makes of it.

His silence is out of the ordinary and I can feel her glancing down at him, unsure if she should introduce herself or not. I don't ever have anyone sitting in my office without them quickly tucking tail and running as soon as their ass hits the seat.

"Oh, are you Benjamin?" she finally says recognizing him.

"I am." He stands up. "And you are...?"

"Hi, I'm Jane. Kenna's roommate."

"Oh, *you're* Jane," he says lowly, I'm sure already trying to charm her. "Nice to finally meet you."

"You, too. I was beginning to think this elusive *Waldorf sibling* was a myth or something."

He chuckles, "I could say the same to you. Tell me something. Are you and my sister...more than friends?"

She full on laughs, and I dart my eyes up for a small peek. I find myself desperate to catch a single glimpse of her wide smile and how they affect her eyes and face. "We pretty much are in a relationship, but not on purpose. We only seem to spend time with each other since we both work so much." I can feel her eyes on me after the last comment, and I'm slightly tempted to bite.

"I see that," my brother drawls out, his eyes now on me as well. Great, now he'll be prying for information that I do not have. "I didn't know interns worked so much."

"Well, your brother and Miranda like to add a little more onto my workload each and every day."

"Huh." He leaves a small pause. "Maybe I can put in a good word with the boss." The flirtatious tone doesn't escape me.

"I would actually love that."

"Come to my office anytime—"

I make a resounding noise clearing my throat and they both grow quiet.

"I was wondering if I could go find Miranda and see what I can do for her today." She keeps desperately trying to get away from me, but it's useless.

"I need you to set the conference room up. Tell Sam we'll be meeting at ten."

She stands there glaring at me for a drawn-out moment. Then she huffs and mutters a goodbye to Benjamin before turning on her heels to leave. My eyes snap up to her ass that always looks so delectable in those pencil skirts. My mouth fills up with saliva thinking about pulling it up and bending her over my desk.

She slams the door shut on her departure, snapping me out of my trance and I quickly remember that my brother is still here. I see him turn back in his chair from watching her leave as well and I grip the pen in my hand wanting to stab him with it.

"Damn. You didn't tell me you hired Jane as your assistant. Nor did you mention the fact that she is fucking *hot*."

I go back to my work before I combust. "She's an intern." He doesn't respond right away, and I can hear the squeaky wheels turning. "Don't even think about it," I warn.

"What?" He puts his hands out feigning innocence.

"I can practically hear your thoughts. That's Kenna's roommate and friend."

"Since when do you care?" I ignore him. "Oh, I see. You're already fucking her, aren't you?"

"No," I respond quickly. Though I do think about it more frequently than I care to admit. So many times, I've lost count. Especially after I found out that she's not only beautiful, but she's intelligent as well. Fully capable to take on more responsibilities as time goes on.

"Then why is she getting you coffee?" Again, I don't give him a response. "Ah, I know what it is. She's Alfred Donahue's daughter. You're punishing her."

"I don't know what you're talking about," I utter under my breath.

He chuckles, "Yes, you do. You're tormenting the poor girl because of your hatred for her father. Shit, Kenna's going to kill you when she finds out you're having her be your little errand girl. Ever since she moved in, it's all Kenna talks about. She really needs a boyfriend or something."

I release a low chuckle and shake my head. My brother is an idiot half the time, but he's the only person who can actually make me laugh. "I've been doing this to her for two months, and she hasn't breathed a word of it to Kenna."

"So, you admit what you're doing to her." I don't answer. "Tell me the truth though." He leans forward. "You want to bang her, don't you?"

"*Bang* her?" I lower my chin with raised brows. "Who says bang past the age of twenty?"

"You're deflecting." He points an accusing finger at me. "Hey, I don't blame you." I occupy myself with my laptop. "She's insanely hot. I would love to drag that sexy skirt of hers up and—"

I slam a fist down on my desk. "Is there a reason you're here?"

He bites back a grin. "I see I've hit a nerve." He stands up and buttons his suit jacket with a smug smirk on his face. "I'll be on my way then." He flicks the pens out of place again then turns to leave and I want to pummel my brother for letting him get a rise out of me. He looks over his shoulder as he reaches the door. "Maybe I'll go and take Jane out for lunch today. Get to know her a little better, since she's quickly becoming a part of the family."

"Fuck off," I mutter, and he bursts out laughing until he shuts the door behind him, knowing that if he didn't leave, I'd give him a long overdue beating.

Jane comes back all too soon. I haven't even begun to push her to the back of my mind since my brother left. "Conference room is all set. Anything else I can do for you, Mr. Waldorf?"

Yes, you can wrap those gorgeous lips around my cock.

"Yes, I need you to look over these papers."

She exhales and plops herself down in a chair. I slide the papers to the edge of my desk, and she takes them in her lap. I found out she double majored in English, so I wanted to see her skills. I gave her something to edit, and she worked fast and didn't miss a single thing. I may be a perfectionist, but I do take on so much more than any person can physically handle, so prompts and documents sometimes get a little sloppy.

Then she once took it upon herself to rewrite an email for me when I only requested her to edit it, and my natural reaction was to be furious with her. To shut her down and remind her of her place. But something made me take a look at it first, and as soon as I read through it, I went ahead and sent it before second guessing.

With her head down, she crosses her legs, attracting my attention. They're long and slender with delicate calves. I wonder if she was ever a dancer? From the way she walks to the way she writes, everything is done so poised and balletic.

Before I'm caught ogling her, I go back to work. I've always enjoyed the quiet confines of my office. It's why I could never have an assistant. I've tried several times to hire one, but always ended up letting them go within a couple of weeks. Anytime I'd make the attempt to put someone in charge of something, I'd end up redoing it myself. Plus, I couldn't have someone following me around like a lost puppy, needing direction and making me feel more uncomfortable than reliant on them. Until Jane.

Not only is she efficient, but she understands how to keep to herself and only speak when necessary. Her questions are never empty, and she takes my sour tone on the chin, no longer letting it get to her.

She pulls a pen out to edit something, once again pulling my attention. She tucks some of her hair behind an ear and bites down on her bottom lip with her perfect teeth. They're almost *too* perfect. "Did you have work done on your teeth?" I blurt out before I can reconsider my word vomit.

Her head snaps up with a frown. "What?"

"Do you have veneers or caps on your teeth?"

"No..." she drawls out. "I had braces as a kid, but these are my real teeth." She holds my gaze with curiosity for a long moment then goes back to work.

"Your hair. Is that your natural color?" *I've already started, why stop now?*

She sets her pen down on the papers in her lap giving me her own scrutiny. She's irritated and I'll admit, I'm a little irritated with myself as well. "Yes, this is my natural hair color. And no, I do not wear colored contacts, and while I may be wearing a pushup bra, these are my natural tits as well." My lips twitch in amusement and I glance down at her said breasts on reaction then back up to her blue-green glare. "Any other questions about my appearance?"

Oh, yes. Too many to count.

"I've never seen anyone with your hair color before. And your teeth..." I trail off wanting to find a muzzle for myself. Clearing my throat, I go back to my current task.

"Are you paying me a compliment?" she asks playfully.

"No," I quip, internally whipping myself for opening my goddamn mouth to begin with.

Thankfully, she drops it and we both work silently, restfully so. When she's finished, she stands up and hands the stack of papers back to me with a sigh. "Alright, if that'll be all, I'll head to the conference room. It's ten to ten," she informs me.

I give her a subtle nod and she exits the room. I keep my eyes trained down this time, unwilling to give into my most basic urge to salivate over her figure. I don't know what this woman is doing to me, but it's driving me insane. The most infuriating part is that it's gone on too long, and there's no stopping it.

I am seized.

I am seized.

EIGHT

Jane

I've already read through the agenda of this meeting, so it's hard to concentrate on what Donavon is saying, but it doesn't stop me from staring at his lips as he talks. Lips I have fantasized about since my first day here. When I had no idea it was Donavon Waldorf, my best friend's brother until his eyes met mine. Those dark blues instantly pulled me so far under.

On top of all that, he's a complete asshole. He's over the top demanding in every aspect of his life. He's rude and condescending and apathetic towards everyone, and orders me around as if I'm hardly human. Not to mention he's seventeen years older than me.

Oh, and he hates me. How can I forget that?

Almost three months here and I've been running around as his personal assistant. At first, it was insulting and demeaning, but now, it's not so terrible. He still talks down to me and easily snaps, but I've learned to quickly brush it off and he even gives me real responsibilities that actually require having an education for. An education I have worked very hard at.

When I'm not picking up his dry cleaning and fetching him his lunch or lattes, he has me editing and even taking notes when he's on a conference call. He might not thank me or tell me I'm doing a good job, but he isn't making me go home holding back tears or ready to bite someone's head off every day. The way I see him treat others day in and day out, I could almost say he's somewhat nice to me. Except when he's not.

"Pst," Nick whispers to me and I lean over. "Are you coming to happy hour for once?"

I smile over at him and nod. I've decided I could live a little. You really are only young once, and I've already had so many precious years of my youth taken from me.

"Awesome." He grins. "I'll wait for you in the lobby after work."

"Okay," I whisper back and straighten my body to pay attention.

"Ms. Donahue, if you don't mind holding off on your flirting until after the meeting, that would be great," Donavon chides out of nowhere and every single eye in the room is now on me. It gives me flashbacks of that day in college my freshman year when my father hit the headlines and I became a spectacle.

My cheeks heat not only in embarrassment, but in rage. His dark eyes clash with mine and he arches one eyebrow in challenge. As if daring me to retaliate, so he can put me in my place and have me hightailing it out of here in defeat. I won't give him the satisfaction though.

I bite my tongue, but I will be telling him off. I'll wait until we're in the privacy of his office though because I can be professional.

Staring daggers back at him, I clench my fists in my lap trying to not blow my lid. "Apologies, sir," I grind out with a tight smile. He holds my stare for a moment longer before addressing the rest of the room again as if nothing ever happened.

I tune every word that comes out of his mouth out while I sit here almost vibrating in ire. What the hell is his problem? Is he trying to embarrass me? If so, he'll have to try much harder than that. But if he was trying to piss me off, mission accomplished. I'm pissed. I've been hazed long enough. It's time for him to back the fuck off.

"I'm so sorry. I had no idea he would single you out like that," Nick says as soon as the meeting is over and Donavon has left the room.

I give him a little smile, wishing I could say the same thing. I'm not at all surprised he found the opportunity to call me out. It wasn't the first time. "It's not your fault. The man hates me."

"How come?" he asks as we both exit the room.

"I think because of who my father is," I mutter.

Nick outwardly grimaces. "Oh, right. Alfred Donahue."

"Yup. He hates him with a passion apparently, so he takes it out on me."

I found that out the hard way not long ago. After a conference call, I made the grave mistake of giving my opinion. His response was, "The only reason you are still here, Ms. *Donahue*, is because of your relationship with my sister. It is not for your intellect and most certainly *despite* being a Donahue." He never apologized for his harsh words, but he did continue to give me more assignments that required my *intellect*.

"That's not okay. You should definitely go to HR about that."

I chuckle humorlessly. "Not worth it." But I am going to confront him personally. "I'll see you after work."

He smiles at me, and I notice how handsome he really is. *And he's not a condescending asshole.* "I'll be waiting."

We part ways and the anger begins to seep back in the closer I get to Donavon's office. I barrel through the door and slam it behind me. "You do not get to speak to me like that," I seethe as I charge through. "I'm already running around like your personal servant and constantly allowing you to demean me, but I will not tolerate you humiliating me." I stop in front of his desk, and he doesn't even have the decency to look at me while I'm speaking to him. "If you hate me so much, then why do you insist on keeping me around? Why not just fire me altogether?"

"I'm sorry," he says pinching the bridge of his nose.

"You're...what?" I ask in utter shock. I have never once heard the man say the words 'I'm sorry' to *anyone* before. I came in here expecting a fight, not an apology.

"I'm having a shitty day, and I shouldn't have taken it out of you, Jane," he says with exhaustion laced in his tone.

I'm not only taken aback by his out-of-character apology, but also by him exposing a sliver of vulnerability. The wind is immediately taken right out of my sails as I watch him sit there genuinely worn down. The angry red haze recedes, and I begin to feel sorry for him. I shouldn't, and yet I do. It's not only sympathy, but there's this nurturing side of myself that I'm slowly discovering rising within me, and for some reason I project it on Donavon.

"Are you alright?" I ask studying the subtle slouch in his posture.

"I'm fine," he grumbles, still not looking directly at me.

"Okay." I back up a couple of steps. "Can I get you anything?"

He decides to go ahead and shock me again. "I need an assistant."

I cross my arms. "Yes, you do." I don't mean to sound so snarky, but is he only now realizing this?

He obviously doesn't appreciate the sassy tone as his eyes roll up to mine with hostility. "I'd like you to be my full-time assistant," he states as if it should've been overtly clear.

I'm instantly offended. "I went to college, Mr. Waldorf. I busted my ass for my degree, not to settle for someone's *assist*—"

"*Executive* assistant," he adds.

I narrow my eyes at him, the tenseness leaving my shoulders. "I'm listening..."

His lips twitch as if he's fighting back a smile, but that can't be. The man doesn't smile, especially around me. I'm pretty sure he's incapable of it. "It pays a lot more than your internship, and if you prove yourself to be proficient, then I'll be sure to pay you more than what you would make here or *anywhere* in marketing."

I stare at him with wide eyes. Is he for real? No, way. There has to be some kind of catch. "And if I'm not *proficient*?"

"I'll let you go back to your intern position."

"Completely back to it? Because technically I am still an intern. At least, I'm still being paid as one."

"I'll leave you alone."

I drop my arms. "Why?"

"Why what?"

"Why would you want me as your executive assistant? You hate me."

"You've been dependable so far. I need things done a certain way, and you've managed to do so without being told how."

He averts his gaze at the last part, and I wonder if he is ashamed of his severe anxiety. I'm no psychiatrist, but having anxiety myself, I can spot someone else with it. Mine isn't nearly as severe as his though, but I do take medicine to help curb it. I find myself wondering if he takes anything. Hell, he might not even know he has anxiety. A lot of people don't know that's what they are feeling. But I can see it in him every day. Specifically, his social anxiety.

I chew on my bottom lip, and I can't help but notice him fixate on my mouth. "Can I think about it?"

His eyes jump back up to mine. "No," he says so quickly it gives me whiplash, then he opens his laptop to focus on the screen. "I need your answer now, or the offer is off the table."

Ugh! Why is he so infuriating?

I clench my fists at my sides and take a deep breath. He certainly knows how to get under my skin, and fast. "Yes," I say blurt out. "I accept." I'd be a fool not to, right?

"Great. Now, go get my lunch."

Not able to resist, I growl through my teeth and spin on my heels. There's no turning back now.

"Oh, and Jane?" I stop in my retreat but don't turn. "Your lunch is on me."

Oh, how kind of you, Mr. Waldorf. I somehow manage not to slam the door behind me on the way out and I freeze just outside of his door, questioning my sanity. Did I seriously just accept? Did I really purposely place myself at his side and be there at his beck and call?

It's shortly after five o'clock, and I'm finally headed down to the lobby ready for a drink. When I let Nick know I'd be running a little late, he insisted on still waiting for me.

I smile when I step off the elevator on the ground floor and find him there patiently waiting. He sees me and returns the smile. "Hey," I say as we meet each other halfway.

"Hey, you ready for a drink?"

"Try several."

He laughs, "One of those days, huh?"

"A very interesting day."

We exit the building walking side by side. "I can only imagine. Mr. Waldorf seem at all remorseful for how he spoke to you in the meeting today?"

I don't know why, but I'm hesitant to tell him about my new position at the company. "He actually apologized."

"Oh," he says sounding surprised. "Then that's good, right?"

I nod. "He also offered me a job."

He looks at me in shock. "Really? That's awesome! In the marketing department?"

I shake my head. "Actually, no. As his executive assistant."

"Seriously?" I nod my head. "Did you accept it?" I nod again, and he looks away. "Hm."

"What?"

He shrugs. "Well, it's just that...I don't know. Why doesn't he already have an assistant?"

I shrug a shoulder. "I don't know. I know he's very particular with how he likes everything done, and I guess I can do that for him."

"And are you really up for it? I mean, look at how he treats you now. You think he'll be treating you any better now that you are officially his assistant?"

"*Executive* assistant," I correct him. "And I don't know. But he said I'll get paid more, so it's worth the chance. And he said if it doesn't work out that I can have my intern spot back."

"Then I guess it is worth it." He places a hand on my lower back and looks at me. "I'm sorry. I didn't mean to put a damper on your evening. You did get a promotion and that's worth celebrating."

I smile up at him. "It's okay. You're just looking out for me. Thank you."

"No problem."

It's Friday and I am ready to let loose a little and enjoy some drinks with Nick, Madison, and some of the other interns. I just got a raise and a more secure position at the company. I can definitely splurge some when there's a good reason to celebrate.

I'm sitting next to Madison and only one and a half drinks in when my phone goes off with a text.

Unknown: I sent you over some emails I need you to go over tonight. I need you to make them more personable.

Motherfucker. Of course, I won't have my weekends off working with him. No wonder why he's offering to pay me so much.

Me: Got it, boss.

I sigh and look over at Madison. "Looks like I'm not exactly off the clock," I whine.

She frowns. "Seriously?"

"Yup." I stand up gathering up my jacket and bag. "I have emails to go through." I glance at my watch seeing that it's already eight o'clock.

"Hey, you leaving?" Nick asks from across the table.

"Yes. Apparently when he said full-time assistant, he really meant it."

"Shit, that sucks."

"Yeah, it really does," Madison whines looking genuinely disappointed. We haven't gotten to hang out much lately. The longer I've been working here, the longer my hours have become.

"I know, I know," I murmur. "I'll see you guys Monday."

"I'll walk you out," Nicks says and reaches me. He shoves his hands inside of his pockets as he walks me out front of the bar. "Are you walking, or...?"

"My feet are killing me, so not today. I'm getting a car." I can't even make it around the block to catch the subway tonight.

"Well, it was nice while it lasted."

"It was," I say smiling up at him.

We stop at the curb. "So, I was wondering if you were free tomorrow night."

"I don't have any plans."

"Would you let me to take you out?"

"Like on a date?"

He laughs. "Yes, like on a date."

"Oh. Okay, yeah. I'd like that." I'm already excited for it. I haven't been out on a date in what feels like forever.

"Yeah?" I nod still smiling up at him. He reaches up and tucks some of my hair behind my ear, giving me goosebumps down that entire side. "Awesome. I'll call you tomorrow then."

We say goodbye as I hop in the back of the car that pulls up to head home to work on a Friday night.

Nine

Jane

I never did get that date with Nick.

Donavon had me working the entire weekend, and every weekend since then. He'll even text me at two in the morning asking if I've finished his emails. What is he still doing awake then? Does the man ever sleep, or even take a single night off? And it's as if the more emails I get through, the faster he sends me more.

Five months in at the company and two months in as his official executive assistant, and I am running myself ragged. But we've fallen into an easy routine because that's what Donavon is; he's routine, and completely predictable. That's why when he does anything even slightly out of character, it's intriguing.

I have him pretty much figured out and I think that's why he wanted me as his executive assistant.

Odd habits of Donavon's:

He doesn't like things set on his desk; needs it handed directly to him. In fact, do not touch anything on his desk.

When you ask him something and he doesn't respond right away, it doesn't mean he's ignoring you. Either he doesn't feel that a response is necessary, or he'll answer you when he is ready to.

He doesn't do small talk, which I don't ever feel is necessary to fill the silence, but I'm great at it when needed. Hence why he has begun to take me with him on business lunch meetings. I fill the silence with small talk charming the potential clients, and he talks strictly business.

He likes his sweets. Any sweets. Sweet lattes, desserts, candies. You name it. I began bringing him a treat with his latte every morning, and he has yet to thank me for it. But he does eat it and hasn't asked me to stop.

Eye contact is distressing for him unless it's for intimidation.

Walking through the door to his office, always without knocking because I have long since earned that right, I go straight to his desk and offer him his second hot latte of the day. He takes them entirely too sweet, but I don't mention that as I hold it and the small bag with a fresh baked cookie out for him.

"You remember the lunch you have with the Moores, right?" I ask him as I sit down with my laptop and cross my legs.

"What time is it again?" he murmurs not looking at me. Always solely focused on work.

"Noon. So, in little over an hour." He sighs and I glance up at him. "Something wrong?"

"I'm a little hungry now."

"You want me to grab you something to hold you over?"

He looks up at me and I quickly cast my eyes back down at the screen. His eyes too intense to stare directly at sometimes. He's an asshole to me half the time and dismissive of me the other half, but he still manages to give me butterflies. I blame his insanely good looks. He could have any personality out there, or none at all. Even a nun would find him sexy.

I spend most of my time with him. Whether here in his office, or at home communicating with him via text and email. I don't know how he's still single, but with the number of hours he dedicates to this place, I can see how it doesn't leave any time for a relationship. He's here before me every day and he's still typing away when I leave close to six in the evening. Then he's up all hours of the night disturbing me with emails and texts.

He glances over at the little bag with the cookie in it. "No, I'll be alright."

We collectively go back to our work, quiet and comfortable. I peek up at him when he once again grabs at the back of his neck and squeezes it. I know his neck must ache day in and day out hunched over like that over his laptop. Why doesn't he get a separate monitor? I pull out my notepad and add a screen monitor to the list of things I feel like Donavon would benefit from. A creature of habit like him, is a creature that is resistant to change.

We're silent up until it's time for his lunch meeting which I attend to take notes and fill in for the polite and friendly aspect.

Donavon continues to call me Jane, but only when no one is around. To clients and colleagues, I'm Ms. Donahue. But he has dropped the venom in in my name finally. I'll sure as hell never make the mistake of ever calling him Donavon again. The one time that I did, he looked like he wanted to rip my head off, and that was at his family's home.

We're riding in the back of the town car when my phone goes off and I see that it's my mom. My gut is already churning because it's been a while since there's been an incident, and I know that we're due for one. I ignore her call, but something tells me she'll keep trying to call until I answer.

As predicted, she calls again and I silence it, also turning the ringer off as I try to keep my mood from souring any further. There's no way I am answering her in front of Donavon.

"You can take your call, Jane," he murmurs grumpily from beside me without taking his eyes off his phone.

"It can wait."

"Take the damn call." He sounds agitated when my phone begins buzzing again.

If I pick it up, I'll have to go to her. I can't ever say no because if I do, something could happen. The guilt quickly outweighs my dignity as I finally answer. "Hey, Mom. What's going on?" I say calmly, not to give away the panic building inside.

"It's your father, Jane," she says through tears. "He's having some sort of episode." That's what she calls his alcohol abuse and the physical abuse it induces. Like he has mental issues when really, he's just a drunken abusive prick. "I can't get him to calm down." I can hear him banging on a door and yelling in the background.

"Mom, I'm at work. I can't help you right now." Regret instantly gnaws at me from the inside. I take a glance at Donavon, and he doesn't seem to be paying my phone call any attention. I hear my father banging on the door again threatening to break it down if she doesn't open it. Naturally, I give in like I always do. "I'll be there as soon as I can. Just don't open the door, okay?"

My mom sniffles into the phone. "Please hurry."

Grinding my teeth together, I exhale noisily through my nose. "Just stay put. I'll be there soon."

I hang up the phone and look to Donavon. Shame painting my cheeks and neck. "Um, Mr. Waldorf, I have a family emergency that I need to take care of."

"Give Ron the address," he says with his focus still on his phone.

"But it's in the opposite direction. You can drop me off here and I can get a car."

He sighs as if annoyed with me. "Just give Ron the damn address, Jane. You can grab a car on your way back."

I lean forward to give Ron my parents' address. "Thank you," I say quietly to Donavon. Presumably he says nothing back.

We turn around and not even ten minutes later, my mom is calling again. "Mom, I'm on my way. I should be there in a few minutes."

She's hysterically crying now and blubbering incoherently.

My teeth ache from gritting them. I am so tired of this shit. She needs to call the fucking cops, not her twenty-two-year-old daughter to help deflect his drunken temper. "I said I'll be there soon," I growl and hang up, ready to throw the phone out the window.

"Everything okay?" Donavon's voice is surprisingly gentle.

I look over at him and find him watching me with concern. I give him a tight smile. "It will be. I'm so sorry for this."

I watch out the window anxiously chewing on my bottom lip the entire rest of the way. As soon as the car stops in front of my parent's brownstone, I throw the door open. "I'll be back at the office as soon as I can." I bolt for the front door as soon as I step out of the vehicle, mentally preparing myself for the shit show.

TEN

Donavon

Something isn't sitting right with me.

I could hear what sounded like her mother through the phone. I couldn't make out what she was saying, but I could hear that she was frantic and maybe even hysterical. Then Jane instructed for her not to open the door. If her mother was in trouble, shouldn't she have called the police?

I don't tell Ron to drive away like I should. Instead, I tell him to wait as I climb out of the car and head towards the front door. There's no need to strain my hearing to make out the fight that's going on inside. I'm on high alert when a man begins shouting and I can faintly hear Jane's voice under it. I act on pure instinct.

The door isn't locked and easily gives way when I try to open it. What I walk into has me charging like a bull, black rimming my vision as I see blood. I witness in slow motion as Alfred Donahue raises his hand and swings, colliding it with the side of Jane's beautiful face. Making her head snap to the side. I lock on my target, every muscle in my body coiled with liquid hot rage.

"Don't you touch her!" I roar with an immense amount of ire.

Jane spins around and plants herself between me and her father. Her arms shooting out to stop me in my tracks. "Please, Donavon. Stop."

I only do so because I would have to use physical force to get to her father. "Jane, move the fuck aside," I seethe, quivering in delirium.

"Who the fuck are you?" her father shouts in sloppy English, sway-ing on his feet in his drunken state.

"Please, Donavon," she begs again and places a gentle hand on my chest. I glance down at it then up at her angelic face. A face pink on one side that sends me into a fit of rage all over again. "Please. This isn't any of your business. Just leave. I'll be fine." There's anger behind her words that is aimed at me.

My nostrils flare and I can feel the vein in the side of my neck throbbing. "The only way I am leaving is if you're with me." It's in no way a threat. I'll toss her ass over my shoulder if I have to.

She looks at me in astonishment. "I can't. I need to take care of this. It's really okay."

Before I get to argue with Jane, her father starts in again. "I said who the fuck are you?! Get the fuck out of my house!"

I keep my eyes trained on Jane as my fists shake at my sides. "I'm telling you right now, Jane. If you do not want me to put your father in an early grave, get your ass moving, or so help me..." I'm barely hanging on by a thread here. Seeing anyone lay a finger on Jane, I can't even form the proper words or emotions of how it makes me feel. Anger like I've never felt before. I could kill her father right here and now. No one touches her like that. No one hurts her.

Her face drops along with her hand. Immediately, I miss her touch. "Mom, I can't stay," she says regretfully looking her in the eye. "You should come, let Dad cool off for a bit."

I finally steal a glance at her mother as she cowers behind her pitiful husband who's barely able to stay upright and continuing to slur some empty threats. The woman can't even look at her own daughter. She's spineless and nothing like Jane who is a force.

"Mom, please," Jane presses desperately.

The right thing to do would be to demand that her mother leave with us, but I owe her mother nothing. She stood idly by and watched her husband strike her daughter. She called Jane when she should have called the police. She knew damn well what would happen by pulling Jane into the middle of her and her husband's squabbling. *Fuck her. Fuck the both of them.*

Her mother says nothing and doesn't make a move to leave with us, and I can feel Jane's guilt. Wrapping a protective arm around her shoulders, I steer us towards the door all the while her father screams in the background making absolutely no sense. I'm kind of hoping he'll try and come after us. *Just one fist to his aging face...*

The only thing keeping me from reacting is the woman tucked into my side. For her, I'll walk away peacefully.

We slip back into the car, and she immediately scoots away from me, turning her head to look out the window. "Let me see."

"I'm fine," she mutters.

"Jane." I gently place two fingers under her chin to turn her face. It's already red and swollen on one side, but it doesn't do a damn thing to taint her beauty. "It'll most likely bruise." My molars groan under the pressure.

Her face tenses in anger as she moves her chin out of my touch. "Why did you follow me?" she snaps.

"I had a feeling." I rub my hands over the tops of my thighs, unsure what to do with them.

"It wasn't any of your business. It still isn't any of your business."

I look at her with flaring nostrils. Rancor rising to the top. "I'm not the one you should be angry with, Jane. I didn't hit you, nor was I the one to put you in that position." *Why the fuck is she mad at me?*

She looks away again. "Just like I have no business being in your family home, you have no business being in mine."

I gape at her then look away shaking my head in disbelief. "You are unbelievable."

She's right. I shouldn't have pushed her to answer her phone in the first place. But the overwhelming need to protect her has my fists furling into balls of furor. The look on her face when her father raised her hand then struck her—she was hurt, but she wasn't shocked. It wasn't the first time this has happened. Thinking back to when she was ignoring her mother's phone calls, her whole demeanor changed. The anxiety was written all over her face and body language. She knew what she would be dealing with.

"How often does this happen?"

"I am not talking to you about this."

"Next time, you're calling the cops. Or I will," I say sternly without room for argument, but she still finds it.

"Then I won't answer the phone around you again."

My eyes burn into the back of her head with molten intensity. I'm used to owning complete rule. What I say goes. But this is new territory for me. She isn't my sister, and as my employee I have no say over her personal life. She isn't mine to dictate. So, I don't, and we ride the rest of the way back to the office in thick silence.

When we enter the building, Jane keeps her head down using her hair as a shield. I'm itching to shelter her with my arm, give her comfort and protection. I should give her the rest of the day off, but I need to care for her first.

We continue our silence the entire elevator ride. "Head inside my office and wait for me there," I say as soon as we step off on our floor. Not waiting for a response, I head to the small kitchen we have up here and grab some paper towels and fill it up with ice from the freezer.

When I return to the office I find Jane's back turned at the windows with her arms hugging herself. I place a hand tentatively at her hip. "Come sit," I say and lead her over to the leather couch.

I crouch down in front of her and gently place the icepack on her cheek. She winces, but doesn't protest. Time ticks by as our eyes lock, and all I can do is admire her beauty. She's so incredibly beautiful, and even more so up close. The unique color of her hair I obsess over. And her smile... God, her smile. Her perfect set of teeth and wide grin.

Those blue-green eyes of hers that pull me in deeper and deeper until I'm infinitely lost. Forever her captive.

"You don't have to do this," she says quietly and tries to replace her hand on the ice, but I refuse to move, so her hand sits there on top of mine.

Our faces are so close, I can feel her light pants hitting my face. "Tell me why you let this happen to you."

It's as if a bucket of ice water is dumped on her head and she yanks the icepack away from me to lean back on the couch, putting more space between us. "Stop looking at me like that," she demands.

Standing up to my full height, I hover over her. "Like what?"

"With pity. I don't need it. My father is a drunken asshole, but I don't need your pity." She glowers up at me, angry tears bubbling in her eyes.

"He doesn't deserve to be called a father."

"What should I call him then?"

"A donor. Your financial support as a child. A drunken bastard. Anything but father. And I am not looking at you with pity." I yank on the hem of my jacket and round my desk to sit and put even more distance between us, so I don't shake the woman.

"Then why are you looking at me like that? And treating me like this?"

I choke on indignance. "You mean why am I not being an asshole to you right now?" She narrows her eyes at me with terse lips. I full on laugh and shake my head. "Your parents really messed you up, haven't they? You are the only woman to ever complain about me being somewhat nice to them." It's either messed up or totally remarkable.

We both stare at each other for several heated moments, then her lips curl into a smile and she breaks the stare. "I'm sure my parents did mess me up."

Eleven

Jane

I make sure to get to the office today before Donavon. I'd rather him not have the chance to smash the shiny new screen on his desk.

I'm a little terrified of his reaction, but I know damn well this will only benefit him. I have an entire speech planned out and everything.

I occupy myself on my laptop when I hear him enter his office. Not even five seconds pass before he says, "What the hell is that?"

I give him a cheerful smile as he approaches. "Good morning to you too, Mr. Waldorf. That there is a monitor."

"What the hell is it doing on my desk?" he growls.

"It's yours, and before you throw a tantrum over it, please let me explain and show you why it's necessary." I close my laptop and stand up as he stands there with several feet between him and his desk as if the monitor is a snake about to lunge. "Come, and I'll show you." I round his desk and wait for him to do the same. "Can I see your laptop, please?"

He's reluctant, but he hands it over and allows me to hook it up to the monitor and I begin showing him how he can split screens with it instead of scrolling back and forth. I go on to explain how this will be much better for his posture and unless he wants to be an old man with a hunchback, he should head my advice and give it a chance. His neck will thank me later, though I expect nothing from him.

He's silent the entire time, I'm sure struggling with the anxiety of something new. But if he were too uncomfortable with it, he would be agitated and would have no qualms with telling me to fuck off and to take the monitor with me before he chucks it in the trash.

"It's also good to switch up between your track pad on your laptop and an actual mouse to help prevent any strain in your wrist." He replies with a grunting noise and begins messing with his new set up. I take the hint and know he needs a minute, so I leave him to it.

I leave praying it's not smashed into pieces when I get back. He's stubborn, but I honestly think I am one of very few that can talk some sense into him. As if I'm a professional trainer with the niche for crabby, stuck-in-their-ways men.

"Jane!" I look over my shoulder to see Nick jogging to catch up to me.

"Hey," I smile and stop for him. "How are you?"

We fall in step together. "Good, and you? I feel like I haven't seen you in a while."

He isn't wrong. I used to eat lunch with him and Madison, but not so much anymore. I'm practically glued to Donavon's side. Not by choice. Every time I walk out of his office, he calls me back for something else. But what did I think I was getting myself into?

I sigh, "I know, I miss seeing you and Madison at work."

He stops with me as we approach Donavon's door. I gave Donavon a good half hour to come to terms with a minor change to his office and routine. "We never did get that date."

I tuck some hair behind my ear. "I know. Sorry about that." And I really am. It's been too many months since I've gotten any, and working so closely with someone as attractive as Donovan isn't exactly helpful. The first thing I do when I get home is pull out my vibrator. Nick would definitely be a good lay. I wouldn't have time for a healthy relationship, but maybe he'd be up for something casual. "I've just been so crazy busy lately."

"What about this weekend? You think you could squeeze me in at all?" He shoves a hand in the pocket of his dress slacks with a charming smile.

Donavon will be out of town on business, so maybe I'll have a little time for myself. "Possibly Saturday, if you're free."

His smile grows. "Saturday then."

I return his smile and open my mouth to respond when Donavon comes out of his office abruptly. "Sorry, but she won't be available this weekend. She'll be on a business trip," he says not looking at either of us as he hands me a stack of paper. "Look these over. Study them."

I'm flabbergasted as I robotically accept the papers, and he walks away. *Was he listening at the door? And...what?*

"I guess maybe another time," Nick says and chuckles nervously, rubbing the scruff on his chin.

"I'm so sorry. I had no idea I was going with him."

He looks in the direction Donavon went in before turning his gaze back on me with accusation in his eyes. "Well, I'll see you around, Jane."

"Yeah..." I whisper as I turn into the office.

"What do you mean I'm going with you?" I ask as soon as he enters a few minutes later.

"You're my assistant. Why wouldn't you?" he says casually, eyes always elsewhere.

"*Executive assistant,*" I correct him like I always do. "And you didn't take me on the last one."

The cheeky bastard tries hiding a smirk, knowing the whole assistant verses executive assistant thing bothers me. "I didn't need you on the last one." He sits down behind his desk, thankfully with the monitor still in one piece.

"And you need me now?"

"Yes. How's your Spanish?"

"I'm fluent," I sigh in defeat, plopping down in the chair that has the shape of my ass imprinted on it. *I guess I'll have a chance of sex next year.* I open my laptop. "I'll book myself a room then."

"No need." I look up at him. "You booked me the two-bedroom suite, correct?"

"Yes..." I know I've lost.

"Good, I'd like you close and not have to track you down." He continues to avoid eye contact as he pretends to be busy.

Makes sense, I guess. Okay, this won't be awkward at all. We spend more time together than not, but this is different. Living together for a couple of days.

Since we'll be flying on his private plane, I don't need to book myself a plane ticket, so all that's left to do is pack and mentally prepare myself.

It's nearing the end of the day, and I close my laptop and stretch my arms above my head. My neck and back so stiff from sitting in this chair working over my laptop every day.

I steal a peek at Donavon eyeing his monitor, deep into work and it makes me smile in satisfaction. My bold gift he actually accepted.

I glance down at my watch and see that it's already six. "Oh, wow. I don't know how it got so late." I'm tired and now starving. Not to mention how much my back hurts. I stand up and begin to gather my things. "I'll see you tomorrow, Mr. Waldorf."

"We leave for Miami in the morning," he throws out there, still concentrated on his work.

"I thought you were planning on leaving in the evening."

He ignores my question. "Ron will be there to pick you up at seven AM."

I take a slow breath in and out of my nose. "Okay." I'm ready to leave when I realize Donavon must be hungry too. "Do you want me to grab you some dinner before I go?"

He looks at me as if shocked I would even offer. I am his EA and taking care of him is part of my job. "I'll be okay. I'll see you in the morning."

When I come out of the building, Ron is smiling as if waiting for me. "Good evening, Ms. Donahue. I was instructed to take you home."

I frown. "Did Mr. Waldorf insist?" I always walk or take the subway home.

"He did," Ron confirms and opens the door for me.

I glance up at the top of the building wondering why the sudden change? But I don't linger on the thought long as I let out a sigh and get into the car.

"Oh, my God. What smells so good?"

Kenna is in the kitchen cooking away when I get home. This girl spoils me. "Just in time!"

I join her and inspect the steaming skillets. "What are you making?"

"Fajitas."

"Oh, then I'll make us some margaritas."

"Perfect."

I start grabbing ingredients. "So, I'm leaving for Miami tomorrow morning for a business trip with your brother."

"How long will you be gone?"

"Till Saturday night, I think."

"You *think*?"

I get to work on squeezing limes. "Well, I'm not sure because your brother likes to spring things on me, apparently. I didn't even know I was going with him until today, and we were supposed to leave tomorrow evening, but now we're leaving in the morning. So, who knows?"

"He didn't tell you until today?"

"Yeah, it was weird. I was talking to that guy at work I told you about." She nods. "And we were actually making plans for that date we never got, and your brother popped up out of nowhere and was like *'Sorry, she can't make it. She'll be in Miami.'*" She giggles at my horrible Donavon impression.

"Are you serious?"

"Yes! So rude, right?"

"I need to have a talk with him. He has you working too much. I hardly see you and you should be able to go out on a date once in a while."

I scoff, "Good luck with that. I swear he likes having me around so much just to have someone to constantly torture."

She spins to face me. "Wait, he's not mean to you, is he?"

I want to laugh out loud. Instead, I shake my head. "No, he's fine. A huge grump, but he's not terrible." Truth is, he isn't as bad as he was to me in the beginning. Still no pleases or thanks yous but he's not demeaning me every chance he gets.

"Good. You tell me if he is though. I'll kick his ass."

I laugh at that. "I'll be sure to do that."

We catch up on life and work and Kenna's new love interest. It's nice to have a normal night in. "So, how's it going with Tom?"

"Good." She smiles. "I really like him."

"Yeah?"

She nods still grinning. "Like butterflies and fireworks."

I return her smile, genuinely happy for her. "When do I get to meet him?"

"You tell me! Tell Donavon to give you a damn night off."

I shrug. "Maybe if I tell him why I need the night off, he might let me."

"Tell him to tag along. We can double date." She waggles her eyebrows.

"I don't think so," I say dryly.

"You don't find my brother attractive?" She watches me carefully over her margarita as she sips it.

"I won't even try to lie to you and say that I don't. I'm not blind. But that would never happen."

"Why not?"

My mouth pops open. "What do you mean why not? I wouldn't even know where to start." She gives me a look, challenging me to go on. "Okay, for one: he's my boss. Two: he's your brother. Three: he's almost twice my age. And four: he's...*him*!"

She giggles. "Yeah, he's *him* for sure."

"Does he date at all?" She gives me a look. "I mean, he's at the office more than me and I don't even have the time to date."

"He's never brought anyone around, but I don't know what he does in his personal time."

"You've never met a girlfriend?"

She shakes her head. "Nope. Not that we know of."

"Like ever?"

"Not even in college. I mean, he's no virgin. When he was younger, supposedly he was a little hellion that indulged in a lot of partying."

"Really?" I ask genuinely surprised to hear that. I can't ever imagine Donavon 'partying'.

"Oh, yeah. I was only a few years old, so I don't remember that side of him, but I've been told. Who knows? Maybe he still does like to party, he's just better at hiding it now. You know, since he has a company to run and a reputation to uphold."

Could that be true? He's up all hours of the night and the morning, emailing me or texting me with work stuff. But maybe that's why he's still up... he has a beautiful woman in his bed next to him.

TWELVE

Donavon

The original plan was not to take Jane with me on this trip.

For days I went back and forth about it. I need a way to distance myself and break the dependency I have built on her. But truth is, I need her. I do not like traveling in any capacity. Temporarily living outside of the comforts of my own home and space leaves me on edge. I like my room a certain way, the bathroom, my meals, knowing who's been there.

But Jane has adapted to my quirks. With her presence, the compulsions are less nagging and less dominating. The incessant thoughts like a merry-go-round in my head are more tolerable. Her sitting across from me on the plane, I'm not so eager to get the trip over and done with so I can fly right back home. She could possibly be the amenity that gives me the complacency I am always missing.

Jane passed out less than an hour into the flight. She was going over some papers while her eyes grew heavier and heavier until she could no longer fight it.

"Can I get you anything, Mr. Waldorf?" the flight attendant asks, and I glance over at Jane across from me to make sure she didn't wake her.

"No, I'm fine. But could you bring Ms. Donahue a blanket?"

A few moments later she comes back with the blanket, and I take it from her, not wanting her to accidentally wake Jane. I feel bad for the way her head is lolled to the side, but a sleep-deprived Jane is a grumpy

Jane. I carefully cover her with it, and it takes me a second to withdraw myself from proximity and sit back.

Willing my focus to my phone instead of the sleeping beauty in front of me, my gaze is still drawn to her every few minutes. How peaceful she is when she's not glaring at me or rolling her eyes or doing whatever she can to run away from me.

Jane sleeps until the plane touches down and jostles her awake. "Oh, my God." She sits up. "I can't believe I slept that whole time." She wipes at her mouth. "Oh, God, I was drooling," she murmurs and inspects her shoulder. "Well, that's embarrassing," she mutters making my lips fight a smile. "Did you get me a blanket?"

"The flight attendant did."

"Oh. Right."

When we get to the resort, I let Jane go ahead to the front desk to check us in as I hang back to take a phone call. I overhear her raising her voice slightly and tune out the person on the phone. It seems there's been an issue with our reservation and while my normal reaction would be to take over the situation, I can't help but find entertainment in watching her take initiative. "We're all set," she says with a satisfying grin as someone comes behind her to grab our bags. "We'll be receiving a nice bottle of champagne for the small inconvenience."

We fall into step together. "And you wondered why I wanted you as my assistant."

"*Executive* assistant," she says through her teeth. "And we both know why you wanted me." She pauses, and I stiffen a little. "At first, it was to torture me. Now, it's because you need me."

"I do?"

"Yes," she chuckles. "Don't even try and deny the fact that you're entirely dependent on me." The tensity in my shoulders is back. "You were fine before, but you can't possibly cope without me." She laughs hoping I'll join her, but I can't. The accuracy of her assumptions is absolute. Thinking about a life without Jane now—it's unimaginable.

"Uh-huh," I humor her.

I allow Jane to walk inside the suite before me as the bellhop trails us with our bags. "Oh, my God," she gasps looking around. "This is beautiful."

I tip the man and dismiss him, leaving us alone. Jane goes to the sliding glass doors and opens them, stepping outside. I watch her for a moment as she basks in the sun. Her hair lightly billowing from the breeze coming off the ocean. She's so pretty, it's almost infuriating.

I go and join her. "You can have a few hours for yourself if you'd like. We can meet up later to go over preparations for tomorrow."

She looks up at me grinning. A real grin. Her eyes squinting and her wide smile showing off her perfect teeth. "If I'd like? Of course, I'd like."

I head back inside, grabbing my bag and going to my room. I toe off my shoes after reorganizing everything to accommodate me when I hear a moan coming from her room across the suite. Her door is wide open, and she makes another noise. Out of curiosity, I cross the open space and stand in her doorway. I watch in amusement as she rolls around on her bed, messing up the covers and pillows.

"Oh, my God," she moans again, bringing my cock to life. "I miss luxury bedding. It's like sleeping on clouds."

"Something wrong with yours?"

"Nothing really." She looks up at me from the bed. Her face a little flush and her hair askew, looking freshly fucked. She hugs a pillow. "I miss having money," she giggles.

"With the amount I pay you, I'm sure you can invest in some new bedding."

"I have student loans and other bills to pay." She sits up and shrugs her shoulders. "Plus, I'm perfectly fine with what I have. I have a different perspective on life now. Needs and wants are a lot more definitive."

I don't respond as I turn to leave. I would love nothing more than to spoil her rotten. Fill her room with the most luxurious pillows and blankets. Have a gift sent to her every single day to watch as her cheeks blush every time she opens them.

It was a pleasure for me to be able to spoil my family, but this is different.

I hear a knock on the main door and get up to go answer it, then halt in my steps right outside my room. Jane beat me to it...in a bathing suit. I'm too entranced by the gorgeous body on display to check who has arrived. Those loose blouses and skirts or slacks at work do well hiding the perfection underneath. Her breasts sit high up on her chest, plump, and filling out the top of her suit. They look good enough to fuck.

I can imagine her plush lips wrapped around my cock, giving me a coy smile around it. Then I'd slip out of her wet heat, my cock lubed up with her saliva, so I can glide it between her breasts until I come all over them.

My cock throbs with urgency.

"Thank you," she says closing the door and now holding an ice bucket with a bottle sticking out of it. "If you need me, I'll be out there enjoying a nice glass of champagne." She grins. "Would you like one?"

I shake myself from my dirty thoughts. "Maybe later," I mutter and go to close myself in my room.

I try dousing my pulsing rod with cold water in the shower, but it does nothing to deter my arousal. Gripping my cock tightly in one hand, I fist it and hiss at the sensitivity. Giving into the vulgar thoughts of Jane. Images of her in her floral bikini, exposing so much of her delicate skin, spins behind my closed lids. Those large breasts, wide mouth, feminine hips, long legs I can see wrapped around my head. I wouldn't know what to do with her first.

Fantasizing about thrusting inside a warm cunt isn't an aberrant thought, though it's startling when there is a distinct face that goes with it. I can imagine myself fucking her, only her. No third part involved. Jane laid back on the bed, her legs spread, a coy smile to her pretty face as she touches herself.

Fuck.

I come harder than I have since I was a teenager using my own hand.

I'm indecisive after I get out of the shower on whether or not to leave my room. Hoping I am fully satiated for the rest of the day if I'm going to see Jane again. Giving into those devious thoughts, I throw on a pair of swim trunks and exit my room. Grabbing myself a glass of champagne, I go ahead and grab the bottle too before joining Jane out on our private patio. She's splayed out on a lounger, soaking up the hot sun.

I refill her empty glass then sit down on the lounger next to hers. It creaks a little when I do and her eyes pop open. "Mind if I join you?" She gapes at my naked torso, speechless. Her eyes ogling me, I know I should've stayed in my room. "Jane?"

She rapidly blinks and looks away. "Sorry," she mutters. "Of course, you can join me, Mr. Waldorf."

I swing my legs up to recline back. "How about for this trip you call me Donavon."

I can feel her studying the side of my face before looking forward again, to my surprise not saying anything about the last time I chewed her head off for calling me by my first name. "I haven't been to the beach in years."

"I haven't either."

"Really? Why? I mean, I know why I haven't been on a vacation in years, but why haven't you?"

"Haven't made time for it." Even sitting next to Jane, not having my phone or my laptop in hand has me antsy, though tolerable.

"That's pretty sad. What's the point of being your own boss if you're not taking advantage of time being your own?"

"Taking time off would mean putting someone else in charge in my absence."

"And you don't trust anyone enough for that."

"It's not that I don't trust anyone…"

"Okay. You can't *rely* on anyone to fill your shoes."

My lips stretch and I reach for her glass to push it at her. "Thank you," she says accepting it and our fingers touch. She retracts the glass too abruptly for my liking, and I wonder if there's more to it than just my presence. She sits up and spins to fold her legs up on her chair. Her knees spread open. *Good God.* "Can I ask you something?" I nod avoiding her direction. Knowing her thighs are open like that. "Do you date at all?"

This makes me look at her, straining my gaze to remain on her face. Not an ounce of makeup on and in the natural spotlight of the bright sun, and she's flawless.

I have yet to find one thing I dislike about her. Which is inconceivable. I've tried dating, but even when I was still a young adult, the smallest thing would aggravate me to the point of anger or something I couldn't possibly ignore. Her *perfection* is the only thing that is aggravating.

"Do I date at all?"

"Yeah, I mean, you work more than I do, and I don't even have time to date."

If she's looking for me to feel sorry for her lackluster sex life, she'll be deeply disappointed. Something about her not with other men is relieving.

"No, I don't date," I say flatly, looking away.

"Don't you want to?"

"I'm fine without it."

"Don't you ever get…lonely?"

I laugh at the subtle innuendo and drain my glass. "I said I don't date. Not that I don't have sex."

"Oh." She grows quiet and looks away.

"What about you? Do you want to date?"

I see her shrugging out of the corner of my eye. "I don't want a relationship or anything, at least not right now. But I do get lonely."

Fuck me. My cock rouses to life as if I didn't just drain it.

I notice her glass is empty and top both of ours off. "Oh, if I drink any more, I won't be any good for work later."

"Then good thing your boss is giving you the rest of the day off."

She looks at me with wide eyes. "You are?"

I nod. "I might just take the day off too." I wait for the panic to overwhelm me, but when I feel Jane's brilliant smile aimed at me, it never comes.

"And what about prepping for tomorrow?"

"We'll wing it." I sip my drink.

She continues to stare at me suspiciously, then she lays back on the lounger again. "Well then, thank you, Donavon."

Silence veils us, and as always, it isn't uneasy.

"After we finish this bottle, want to go for a swim?" Her voice is quiet and unsure.

"The pool or the ocean?"

The first day I have taken off work in years, and it was exactly what I didn't know I needed. Spending time with Jane outside of the office is enjoyable. She makes great company. She doesn't prattle on, needing to fill the silence and to talk just to talk. When we are silent, it's comfortable. Not that it was ever uncomfortable for me, but my silence can be more intimidating than when I am chastising someone. She seems content with it.

I'm unsure how it's possible, but every time I look at her, I am astounded by her beauty. I can't believe I was judging her based on her worthless father, thinking she would be anything like that scum. Jane's beauty also radiates from within. She's patient with me, anticipates every want and need. I know she's only doing her job, but I can't fight the satisfaction I get being on the receiving end of her nurturing side.

The day flies by all too quickly and the sun is already going down. "Oh, my goodness. I am so stuffed." She groans and leans back in the chair on our patio. "Good thing I won't be getting into a bikini tomorrow."

I snort and glance over at her on instinct. The woman couldn't have a more feminine shape to her. Pretty sure everything she eats goes straight to her hips and breasts. Fuck, I cannot stop staring at them. Her skin is already kissed by the sun, and I imagine pulling the small fabric off her body to see the tan lines it's left her.

My jaw tenses when I tear my eyes from her perfect figure, trying to focus on anything else. Then she rolls over to her side, and I know her breasts are pushed together, and my cock rises.

"You should do this more often," she says.

"What's that?"

"Take a vacation. You look good when you're relaxed. Not so tightly wound and one straw away from breaking."

I smile and shake my head. "Well, don't get used to it."

"That's too bad," she sighs, and I cave, turning my head to look back at her. Our eyes lock and her smile fades, but she doesn't break the stare. There's a moment there between us. I have no idea what it is. Never have I felt so relaxed looking at anyone in the eye like this. It's always made me restless. That's why it's easier for me to act as if I'm too big of an asshole to look at someone when speaking. The reason is, I can't. But looking into Jane's eyes, I feel like I can clear my mind. She has my mind spinning, but it's not on the next hour or the next business meeting or the next email or phone call. It's just here in this moment.

She shakes her head and diverts her eyes as if snapping herself from the trance we were both spellbound into. As if remembering where she is. "Well, it's getting late."

Her and I swing our legs off the loungers and stand up in tandem. Our bodies only inches away from being pressed together. It takes her by surprise, and she tries to take a step back but bumps into the lounger. My hand flinches out to grip her hip to steady her. The movement now has our bodies compressed with my erection pushed against her lower stomach.

Those blue-green eyes brighten, and she gasps. I don't move a muscle. I can't. If I do...

I slowly lean my head in some. Just enough to crowd her and catch her scent. "Run along, Jane, or I'll have you pinned underneath me on this chair," I say tightly, grasping at any restraint I can muster up.

She licks her lips, hypnotizing me. "What if I want that?" she whispers.

My eyes jump back up to hers and my hand flexes on her hip. No matter how much I want this, I can't. I can't do intimacy, and I also cannot lose Jane. And that's what would happen if I act on this. "I said run, Jane."

She stares up at me blinking. Five times. She blinks five times before turning her body making me drop my hand from her feminine curve. "Goodnight, Donavon," she says in a breathy tone. *Is she trying to provoke me into dragging her ass to my bedroom for the night?*

I hold my tongue. Not trusting myself with words or actions at this moment. I let her walk inside as I shamelessly watch her backside the entire way.

I swear I can still feel the heat of her skin in my hand as it flexes and furls at my side while I stand there motionless.

I have never denied myself anything. Never felt the need to. And Jane isn't only something I want, she's an obsession. Yes, I've had to redirect my obsessions when they were unhealthy, but Jane is anything but bad for me. Why should I deny myself? I cannot think of a single good reason as to why I should.

I want Jane.

It's time I admit to myself that she's mine.

Then soon, she'll see it too.

Thirteen

Jane

Donavon's mild temperament only lasted that one day.

I hardly slept at all that night, thinking and fantasizing about him pinning me to the chair like he threatened. But like the heated moment at his family's house in the bathroom, he acted as if it never happened, and I had no choice but to do the same.

Once we woke up Saturday morning, he was right back to his restive self. Right back to a strict schedule with demanding requests while still micromanaging every single thing. But the images of Donavon shirtless with sweat trickling down his impeccable torso stained in my brain kept my mood up.

I wanted to lick the sweat right off his body. Follow the trails of it and continue downwards. *Damnit, I am so horny.* I could come from my pants being too tight these days. I thought it was the alcohol I'd been sipping on all day, but I felt like he kept checking me out. I swore it was all in my head. Then he touched me, and I even felt the large bulge straining his swim trunks.

But what if it was all in my head? The thought of Donavon Waldorf; wealthy entrepreneur, intelligent, family man, New York's most eligible bachelor, and the city's finest man to ever walk the streets; looking at *me.* Wanting *me.* A woman seventeen years younger than him that comes from a fallen empire? It's ludicrous. No, in any version of that situation he will always be the sun and I will always be Icarus, flying too close and always getting burned. It was just his way of messing with me, his display of authority and dominance. Reminding me how he holds all the power.

"Don't worry about coming into work tomorrow, Jane," he says from next to me in the back of the town car on our way back from the airport.

A sudden panic rises within me. "What? Why?"

He gives me a slight glance with delight in his dark eyes. "Because you worked all weekend."

It's instant relief, and I feel a bit silly thinking he was going to fire me. I should want him to fire me. Of course, the job pays well, and I honestly do like working for him. Not just working, but being around him all the time. It muddles my brain and has these childish fantasies keeping me awake at night.

"I always work weekends."

He smirks and faces away. "Well, you've earned the day off."

"Is it because you're getting sick of me?" I ask playfully.

He fights his smile this time. "Yes, I am sick of you. But that isn't why I am giving you the day off."

"By day, do you really mean I don't have to come into the office, but you're still going to send me a shit ton of emails and texts?"

"I won't contact you unless it's an emergency."

I don't believe him for a second. "Seriously?"

"Seriously."

"You sure you can survive without me?" I tease. "Do you even remember how to get yourself lunch anymore?"

"I'm sure Maggie will remember how to."

My mouth falls open in aghast. "So, you never needed me to do those things?" He doesn't respond and I shake my head in amusement.

I am so getting laid tonight. I'm not typically a one-night-stand kind of girl, but that's all I have time for these days. It's all I really want, to be honest. I also haven't seen Bonnie in forever. She'll be thrilled to hear that I have a day off and come out with me.

I pull up my messages on my phone and begin texting the girls.

Me: Ladies! I have tomorrow off, and I am in need of a drink tonight. Dinner and bar?

BonBon: Hell yes! About damn time! What's the point of living in the city if you don't enjoy it?!

Kenna: Yes! Who needs sleep anyways?!

Madison: What Bonnie and Kenna said! I'm in!

Bonnie texts me separately.

BonBon: I have to ask. Are you banging 'Mr. Waldorf'?

My cheeks heat with too many emotions and I glance over at Donavon to make sure he isn't paying my phone screen any attention.

Me: No, I am not banging my boss. And who says banging anymore? Loser.

BonBon: I say banging, and I'm cool, which makes it still cool.

BonBon: I'm packing an overnight bag as we speak. Get ready to hoe it up! I've been in a wicked dry spell and I'm ending it tonight!

I bite back a giggle.

Me: Girl, same. You know it's been too long for me.

BonBon: How many months are we going on now?

I send her an angry emoji face and the finger.

BonBon: Like a year now?

Me: Ha ha. Hilarious. No. Though it feels like it.

BonBon: So, why don't you just bang your boss? You have to want to. He's the hottest guy in all of New York.

BonBon: Oh, the things I would do to that man...

Me: Stop! I'm literally sitting next to him right now!

BonBon: If I were you, I'd be sitting ON him.

I choke on a laugh and cough a little into my fist. "You alright?" Donavon asks from beside me.

I nod. "I'm fine. I'm just talking to my friend."

Me: I hate you.

BonBon: Well, if you're not going to fuck the sexiest man ever, then you should invite that guy Nick from work you told me about. You said he was pretty hot, right?

Me: Yes.

BonBon: Tell him to bring some hot friends too.

I agree to invite Nick out and tell him to bring a friend or two, and he doesn't take long to respond telling me to give him the time and place. I'm genuinely looking forward to hanging out with him. He might not have the intense effect on me that Donavon does, but who can really compare?

I bite my lip smiling when Donavon draws my attention. "Jane?"

"Hm?" I look over at him and find him watching me with his eyebrows drawn in.

"We're home."

I look past him to see out his window that we're in fact in front of my building. I didn't realize the car stopped moving. "Oh! Sorry."

He studies me closely as I gather my things. "Everything okay?"

I nod my head grinning. "I'm great. Thanks again for the day off."

His forehead relaxes. "Already made plans?"

"Sure did." My door opens. "I guess I'll see you Tuesday." I slip out of the car and take my bag from Ron, thanking him and making a beeline inside, afraid he might take it all back and tell me to be at the office tomorrow morning.

The apartment is quiet when I get in. Kenna said she was at her boyfriend's but will head home soon. I greet Luna and head back to my bedroom. As soon as I drop my bag, I spot the two large boxes waiting for me at the end of my bed.

I check to make sure they're mine, which they are, though I don't remember ordering anything. Mistake or not, I'm opening them. I recognize the name of the department stores on each box and grin from ear to ear knowing that whatever it is, it's good.

I tear into the first box and find two luxurious pillows with a note attached.

Since your asshole boss works you so hard, you should at least get a good night's rest.

Yes, I know what you call me when you think I'm not around.

Donavon

A grin somehow takes over my entire face and those butterflies swarm, taking up all of my insides. I rip open the next box, which is just as large, and I cannot believe what I find. More luxury bedding, and in my favorite color; Dusty rose. It's not a common color and I have no idea how he would know it's my favorite. Maybe he asked Kenna? Either way, I can't believe he did this.

It means nothing; I know that. He has a nice side. The way he is with his family proves that. A nice gesture is not completely unimaginable. Out of character yes, but not unreasonably so.

I'm just finishing up making my bed when I hear Kenna get home. I'm ironing out the comforter with my hands when she appears in my doorway. "Oh, you got new bedding?"

So, she didn't know…

"My boss actually did."

Her eyes widen in surprise, and she comes in to run her hand along the soft fabric. "Don got you this?" I nod, trying to avoid looking at her. But her eyes are singing holes into me.

"Don't look at me like that," I mutter. "It doesn't mean anything. I only mentioned how amazing the pillows and stuff were at the resort and I guess he felt like doing something nice for me." I shrug. "For being the best executive assistant ever."

"First of all." She lays back on my bed and I join her. "You're the first assistant, executive or not, he's ever had. And second," she rolls onto her side to face me, "he doesn't get his employees gifts."

"I'm sure he has," I argue weakly, not wanting to think that I'm in some way special.

"I'm telling you, Jane," she says sternly. "He doesn't."

I roll my head to the side to meet her gaze. "I can't believe he's never really had an assistant. It's hard to think about him doing everything himself. I know Benjamin works for him, but it seems like all he does for him is do most of the traveling." And now I know why.

Most people must think he's a neat freak, but it's beyond that. He has OCD on top if his anxiety. After some research, I found that those two together can be crippling. I don't think his family knows though, and it's not my story to tell. It's obvious he does his best to try and hide it, pretending it doesn't exist, so it isn't my place to bring it up. Mental health is important and nothing to be ashamed of, but it can be a sensitive subject.

"If you haven't noticed, he has difficulty trusting people."

"Do you think that's why he hasn't had a serious relationship?"

"I'm sure it's part of it."

When Donavon first began having me check emails for him, he would continue to change his password, so that I would have to have him log me in every single time. It wasn't until a week ago that I went to log in, and it didn't tell me the password had been changed, and it hasn't since.

It doesn't mean anything though, right?

"I'm pretty sure my brother has a thing for you," Kenna says breaking me from my thoughts.

"What! No, he doesn't," I say defensively, and she bites back a grin. "Stop it," I mutter and face the ceiling, refusing to let her get into my head. God knows he's already gotten in there.

"Yes, he does, Jane." I shake my head stubbornly. "Okay, then explain this. How much time do you spend in his office a day?" I don't answer because she knows the answer to that question. I've bitched and complained to her several times about it. Sugar coating it, of course. "Exactly. Donavon does not do well with his personal space invaded. I'm pretty sure he has social anxiety, though he would never admit it." He definitely does, but again, I keep my opinions to myself. "You being in his office all the time—his precious office at his precious company, it speaks volumes." As if she isn't muddling my brain enough, she continues. "How often were you in his hotel room this weekend?" she questions in a presuming tone.

"I wasn't," I murmur. "We had a two-bedroom suite," I say just above a whisper.

"What!" she shrieks, sitting up abruptly. "Oh, my God!" She flops back laughing, finding way too much humor in this than necessary. "Don is totally into you!"

"No, he's not!" I shout half-heartedly. My cheeks aching from fighting back a goofy grin. "Stop it." I give her a swat with the back of my hand.

"Jane!" She rolls over to her belly, but I refuse to face her. "How can you not see it? He hates being around people for any length of time, including his own damn family. Why do you think he's never had an assistant last more than a couple weeks? And why do you think he has meetings anywhere but in his office? So, he can make a quick escape." I mull over her words, but no! I won't let her confuse me like this. "And sharing a suite? He doesn't even let people inside his home!"

I turn my head. "Seriously?" She nods. "So, you've never been inside his house?"

She rolls her eyes. "Of course, I have. But not invited, and it's obvious when I quickly wear out my welcome only after minutes of being there."

I look away. "Well, I've never been there."

"Yet," she teases. "And this?" She gestures to the bed. "I'm not kidding, Jane. He likes you."

I sigh. "Maybe he's grown a soft spot for me, Kenna, but your brother does not see me in that way."

"Why not?"

I choke on a laugh. "Why not? Your brother is..." I wave my hands around trying to find the right words. But it's ineffable. "He's..." I try again. "He's Donavon Waldorf!"

"And...?"

I shake my head. "And I'm just me."

"Jane, do you know what I said to him when he hired you?" I don't answer and wait patiently. "I told him he better not fuck you."

"Ew, why would you even say that?" I mutter—not at all thinking about fucking him.

"Because you're stunning!" I chew on my lip, not always receptive of compliments. "And yes, he can get basically anyone he wants, but I don't know. I had a feeling or something. Like if he had a type, it would be you. But I don't think he just wants to fuck you." She pauses and we both sit up. "I really think he likes you."

I sigh and stand up to look for something to occupy myself with. "It doesn't matter anyway. He's my boss and your brother. I would never go there. So, let's just put a pin in it."

"For now," she says grinning and walks away as if she didn't drop a bomb.

I'm already insanely attracted to him in practically every extent. Even when he's an asshole, he still has my skin tingling. I could go on and on about every flaw in his personality, but I could still name twice as many qualities about him that I happen to really appreciate and find amazing. Pros heavily outweighing every con to the point they are irrelevant.

It's bad enough that fantasies flood my mind every time we're in the same space. Now I have his sister here making those fanciful thoughts ceaseless.

Could there be any truth to it?

Fourteen

Donavon

It was an instant regret of mine to give Jane the day off.

The thought of not seeing her, not having her there, not able to rely on her...that anxious edge is back and sharper than ever. Piercing through my chest like a jagged knife. I didn't realize how quickly she would make plans until the flush in her face while talking to whomever via text making this ugly feeling churn in my gut. I can't help but to think it was that blonde headed boy that continues to sniff around her at the office.

It's after nine and I pull up the tracking app I have on my phone that's connected to hers for the umpteenth time in the last half hour. She's finally on the move, heading further into the city. I'm irrationally tempted to text Kenna and ask what she's up to tonight, to fish for some information, but it wouldn't go without suspicion. I'd only expose myself as a man obsessed.

It started that first day I saw her on the elevator. I assumed it was something I could fuck out of my system. That I needed to fuck *her* out of my system. But I do not fuck employees, nor do I fuck women seventeen years younger than me. So, I tried to counteract my cravings by fucking more women than usual. Remind myself of the real beast inside. The one that's selfish and content with touch deprivation. I use women to assist me in getting off. I don't crave sex, I crave the arousal that is painfully difficult to procure.

But nothing could satiate that carnal need that Jane has awakened in me. It's beyond insatiable. I yearn for her physical touch. One hand on my cock could have my thick rod throbbing, my balls ready to jump up.

My preference has always been at least two women putting on a show for me to get me started, then I would let them finish me off. Mouth, pussy, ass. Didn't matter. As long as I was already close.

I want Jane, and only Jane. I want to idolize her, explore every piece of her, taste every inch of her. And I want her to see me as me. Not only the surly businessman that portrays apathy, but the mess inside that feels too much. I want her to know me and accept me for it.

But who could?

I'm hardly comfortable in my own skin, how could I expect someone else to endure my mental instability?

Jane is turning me into a man I'm unfamiliar with, and it honestly scares the fuck out of me. Yet I keep asking for it.

It's now going on one in the morning and I am no less immersed in tracking her whereabouts as she's once again on the move. She was first at a restaurant, then moved onto a small nightclub around eleven. Still no knowledge of who she's with. It's the most frustrating thing of it all. I know she isn't the type of woman to feel comfortable going home with a man she just met on the first night, but somehow knowing she might be out with that one intern is a far worse scenario because it could possibly turn into something.

She seems to be heading in the direction of her home and I pray that she's going home with only my sister. But minutes tick by and the car she is in takes her past her place. That fucking instant paranoia has my nails biting into my palms and my heart thundering in my chest. She could be going anywhere. She could be inebriated and abducted for all I know.

Then it dawns on me. She's headed in her parents' direction.

Without much thinking, I pull up her contact and call her. She lets it ring until I'm sent to voicemail, which only has me even more peeved. I immediately dial her again, and she answers after three rings. "Hello?" she answers way too cheerfully.

"Jane, where are you?"

"Um, out? Well, I was out, but now I'm headed home."

My fists tighten to the point my joints creak. "Don't lie to me," I scathingly snap, grabbing my keys, and heading for the door.

"What?" she squeaks.

"I know you're headed to your parents' house."

"Oh, my God, Donavon! Are you following me?!" she shrieks incredulously.

I pause for half a moment to think. "Kenna told me."

"Oh," she says sounding with a little embarrassment. If she only knew the truth, she'd be horrified knowing that her boss is practically stalking her. "Look, I'm fine. My mom said that my father is already passed out and—"

"Turn your ass around, Jane," I growl, still riding the elevator down.

"Donavon, this is none of your business."

"Turn around or I will come there myself to make sure you do," I threaten, and not lightly. "And your safety is most certainly my business." I hit the ground floor.

"How do you figure?"

"You're my assistant and my sister's best friend."

"Executive assistant," she exasperatingly says making one side of my mouth tick.

"Do I need to come get you myself, or will you be a good girl and turn around?" She's silent. "Jane," I growl her name as I enter the car garage under my building.

"I don't know how to say no to her," she says quietly.

"Now could be a good time to start."

"What do I say?"

I stop outside of my car. "You tell her to grow the fuck up and start acting like a mother and not the child."

She giggles and I cannot say how it makes me feel. "I can't say that."

"Yes, you can, Jane. You've showed me your backbone time and time again. I know you have one. It's time you show it to her."

She's quiet for too long. I open my car door and she finally responds, "I can't."

"Jane, you can, and you will. Tell the driver to turn around, or I will deal with your mother myself," I seethe, now sitting in my car.

"Fine," she snaps. "I'll go home." She pulls the phone away from her mouth and I can hardly make out her mumbling, hopefully telling the driver to change directions. "I'm going home. Happy?"

"Straight home."

"Yes, sir," she mocks, and I actually smile.

"Good girl," I say lowly, and I swear I can hear her smile through the phone.

"Any other demands, Mr. Waldorf?" she says in a sultry voice I've only ever dreamt of.

Yes, get your beautiful ass over here, so I can put you over my knee and—

"Just get home safely."

"Yes, sir. Goodnight, Mr. Waldorf."

"Goodnight, Jane."

I smile down at the phone after we hang up. Rapidly blinking to clear the glamour I was stuck in, I head back up to my condo. All the while checking my phone to make sure she's heading home and pleased to see that she is.

Me: If Jane asks, tell her you told me about her leaving to go to her parents.'

Kenna: What? Why?

Me: Just do it, okay?

Kenna: Only if you admit you like her ☺

Me: Don't start with me. Just do it.

Kenna: You first...

I don't say anything.

Kenna: Fine. I'll make it easy for you.

Kenna: If you don't like her, then say so. If you do like her—like I know you do—then say nothing.

I stare down at my phone debating on what to do here. My thumb hovers over the keyboard. Kenna is the last person to provoke. She'll create this elaborate romance that I'm not even sure is possible.

Kenna: I knew it!

Kenna: If she asks, I will tell Jane that I told you how she left us and her hot date because her mom wouldn't stop calling.

Kenna: Have a good night, brother!

Me: Be safe.

Hot date? I'm going to have to do something about that. Or maybe it's time for me to finally claim what I know is mine.

Fifteen

Jane

I'm walking into work Tuesday morning feeling so refreshed.

Bonnie being the best friend that she is, called into work sick so that we could have an entire day together. We went shopping, got our hair done, got pedicures. It was an amazing day off, but Donavon was on my mind the entire time.

He called me, furious knowing I was going to my mom's after he tried to forbid me to put myself in that position again. Like I was his to control. It only feeds those fanciful thoughts Kenna already put inside my head. That Donavon might actually have feelings for me.

The couple of heated moments we've had, the protectiveness he exuded when my father hit me.

No. He's protective over me because he's protective by nature. And those heated moments, most likely all in my head. This is how he is with his family, and by working so closely with him and being close with his sister, I'm almost like family too.

If Donavon wanted me, he would make it happen. That's the kind of man he is. What he wants, he goes for it, and he gets it. He isn't the type to hesitate and he'll bulldoze over anything in his way.

Breezing right into his office with his latte in hand, I put all feelings aside. "Morning, Mr. Waldorf."

"Morning, Jane," he murmurs and glances up to accept the latte from me. I go to sit down and he stops me. "Don't bother sitting." He stands up and buttons his suit jacket. "Come with me, I have something to show you. And bring your things." I frown and follow him out of his office. He glances over at me as I walk beside him. "Did you do something to your hair?"

"I got it trimmed yesterday." I can't believe he would notice that. *I* hardly do.

"It looks nice," he says without looking at me.

Damnit. Those butterflies. "Thank you."

After making a right out of his office, we stop at the next door, and I almost gasp. There's a new shiny plaque next to the closed door that reads, *Jane Donahue - Executive Assistant*. I gape at him, and he opens the door, letting me enter first.

I'm speechless as I make a step inside and take in the new office. It's the prettiest room I have ever seen. All the décor is chic and feminine with light colors and creams and plants scattered throughout. Some at the windows, some on the desk, a large one in one corner. Then I notice the array of fresh cut flowers in a crystal vase. I'm too overwhelmed to acknowledge it and the note attached with him hovering in the room.

I turn to Donavon, wide-eyed and tongue-tied. He's hovering at the door with his hands in his pockets. "Is this really for me?"

He nods his head. "If you don't like something, feel free to change it. I had a decorator come in over the weekend, but I can have her come back and make adjustments."

I look down at the plant on my desk and finger a leaf, knowing he did more than that. He either talked to Kenna about what I might like, or he knows me a lot better than I ever thought. "I love it." I wouldn't change a thing. I face him with a smirk and plant my hands on my hips. "Is this your nice way of kicking me out of your office?"

He lets himself smile, not fighting it like he always does. God forbid anyone see his gorgeous smile. It's panty melting. "I knew you couldn't be comfortable sitting in that chair hunched over your laptop all day."

He reaches up to rub the back of his neck. "Don't tell me you'll miss me." I toss my head back and laugh out loud.

When I find my composure, the flutters in my stomach intensify to a thunderous beat from the way he's gazing at me. It's too much and I have to look away. "Well, thank you so much for this. Seriously. It's perfect."

He's quiet for a drawn-out moment before saying, "You're welcome, Jane." The cadence in his voice has me peeking up at him. His dark gaze is still heavy on me, holding me hostage.

I want to kiss him so badly it hurts. Or just once, wrap my arms around him for a hug. I'd do anything to feel his strong embrace, my face buried in his chest, breathing him in. I could die in his arms and feel at peace. The absurdity of that mental picture isn't lost on me.

I can tell he feels my uneasiness as he holds my stare for a moment too long to make me squirm. I know he takes pleasure in it, asserting his dominance and flaunting his absolute control. Once he's satisfied with my restiveness, he takes his leave, letting me breathe again.

I take a seat in the ergonomic-yet-chic desk chair and I stare at the white paper sticking out of the flowers. I know I'm overthinking this.

I pluck the card out and open it before hesitating a second more.
Merry Christmas

Donavon

I smile and then cover my mouth when a girlish giggle comes out. It's a reciprocal of the card I left in his desk for the monitor I got him. All it said was 'Merry Christmas –Jane'. Still cheesing like a fool, I fold the note back up and put it in a random drawer of my brand-new desk.

It's hardly halfway through the day when Madison waltzes right into my office with a brazen grin. "You bitch." The door clamors when she harshly shuts it. "I cannot believe you got your own office, on the top floor, right next to the boss."

I had texted her not too long ago saying I had a surprise to show her, and of course she couldn't wait. I watch as she gawks at the space then she pins me with a stare. "You're fucking him, aren't you?"

My smile deflates and I narrow my eyes at her. "No, I am not."

"Oh, come on!" She plops herself down in one of the velvet chairs in front of my desk. "You two are together twenty-four-seven and he gives you this beautiful office right next to his?"

"I'm his executive assistant. We're supposed to work closely together and with the amount of work I do for him, I kind of needed my own space."

"Jane. Look around you. If you guys aren't fucking, he definitely wants to."

I groan and cover my face with my hands. Not this again. First Bonnie, then Kenna, and now Madison. "I'll tell you exactly what I told Kenna and Bonnie." I drop my hands. "I am not fucking him, nor will I ever because of a list of reasons."

"Jane—"

"No." I put a hand up and shake my head. "Please, stop. He's my boss, Madison. That's it. Believe me, he doesn't want his little assistant."

"Good God, woman." She shakes her head. "You are clueless."

I roll my eyes. "Whatever."

"Jane?" Donavon's voice projects over the speaker from my desk phone.

I press the button. "Yes, Satan?"

"Very funny. I need you in here."

"Be right there."

Madison stands up when I do, and I can feel her grinning at me. "Stop it," I half mutter, half growl.

"Can I be a bridesmaid at your multimillion-dollar wedding?"

I laugh and literally push her out of my office. "Get out of here with that."

"See you later, *Mrs. Waldorf*," she whispers the last part and I shake my head at her, ignoring her laughter down the hall as we part ways.

I walk into his office and have a seat with my laptop ready. "Did you finish with those emails from this morning?" he asks right away.

"I was just finishing up when someone came to my office."

His head snaps up. "Who?"

"Madison." *Shit, am I going to get her in trouble?* "She's an intern here. We're friends, so she just wanted to come by to see my office and say hi. She didn't stay too long."

His face relaxes. "It's fine, Jane."

His phone rings and by the way he answers it and how he speaks, I can tell it's Maggie on the other end. "Bring it in."

He hangs up and goes back to his work, ignoring me. Maggie walks in with a large brown paper bag. "Just set it over on the table."

"Sure, Mr. Waldorf." She places the bag down then leaves.

"Why didn't you ever hire Maggie as your assistant?."

He blatantly ignores my question as he sighs and gets up. "Ready for lunch?" I give him a funny look and watch him go over to the coffee table and couch. "I ordered from that Mexican place you like." He sits down nonchalantly while I stare at him. "Come get it while it's still warm, Jane." He begins pulling out the containers from the bag.

Not entirely understanding what's going on here, I move on autopilot as I go and join him. "You don't eat Mexican food," I point out. He's the pickiest eater I've ever met, actually. He also doesn't ask me to join him for lunch unless it's a lunch meeting with clients. He usually tells me, "Go get yourself some lunch, Jane." I feel like it's a way to get rid of me and give himself some alone time.

He's not only having me join him for lunch in his office, but he knows the Mexican restaurant I like. No, this is all fucking with my head.

Be cool, Jane. This isn't a fucking marriage proposal. It's lunch. Just a nice gesture. It means nothing.

"Thank you," I finally say when he chooses to ignore me yet again.

We eat in a comfortable silence as we both scroll through our phones. Neither of us willing to waste a single moment. I never thought I would like this job. Never thought I would be good at it, but here I am. Donavon Waldorf's executive assistant. Helping make his life easier and taking on some of his workload. It's more responsibility than marketing would ever be, and I thrive on it. I love the dependence he has on me. I honestly do not know how he went so long without any kind of support, or at least interns doing some of his mundane everyday tasks.

The rest of the week flies by much the same. We have lunch together again on Wednesday, Thursday we have a lunch meeting at his usual spot, and today we again did lunch in his office. It feels intimate, but without the actual intimacy.

"Hey, Jane!" I turn to see Nick quickening his steps to catch up to me just as I'm about to head into my office.

I smile. "Hey. How are you?"

"I'm good." He peers over my shoulder. "Do I get to see your new office?"

"Of course. Come in."

"Wow. Really nice. Sucks I had to hear about it through Madison though."

I cringe as I take a seat behind my desk. "I know, I'm so sorry. To be honest, I'm a little embarrassed with how I had to abruptly leave the other night. You were so sweet to stay out with us so late when you had work in the morning, and I up and left you."

"It's alright. You had something going on with your family, right?"

"Yes."

"Then I completely understand. Family is important."

"You really aren't upset?"

He stuffs his hands in his pockets standing in front of my desk. "I mean, I was a little disappointed I didn't get to take you home, but I'm not mad."

I give him a smirk. "A little presumptuous, don't you think?"

"Don't lie. You wore that dress for me," he teases making me giggle.

"No, I wore that dress for myself. Glad you appreciated it though."

His smile stretches. "I did. You're beautiful, I bet you look great in everything." I glance down bashfully. "So, a bunch of us are going out for happy hour after work tonight. You think you'll be able to make it?"

I open my mouth to respond when Donavon literally comes out of nowhere, standing at the threshold of my office. "Unfortunately, Jane will be working here pretty late this evening." Nick turns to face Donavon as I sit completely stunned. *This is the last-minute Miami trip all over again.* "Don't you have somewhere to be?" he says to Nick, and my mouth falls open in shock. I'm used to his mood swings and impudence, but this is totally uncalled for.

"Yes, sir. I was only giving Jane a quick hello and congratulating her on her new office." Nick looks back at me as I try to recover some level of composure. "I'll see you later, Jane."

I give him a tight smile. "Bye, Nick."

To insert his dominance even more, Donavon doesn't move so that Nick has to basically squeeze past him to leave. Once he does, Donavon steps in and closes the door behind him. "That guy just wants to fuck you," he says abruptly, unfazed by the scowl I'm forcing on him.

"So?" I lean back in my chair and cross my arms over my chest. "Is there a rule I somehow missed about fraternizing with interns?"

"You're not an intern anymore."

"Again: Did I miss some rule about who I can and can't have sex with?"

His jaw ticks and his fists clench at his sides before he stuffs them into his pockets. "It's unprofessional."

My mouth pops open again. "Unprofessional? Really? It's not like I work closely with him and I'm pretty sure that unless I plan on sleeping with him at the office—which I don't—it's not any of your concern what I do with my free time." I know exactly what I'm doing. I'm baiting him and I can't help myself. Especially since I can physically see how worked up he's getting. Nice to ruffle *his* feathers for once.

"So, that's what you do? It doesn't matter who it is, so long as they're willing?"

I can feel my face ruddled with anger. "Not that it's any of your business," I bite out. "But no, I am not a whore. I don't sleep around. And honestly, between my life being a shit show for the past few years and my super needy boss, I don't exactly have time for a relationship. So yeah—it's been a while. So, if a handsome guy just wants to hook up, then that surely works for me. Just because I don't have a dick doesn't mean I don't have needs. Now, if we're done discussing my sex life, I'd like to get some work done so maybe I can actually have one." I'm practically shaking once I'm done with my rant.

The nerve of him! Accusing me of sleeping with whoever is *willing*. He's one to talk! His reputation precedes him; all he does is sleep around. But is that any of my business? No.

He holds my glare for another uncomfortable moment, then without a word, he opens the door and leaves.

Sixteen

Jane

Clearly, going off on Donavon was not well received.

It's not like the first time I've done it, and I'm sure it won't be the last. I guess this time was a little different though. Both of us approaching new territory with talk of our personal life.

Now he's punishing me with fetching his dry cleaning and adding to my never-ending agenda all so he can keep me here longer. I see what he's doing. Question is, why?

Seven o'clock rolls around and I am done. We're going on twelve hours, and he cannot continue to keep me here. "Unless you need me to polish your shoes or wipe your ass, I'm done with everything you have asked of me and I am leaving," I say bitterly, and his lips twitch. I'm glad he thinks all of this is funny.

"Fine. You can go." I wasn't exactly asking but I get up to grab my things from my office, nonetheless. "You still going out?" he calls after me.

I stop and turn around. "Not that it's any of your business, but yes, I am."

"Great," He stands and slips his jacket on, "I'll join you."

"What? You can't come hang out with the interns," I protest lamely.

"You're not an intern anymore," he points out for the second time today. "And sure, I can. I am the boss after all."

He packs up his laptop as I stand there frozen. "Seriously?"

"Yes." He walks to me smugly.

"Well..." I trail off trying to find my voice. "You can't walk in with me."

He stops only inches from me with a devious grin. "Are you embarrassed to be seen with me, Jane?"

I scoff and roll my eyes. "No, it's just that between the new office and all the time we spend together I don't think we need to add any fuel to the rumor that we may or may not be fucking."

He bites back a grin. "You care too much about what others think."

"Maybe. But I'm serious; we are not walking in together."

"Fine. I'll walk in a whole five minutes after you."

We stand there for a while. "You're really doing this?" He nods. Huffing like a child, I walk out and go to my office for my things. "Have you ever gone out with any of your employees before?" I ask when we're in the elevator.

"It's been a while."

He's totally lying. I don't even think he goes out at all with anyone.

It's officially cold in the city, the wind ripping through the tall buildings to make it miserably cold. Walking in silence, he casually strolls beside me until we get to the bar down a couple of blocks. I turn and look at him and I loathe the smirk he wears. So proud of himself for messing with me like this.

"Hang back," I say sternly, and he gestures for me to go ahead.

I look around when I walk inside the bar, and I spot Madison and Nick with a bunch of other interns. Madison spots me first and waves me over. Nick turns his head and smiles when he sees me, then both of their expressions change, and other heads begin to turn.

I don't need to look and see that Donavon is now standing next to me, but I do anyways. He shrugs his shoulders. "It was getting a little chilly out," he says innocently making me roll my eyes at him.

Everyone is shocked to see *Mr. Waldorf* joining us, but they all faun over him and all too eager to ass kiss. Someone immediately jumps up to give their seat to him, and I take the spot between Madison and Nick that happens to be directly across from Donavon.

"Sorry I brought the boss. He sort of invited himself," I mutter to Madison.

She predictably gives me that knowing look. "I'm sure he did."

I narrow my eyes at her. "Don't start with me," I warn.

"Hey, what do you want to drink?" Nick leans over to ask me.

"We got a pitcher of margaritas if you want in on it," Madison offers.

"Absolutely."

He gets up to fetch me a glass and I finally give in to look at Donavon that is staring daggers at me as if I've done something wrong. I glower right back at him and purposely turn away to talk to Madison.

I get lost in conversation with her as everyone else fights over Donavon's attention. His little game is totally backfiring on him. He absolutely *hates* socializing and detests being center of attention.

In the thick of my father's trial, reporters were coming after my mom and me. I couldn't go anywhere without cameras in my face and asking me all these questions I didn't have the answers to. I always had anxiety, but never social anxiety until then. It's still difficult for me to be in a large group of people, and I cannot stand being the focus of attention.

"Glad you could finally make it out with us," Nick says as he hands me a drink.

"Seriously, the boss is constantly riding you," Madison says covering her smirk up with her drink.

I give her a look of warning, telling her to cool it. "So, how was *your* date, Mads?" I bat my lashes at her, forcing the change of subject, but it's just my luck that it doesn't stick.

"So, what's up with you and the boss man?" Nick whispers into my ear and I almost choke on my tongue.

"What do you mean?" My heart begins beating rapidly in my chest.

"You guys have a thing going on or something?"

My initial reaction is to tell him to mind his own business, like I said to Donavon earlier. But I opt for a more nonconfrontational tone. "No, there isn't," I say evenly and sip my drink when I kind of want to throw it in his face. *Or maybe I should throw it in Donavon's face.* I told him I didn't want us to show up together and give anyone the wrong idea. Now, I feel like more eyes are on me and people whispering to each other wondering if Mr. Waldorf is fucking his assistant. "Why would you even think that?"

"Because he keeps looking at me like he wants to kill me. Especially when I talk to you."

I smile at him, but it's mainly to poke at Donavon. "There is absolutely nothing going on between me and our boss."

"Good, because I don't think I'd be able to compete with him."

"Well, good thing it isn't a competition."

With Nick's eyes on me and the weight of Donavon's stare, I drain the rest of my drink feeling suddenly parched. Madison fills my glass back up, and I give her the majority of my attention.

It's already going on eleven o'clock and all the margaritas did for me is make me tired. The bar is filling up, and without a good buzz to take the edge off, I'd rather be anywhere else than here. Too many people, too much noise. Either I'll begin downing shots to drown it all out—which is not an option with Donavon and other coworkers around—or I need to go home.

"Hey, I'm going to get going," I raise my voice above the music and chatter.

"Noooooo," Madison pouts.

I smile, grabbing my jacket and bag. "I know, I know. We'll get together again soon. I promise." She tries giving me puppy dog eyes. "If I don't leave, I will fall asleep right here on the floor!"

Nick chuckles beside me, "I'll walk you home."

"That's okay, you don't have to."

"I was already planning on calling it a night myself."

"You sure?"

"I am." He places his hand on the small of my back and helps me out of my seat.

"Let's do brunch this weekend at some point," I say giving Madison a hug.

"Oh, I'm there," she replies.

I turn to the gleaming pair of dark blues. Donavon looks like he's about to explode, and maybe it's the alcohol mixed with exhaustion, but he seems...jealous.

You want me? Come and get me.

"Goodnight, Mr. Waldorf," I say with Nick at my side, still touching my lower back.

I genuinely enjoy the small talk we have for the eight-block walk to my building. Though I kind of wish I were alone with my own thoughts. Things are changing between Donavon and me.

I kept thinking those little moments were all in my head, but he's been different around me. More possessive and needy than ever, always finding reasons to keep me around. I honestly think he might miss me working in his office and may slightly regret giving me my own.

"Well, this is me." We stop in front of my building, and I take another glance behind me, thinking I might find Donavon stalking in the shadows.

"Damn, this is you?" he asks craning his neck back to look up at the building.

"Yeah," I say abashedly. "My roommate is Mr. Waldorf's sister, remember?" Ugh, I hate the way that sounds. Like I might be getting special privileges or something because of it.

"Right—Kenna."

"Yup."

He inches forward, smiling down at me. "You think we'll ever get that date?"

"I wish I could tell you."

"I do like you, Jane. I'd still love to take you out properly."

Oh, I would love a proper date.

"I'm afraid I might be a lost cause, Nick."

He threads his fingers into my hair and bends his head down towards me. "I think you'd be worth the wait."

"You shouldn't have to," I whisper right before his lips descend onto mine.

As soon as his lips start moving, I think of Donavon. I don't know why and I kind of hate myself for doing it. Here's this attractive, perfectly nice guy who has been asking me out for months, and finally we get our first kiss, and I can't stop thinking about my asshole boss. No, I need to enjoy this kiss from this guy right here. He's someone I'd be a lot safer with anyway.

His lips gently part mine and he sweeps his tongue in. He tastes like tequila and mint. A strangely pleasant combination. The kiss doesn't steal my breath away, and my toes aren't curling, but his lips are soft and he's surely a deft kisser.

Before we get too carried away, he pulls back respectively.

Smiling down at me, he strokes my cheek with his thumb. "Goodnight, Jane."

I smile up at him and step back towards the entrance. "Goodnight, Nick."

Spinning on my heels, I head inside. Once on the elevator, I brush my fingers across my lips and smile. But then Donavon's face haunts me, and a sense of guilt has my stomach sick. *Why in the hell should I feel guilty for kissing Nick?* Donavon is my boss. My best friend's brother. The untouchable bachelor of New York. He could care less about who I kiss, and I shouldn't even think about him when I do. He most certainly does not think about *me* when he's balls deep in whatever woman he's with.

It's dark and quiet inside when I enter. Luna comes to greet me as always and there's no sign of Kenna. Tom, the guy she's been seeing lives alone, so they go to his place a lot. New relationship and all. That sweet honeymoon phase.

I go to walk towards my bedroom when there's a firm knock at the door. My eyes widen and I go back to glance through the peephole and sure enough, it's Donavon standing on the other side. A very pissed of Donavon. "Open the door, Jane," he orders.

What the hell?!

I open the door and before I can open my mouth, he steps inside and closes the door behind him, even locking it. "You let him kiss you," he snaps.

"What?" My eyes widen as I retreat from his advance. "Oh, my God! Were you watching me?" I shriek incredulously.

"Tell me. Why did you kiss him?" He steps forward and I step back.

"Why not?" I retort, crossing my arms.

"I don't want you with him."

I come to a halt, and he stands dangerously close to me, his chest rising and falling with shallow and uneven breaths. Holy shit. Everyone was right. He wants me. Donavon Waldorf wants *me*. The man I fantasize about, knowing that's all he'll ever be, was jealous that I kissed someone. I feel so empowered by this revelation.

I'm imbued with new confidence and plaster on a seductive grin. "And why not, Mr. Waldorf?"

He begins to advance on me once again and I respond by moving backwards. "Because he's a tool and you can do better."

"I think I can decide that for myself, thank you very much. And like I said before, I don't want to be with him, I want to fuck him, if that's what he's offering."

His teeth grind as I lure him down the hallway toward my bedroom. "Say you won't touch him again."

"And why would I do that?"

"Say it."

I cant my head to one side with a pensive look. "I don't like games, Mr. Waldorf. You're going to have to give me a good reason why you don't want me kissing Nick."

"I don't want you *kissing* anyone."

I stop in the doorway to my bedroom. This is it. The moment of truth. "What do you want?"

"I can't say it," he growls.

"Sure, you can. You're Donavon Waldorf. A man who demands what he wants and gets exactly that."

"You know what I want," he says in a low and menacing tone.

"I'm afraid you won't be getting it unless you say exactly what that is." I have no idea where this confidence is coming from, but I'm rolling with it.

He seethes, his nostrils flaring. "I want you."

The frantic flutters in my belly turn into a vortex. "You want me to...what?" I begin the dance again. Moving back as he stalks me. "To do your taxes? Wash your car? What?"

"I want *you*, Jane." He pauses and we stop in the middle of my room. "I'm going to fuck you."

My bravado falters slightly. "Now, was that so hard?" I peel my jacket off and he does the same. "You're my boss, Mr. Waldorf."

Our clothing begins to hit the floor. "Yeah." His voice is low and husky. His eyelids are heavy as he watches my every move like a hawk.

"Your sister is my best friend."

"Yeah," he rasps as my shirt is being removed. His eyes darker than ever.

It's difficult to swallow when his shirt hits the floor. His torso solid muscle. "You're seventeen years older than me." All the valor is suddenly drained from my voice.

"I am."

My pants go next.

"You hate me."

He snorts but doesn't deny it.

"Yet you want to fuck me."

We've stripped down to our underwear.

"Yes."

"Then what are you waiting for, Mr. Waldorf?" I taunt.

SEVENTEEN

Donavon

The pent-up aggression we both share for one another is palpable.

She meets me halfway when I go in for the first kiss. We attack each other causing our teeth to clank as we sloppily kiss and try to swallow each other whole. Our hands everywhere.

I reach for the clasp of her bra and pinch it to release it from her body and down to the floor. I'm only slightly reluctant to break from the kiss to devour her prefect breasts with my eyes. Fucking remarkable.

My mouth is watering and I'm much too eager to prolong this. Dropping to my knees, I latch onto one of her breasts with a firm hand to her back, forcing her to arch against me. She moans and I have to stifle a groan when her hands fist at my hair as her nipple hardens inside my mouth.

She's panting above me as I toy with her astounding breasts with my lips, tongue, teeth, and hand, quickly familiarizing myself with the feel and taste of them. Their weight, their shape, their color. Everything about them.

I pull her nipple harshly into my mouth and she gasps and quivers. *Why in the fuck did I wait so long to take to her?* No more waiting though.

With my mouth still firmly attached to one breast, I back her up to the bed until we go tumbling down onto it. I switch to her other breast to nip at her and have her sucking in air through her teeth and arching off the mattress.

She moans again and my erection is actually painful. I need to be inside of her. I pull back to ogle her breasts and her body becomes restless under me. My gaze snaps up to hers and she gives me a sleepy smile. "I'm going to fuck you hard and fast, darling. Then I'm going to worship every inch of your body like I've been longing for and take my sweet time fucking you again."

Her eyes light up as she stares at me with anticipation. She licks her lips before speaking. "Condoms are in the side drawer," she rasps, her voice already hoarse.

I spring up her body to reach the nightstand and dig in it for a condom. The sound of the wrapper and our panting pair well together as I rip it open and sheath myself with it. I roughly yank her panties down her long legs and toss them aside. Nestling my hips between her upper thighs, my cock bumps against her and I can feel her slickness through the latex.

Her breath hitches as I observe her face and rub my cock against her cunt a few more times. I can't hold myself back a moment more. Maneuvering my hips, I impale her with one long thrust forward.

She moans and whines, her back bowing and I rut into her. I inhale her mouth with hungry kisses, and her arms wrap tightly around me; her breasts move against my bare chest with every blunt thrust.

Her cunt is fucking dripping, causing lewd noises and covering my balls. I can't wait to eat her fucking pussy. It'll be nice and puffy for me by the time I get down there. I said I'd fuck her hard and fast, but I didn't mean fast as in it ending so quickly.

She whimpers inside my mouth when the muscles of her cunt begin to quake, then they quiver around my cock as she shudders beneath me. Fucking hell. So fucking good. I knew it would be ethereal, but goddamn.

Tearing my lips from hers, I sit up and wrap a hand around her slender neck and squeeze. She doesn't miss a beat as her eyes flutter, and she exposes her neck more to me. With her face flush, her chest pink, her nipples raw and angry, her breasts bouncing, the dip of her waist and seeing my cock thump in and out of her wet cunt, it has me finding myself too close to the edge. I'm not ready to lose myself inside of her yet. I've only just begun.

Growling through my teeth, I change the angle of my hips slightly and squeeze her neck even more. Her hand snaps up to my wrist, but she doesn't try to remove it. She uses it to brace herself and she arches her body, throwing her head back with her mouth agape. I can't wait to fuck her beautiful mouth. To fill it up and watch my cum dribble from those lips.

Her whimpers come in rhythmic chanting and her body begins to squirm. "Don," she pants and tries to wiggle free.

I lean down and force her to look at me with my hand cutting off her air supply and turning her face red. She looks at me with glazed eyes as she watches me. When her eyes begin to roll back, her pussy flutters and I back off to allow her to breathe and to release a cry and gasp for air when she comes again.

I couldn't hold back any longer even if I wanted to. My balls tighten up as the base of my spine tingles and I fill up the condom with bursts of my cum. All the while her pussy milks me of every drop. I wish I could pull out and watch me drip from her, but fucking condoms.

I grunt as the last drop spills from me and I still my hips. We stare at each other with labored breathing and a bit of astonishment. We made fucking stars.

"Don't move, darling," I murmur and climb off her. I head into the bathroom to dispose of the condom and when I come back, she's in the same exact position I left her in. "Good girl." I grin and she shudders. "Keep those legs wide open for me." I kneel in the end of the bed and start to lower myself, keeping my eyes locked with hers.

"Touch your beautiful breasts for me, darling. Then I want you to watch yourself come all over my face."

Her eyes rapidly blink then she obeys. Her dainty hands squeezing her breasts. I give a grunt of approval and lower my mouth on her shimmering pussy. It's bare and sparkling for me. And just as I'd imagined, it's scrumptious, hitting every taste bud on my tongue in pleasure.

Her pants come in short winds as I suck her pussy into my mouth and hold it there while my tongue lashes her sensitive rosebud. Every muscle in her body contracts and she resists the urge to lift her hips off the bed as she grits her teeth.

A suction noise resounds when I release her pink pussy and flatten my tongue against it to drag upwards. She lets out a pained whimper and her knees wobble. Her hands delve into my hair and clench. Growling, I rub my mouth and tongue all over her. She jolts her body and cries out.

When I shove my tongue inside of her and rub the tip of my nose on her bundle of nerves, she uses my hair to bend herself in half into a sitting position and scream through her teeth in ecstasy.

She flops back to the mattress the same time her muscles give out and I suck up her juices before sitting back. She's breathing hard as I slowly crawl up her body and level with her glorious breasts.

"I'm going to fuck these," I mutter, fondling them. She stares down at me, her cheeks fuchsia from pleasure. I slap one to make it jiggle and she gasps, her eyes trying not to roll back. "But not now. I haven't had enough of this pussy yet."

Slipping my fingers between the swollen flesh between her legs, she chomps down on that bottom lip of hers. Her teeth digging into it causing the skin to turn white from the pressure.

I suck a nipple into my mouth as I play with her, teasing her and taunting her. "Don," she rasps, her fingers still digging through my hair, and she throws her head back.

Practically snarling in response, I roughly feast on her breast and shove two fingers deep inside of her. She whimpers and fists my hair harder. I didn't plan on being so bearish, but there's this uncontrollable urgency to explore her inside and out in a timely manner.

I alternate to the neglected breast until she creams all over my hand, causing a sloppy wet sound to slap off my palm.

There's no time for her to recover as I remove myself from her breasts and kiss her hard on the mouth. Choking her with my tongue and sucking on hers. Ripping myself away, I flip her over to her stomach and grip her ass cheeks, molding the tender flesh in my fists. Getting to know that better as well.

Jerking her hips upwards, I smack her ass hard as she settles in on her knees. She bites back a cry and moans as she rocks back at me. She needs more, and I am all too willing to give it to her.

"Greedy cunt," I rasp before I'm face down in her dripping pussy. Grasping hard on each ass cheek, I spread them wide so that there is not a single barricade in the way of my tongue. The rim of her tight hole is pulled taunt. I will be fucking that too. Maybe not tonight, but that belongs to me.

I lick from the top of her pussy to the top of her ass crack over and over again. I mumble against her cunt, using vibration from the baritone in my throat to drive her wild. She's torn between trying to squirm away to shoving herself in my face and suffocating me. I grip her ass tightly, to the point of pain, letting her know not to go anywhere.

She's close so I flick the tip of my tongue over the most sensitive part of her moistness, and she begins to shake and shiver as her screams are muffled by the blankets. I again savor every drip, sucking and laving it all up before getting up on my knees. My cock aching for her as I stroke it and admire her from this position. Ass up, pussy red and dripping, my handprint on one cheek. I give the other one a good smack to match and she only jolts forward on reaction, then rocks her hips right back into place.

I grin. "Such a good fucking girl." I give each cheek another slap to make sure they keep their color. "Don't you dare fucking move," I growl.

I scoot up beside her to grab another condom, shoving it down my cock, overwhelmed with zeal to be inside of her again. Pulling her cheeks apart, I nudge the entrance with the tip of my length, and she moans, thrusting her hips back to meet me.

I smack her ass and grin. "Patience, darling. I'll feed you my cock as much as you want."

Shoving my length inside in one jerk, my pelvis meets her ass and my breath catches in my lungs. Gritting my teeth, I slide out to slam back in. I don't rut into her like I did the first time. I let every inch of my cock feel the tight muscles of her cunt as I make languid but violent movements.

She cries out and moans, burying her face in the mattress, and I feel barbaric when I start fucking her as hard as I can. I slam into her over and over until she can't take it anymore and explodes around me.

I grunt and chase my own high that is not far behind, filling up another condom and seeing stars.

I practically collapse on top of her. Our skin sticking together from a sheen of sweat. "Just give me a second, baby," I murmur causing her to giggle into the sheets. I smile as my heart beats against her back. I give her damp skin a kiss then gently pull out of her.

She gives the faintest moan that goes straight to my sensitive cock. Giving her ass another slap, I get up to dispose of the second condom of the night. Not at all the last.

When I come back to her room, she's already curled up under the blankets, her eyes hardly able to remain open as she watches me turn the light off and head in her direction. I only hesitate for a split second before lifting up the blankets and joining her under the covers.

"Come here," I mumble, and pull her body against mine.

She looks up at me from where she's curled into my side. "You're staying?"

She seems apprehensive when I nod my head. "I am." I tip my head to kiss her forehead, savoring my lips there for a moment. Then I rest my head back to close my eyes.

I should be too roused to lie still. Too overwhelmed with the anxiety of being completely out of my comfort zone here. In someone else's bed, another body pressed against mine.

My nightly routine.

My morning routine.

My bed.

My room.

My familiar.

Maybe it's because we're laying in the linens I bought her. Maybe because this is the apartment I bought for my sister. Maybe it's Jane. But I'm at ease. I'm okay.

Eighteen

Donavon

My mental clock still awakes me at four in the morning.

When I'm not too deprived of sleep, I hit the gym for an hour or two. Recently, I've gone to the gym almost every morning since I've hardly been making any appearances at the club. Again, proving that Jane is salubrious and healthy for me.

I open my eyes to find Jane still tucked into my side. Her head now resting on my shoulder where I have an unobstructed view of her face. She's tender and pure. At the same time so wicked with the way her leg is wrapped around one of mine, heat radiating from between her thighs. My cock stiffens and I know I can work up a good sweat right here. *Fuck the gym.*

Gently moving over her, so that I don't startle her awake, I move the hair away from her neck and start kissing her there as I reach over into the nightstand to get another condom.

She hums a feminine sound and winds her arms around my neck. I grip the condom in my fist as I reach down between us and find her wet heat swollen, as I intended it to be. She moans as I start playing with her, sliding my fingers up and down her most delicate flesh and then thrusting a finger inside of her. She moans again and arches her back as I trail a line of kisses up her throat then press my mouth against hers. She still tastes like margaritas.

Her legs fall open for me as I add a second finger, then a third. She mewls and rubs her legs up and down mine, just as eager as I am to be inside of her. Though she must be sore, she gives me no signs of refusal as she not so subtly begs me with her body.

I pull back from our kiss so I can tear the condom open with my teeth and encase myself with the rubber, before I'm moving inside of her. The feel of her cunt hugging my cock, it's a cunt I could sink myself into every day for the unforeseeable future. Never has my cock been so pleased.

Hooking an arm under one of her knees, I crank it up and toss her leg over one shoulder without pause, hitting spots I haven't yet touched.

"Ah!" she cries out and pulls at me to get closer.

I clutch one of her ass cheeks harshly with one rough hand and my other hand snakes up her spine to grip the back of her hair at the nape. She hisses when I yank on it and kiss her in the mouth. Both hands fist harder as she nears her climax. She claws at my sides, and I lose restraint.

I pound into her with violent momentum, driving my hips forward through her orgasm. I drop her leg from my shoulder and take her body with me when I sit back on my haunches. She takes over with her hips moving them up and down in my lap as our tongues continue to entwine. My hands remain where they were. One hand pulling and squeezing one beautiful cheek and the other hand still tangled in the back of her hair.

Everything begins to slow down as we sensually kiss and she rises up and down on my cock. My arms constrict around her entire body and I squeeze, not wanting her to ever slip away. She's becoming my foundation. My anchor.

I lay her back to the mattress and angle one hip up. She gasps for air and moans loudly as her head rolls back. Using my teeth, I scrape them down the column of her throat and her panting picks up to match my racing heart and my rolling pelvis.

I hit her harder and harder until she chokes the life out of my cock, triggering the explosion. We both hiss through clenched teeth riding the tidal wave until we finally crash together.

She lazily grins, her arms and legs still holding onto me. Her beauty never ceases to amaze me. Her hair a mess and her makeup smeared, and she's still breathtaking.

I kiss her and tell her I'll be right back before depositing her back on the mattress. When I come back from the bathroom, she's already passed out again with the faintest smile on her face.

I could slip out now but I can't seem to leave. I climb right back into bed and wrap my body around hers, burying my nose in her soft hair. Taking a deep breath, I find relaxation easily and fall back asleep.

Nineteen

Jane

Waking up with the sexiest man's mouth around your nipple is like waking up from the best dream ever, only to realize you aren't dreaming.

He grins up at me and rumbles, "Morning," with my nipple still in his mouth.

I shiver in pleasure and rasp, "Morning." I rake my fingers through his soft hair as he ravishes my breasts. Obviously, his favorite thing about my body.

My eyes pop wide open when I hear the front door open and then close, announcing Kenna's arrival home. "Shit, that's your sister," I hiss panicked.

He doesn't seem even slightly perturbed as he coolly scoots up on the bed to place a sweet kiss on my lips before casually settling in next to me. Pulling the covers around me to make sure my nakedness is concealed, he tucks an arm under me and folds the other one behind his head. All the while wearing a smirk. I gape at him hearing Kenna get closer and closer.

When I know she's about to walk past my room with the door left wide open, I dart my head under the covers to hide causing Donavon to chuckle, his chest vibrating under my cheek. "Oh, my God! Ew!" Kenna cries out, but there's no malice behind her tone.

"Morning, Kenna," Donavon says.

"Okay, I know I totally called this, but I did *not* want to actually see it," Kenna says.

I peek out from under the covers to look at her. Absolutely mortified. "I'm sorry. We should have closed the door," I mutter.

She smiles and shakes her head in amusement. "Here, allow me." She grabs the door and closes it.

I bury my face in his chest and groan. "Oh, my God."

He chuckles again, and I am enamored with the sound and the feel of it. "What's wrong?"

I look up at him in outrage. "What's wrong? You seriously do not care that your sister knows we hooked up?"

He shakes his head still smirking. "I don't. Do you?"

I think for a moment. "I guess I don't, but I thought that you would."

"Nope." He gently pushes me off him so he can roll out of bed. When he stands up, I bite my lip while ogling his backside. Holy mother Mary. He is perfection. From his broad shoulders to his trimmed waist, his round and rock-hard ass to his thick thighs with dark hair scattered. He's so manly and so beautiful.

He confidently strides over to the clothing thrown around on the floor and begins collecting his. "I have to get going, darling."

Darling.

"Okay, I'll see you Monday," I say feeling the veil lift and realizing I won't know how to act around him now.

I never thought last night would happen, so, I never considered the ramifications.

He pulls on his underwear and looks back at me with an eyebrow raised. "Oh, yeah? It's like that?" I frown at him, still not knowing what to say or even do. "You got what you wanted and that's it?" He's teasing me, and there's only one other time he was this light around me, and that was the one day in Miami.

I chuckle, shaking my head. I have no response for that. Of course, that's not how it is. At least not for me. So, what about him?

I pull my knees up and wrap my arms around them as he finishes getting dressed, somehow missing him already. He comes over to the side of the bed and slips his hands inside his pockets. "I'm going to take you out tonight." Why does he seem nervous right now? How can he be nervous around me? Doesn't he know that I'm like, in love with him?

Holy Hell. I'm in love with him.

"Like a date?"

His smile is slow. "Yes, exactly like a date."

I suddenly feel so puerile around him. I've never been on a date with anyone like Donavon before. Because there is no one like Donavon. "Do you even know how to date?" I tease.

He leans down to hover his lips over mine. "I think I can figure it out," he rasps then takes me completely by surprise when he locks his lips with mine.

It's a prolonged goodbye kiss, being sure to deepen and delve his tongue in my mouth to massage mine. His fingers thread through my hair, holding me hostage, as if I could move if I wanted to. Everything locks up and I'm spellbound, my mind light and my skin prickling with electricity.

I moan right before he pulls away and it's difficult for me to open my eyes. "I'll pick you up at six," he says then grabs his jacket and shoes.

"Any clue as to where we're going?" I ask still a bit dazed as he reaches the threshold.

"Be hungry." He grins then slips out the door, closing it behind him.

The giddiness bubbles over as I slap a hand over my mouth when a squeal bursts out and I fall back to my pillow. I'm grinning so hard my face hurts. This is all so surreal.

There's a knock on my door. "Are you decent?" Kenna calls out.

I sit up. "I'm covered, yes."

She pokes her head in with a Cheshire grin. "Get your hoe ass dressed and out here. We're doing brunch."

"Brunch? What time is it?" I look around for my phone.

"It's ten. Get dressed." She closes the door.

I swing my legs off the bed to go get some clothes on. I never sleep in this late, and I know damn well Donavon doesn't either. He's always up at the crack ass of dawn. If the man even sleeps at all. I've learned that most mental health diagnoses come in threes with insomnia being a common co-occurrent.

After throwing on some comfy clothes, I dart over to the bathroom to wash up some and tie my hair up on top of my head. The scent of sex clings to me and I smile at myself in the mirror. I haven't felt happiness like this in years. Maybe not ever. If it was only a one-night fling with him—it was an amazing one night... And morning.

"Pop a bottle of champagne. We're celebrating," Kenna says from the stovetop.

I grab a bottle from the wine cooler. "What exactly are we celebrating?"

She laughs and eyes me over her shoulder. "Seriously? You and my brother finally getting together, of course!"

I pop the cork. "Kenna. We hooked up last night, I'd hardly say we're *together*." At least, I don't think he would say we were. He told me he wanted me and was going to fuck me. He never said anything about a relationship afterward. I pour two glasses and top it off with orange juice.

"I'm telling you, Jane," she sings out. "He does not do this. He doesn't stay over, and the fact that he didn't give a single fuck that his own *sister* caught him says everything."

"I don't think that meant anything, Kenna. He's arrogant like that." He's the type to not care what anyone thinks or their opinions, including his own sister. He does what he wants, and he never apologizes for it. Apologizing would be admitting he's in the wrong, and that man never is.

She turns the burners off and begins plating our food. "No. My brother may be a jerk half the time, and an asshole the other half, but he's always been the best brother. I asked him not to fuck you—made him promise—and he did. So, it can't be just a hook-up. It's more."

"He did ask me out tonight," I murmur into my drink as we sit down.

Her eyes somehow widen ever more. "What! Oh, my God! I cannot wait to tell Allison and mom."

"Please don't tell anyone yet, Kenna."

I want to believe her, and believe Donavon wants more than just sex, but it's practically unfathomable. Donavon is a god among mortals! A *billionaire* and one hell of a lover. And he wants to be with me? After not dating for over a decade and never been married and he's almost forty—and he wants...*me*. Jane Donahue. Daughter of a criminal. With loads of baggage. Almost young enough to be his daughter.

He could have anyone. A model, an actress, a doctor, literally anyone. Why would he want someone with a measly marketing degree and a messy background like mine?

"Hey, you okay?" Kenna asks, shaking me from my disconsolate thoughts.

I nod my head. "Yeah, I'm fine. Thanks for this, it's delicious."

"No, no, no. Tell me what you're thinking. I can see those wheels turning, and I know it's you now doubting yourself."

"Am I really so transparent?" I mutter.

"Only because I'm your best friend." She grins. "So, tell me. What's going on?"

"Okay, I know I'm not an ugg-o or anything, but I feel so...inadequate compared to him," I sigh and stab at my food.

Kenna's eyes bug out as her head jolts forward. "Inadequate? Jane, my brother may be attractive and wildly successful, but he's a very closed off person. It's nearly impossible to get close to him, even us as his family. Sometimes I wonder if he's a robot," she jokes. "Seriously, women may line up hoping they'll stand a chance with him, but they're looking for something out of it. They use him just as much as he uses them."

I hate hearing that. Yes, Donavon is reserved and an introvert by nature, but he's not at all the heartless, emotionless robot everyone thinks. He treats his family the way he does because of how much he loves them.

He portrays himself as a ruthless tyrant, but what most people don't know is how much money he donates to charity without wanting any publicity for it. *I* only know this because of being his executive assistant now and I sometimes have to get his finances in order.

The man has a bigger heart than most.

He does have his secrets about his mental health. I still don't know if he's aware of them or not. I did learn that one can feel trapped when in a place where their compulsiveness will be noticed. It's why he hates being around people. Why he can't stand anyone in his home or anyone in his office for very long.

After I help with the dishes, I excuse myself to go shower up. I regret having to wash the scent of him from me, but I do have a date tonight.

I go through the routine of washing my hair first and then sitting down to wash my body and shave. When I wash between my legs, I bite down from the tenderness there. But that tenderness reminds me of Donavon and the way he fucked me.

His mouth was heavenly on me, but the fullness from the intrusion of his fat cock has me touching myself to the erotic memories. My pussy is a little raw, yet it feels so good. I rub myself and bite back a moan at the slight burn and ache.

I can picture him above me, fucking me, his hair out of place, his lips parted, his eyes heavy. *Yesssss. So good.* It was so good, and I crave more. Rolling my lips in, my orgasm abruptly shatters me.

I'm panting as I drop my hand and stare up at the steam billowing up and grin.

Twenty

Donavon

For the first time in my thirty-nine years of life—I want a companion.

Not any companion, but Jane. To not only want for my own pleasure but strive to bring her the most pleasure as humanly possible. Her pleasure gives me mine.

I told Jane I would wing it tonight, but truth is, I've been thinking of ways to spoil her for weeks. I've thought about presents and trips, but until now I hadn't given much thought to dates. Where do you take a woman out on a first date when you've known each other for so long? A relationship that has been going on without the romance and sex.

The sex.

Sex has always been only that for me. Women only present as a means to an end. Stroke myself while watching live porn, then having them get me off. That's all. That has been my sex life since I've had one. No desire for dates or romance or love.

Jane is the first woman I fervently desire. The first to arouse me with an innocent smile and awaken that craving inside of me I feared I was incapable of feeling. The yearn for touch and affection and passion. The need to enrapture and pamper and cosset her. To give her the security and life she most deserves.

Maybe I do need a little help with the first date tonight. No way in hell am I calling Kenna. She already hears wedding bells, and although

Jane is more than significant to me, I don't need her getting carried away and encouraging the rest of the women in my life.

I pick up the phone and dial Allison. "Is it true that you're taking Jane out tonight?" she says as soon she answers.

I shake my head. "News travels fast," I mutter. "And hello to you too, Allison."

"Sorry, hi. I just got off the phone with Kenna." Of course, she did. "So, is it true?"

"Yes, and that's why I'm calling." I clear my throat, feeling discomfort rushing through my veins. "I'd like some suggestions for a first date."

"Wait, have you never had a first date?"

"It's been a long time."

"How long are we talking?"

"Can you help me or not?" I'm quickly growing irascible.

"Dear Lord. How do I not know this about you?"

I sigh, feeling overly aggravated and irritable. Dating was always more vexatious than enjoyable for me. Spending one-on-one time in an intimate setting, the pressure solely on you as the male. Just the thought makes my skin itch.

"So you get laid without putting any effort in at all?" she accuses.

"I'd prefer not to answer that," I grumble.

"Okay, okay. I won't pry. So, first date. Do you have any ideas?"

I tell her about my plans to fly us to Italy for a couple days, or somewhere closer like Aspen, but she instantly shut that idea down and told me to pump the brakes. First dates should be simple. A quiet and cozy setting to get to know each other. Although I know enough about Jane to know that I want her in my life. And the woman knows more than enough about me.

I demanded Kenna make herself scarce when I arrived to pick Jane up. I don't need her grinning at us like I'm there to take her to prom.

Knocking on the door at five-fifty-nine, it swings open hardly a minute later. I devour her with my eyes, and all the blood rushes to my cock. I see her in her professional attire and when she dressed down on our work trip, but I have never seen her like this. And she'll never dress like this for anyone but me. This will be her last first date. Every moment with her, I'm more certain about that.

The ordinary black dress molds to her shape, stopping midthigh, with long sleeves covering her arms. Her legs look twice as long in the high heeled boots adorning her feet. Her hair is all down, hanging in waves that shine, and her makeup is a bit darker than she wears it for work.

"Darling, you look incredible." I step over the threshold. A hand lands on her hip as I dip my head down to kiss her lips.

She's beaming up at me with stars in her eyes when I pry myself away from her. "Thank you. You look pretty good yourself, but you always do." She looks down at the small gift I brought with me. "Did you bring me flowers?"

"I did." I hand her the bouquet I picked up on the way here.

Her grin broadens as she politely accepts them and places them under her nose to smell them. "Thank you, I love them. Let me find a vase, then we can go."

I help her with her coat, and we head out. Once she locks the door behind us, I take her hand in mine, lacing our fingers together. She peeks up at me with a smile and tucks some hair behind an ear. Something she does when she's nervous.

I don't *do* this, holding hands. I have no idea how anyone casually does this. It's all I can concentrate on. I don't know how long I could do this for, but I'm not nearly as distressed as I thought I would be. Jane seems to be able to quell so much of my deep-rooted insecurities that I've lived with my whole life that have only festered and worsened as I've gotten older.

Her hand gives me a slight squeeze for comfort, and I take an imperceptible soothing breath, letting it all go. I'll never be able to find the words to express to this woman the effect she has on me.

Once we're in the elevator, I hit the button and lean back against the wall taking Jane by the hips. Her delicate hands flatten against my chest when I pull her into me, and I capture her lips with mine. Prying her lips apart to thrust my tongue inside. Her mouth such a warm, welcoming paradise.

The few hours away from her felt like days. I've always looked forward to seeing her at work, but anticipating seeing her tonight gave me eagerness I could hardly contain.

The elevator stops and I don't pull away until the doors open to the ground floor. She stares up at me, and I would do anything to have her look at me this way every day. To be able to keep that look there.

A couple people step inside and unless we want to ride it back up, we need to exit. "Let's go, darling." I take her hand in mine again, already feeling more natural.

Ron is there waiting with the back door open for us and we slip inside. We've sat in the back seat next to each other of this car countless times, but not like this. Not where I could touch her. Where I can't seem to not touch her.

"So, where are you taking me?" she asks with our lips only inches apart and I'm running my fingers through her hair and caressing her face.

"Daniel. I hope you like French cuisine." I stroke her hair some more. Her latte-colored hair.

"I do. I've been there once with my parents years ago." Her eyes bounce between my eyes and my mouth. "I'm surprised you like it." Her lips twitch. "You might be the pickiest man I've ever known."

"I know what I like." Jane has seen me eat dozens of meals, and how I eat them. Shortly after she first started at the company, it was her who brought me lunch. She's a sagacious learner and quickly discovered my finicky appetite. It doesn't only pertain to food. My need for perfection and my acquired tastes revolve around all facets of my life. Women, booze, money.

"Hey." She frowns, moving her head back a little. "You didn't send me many emails today."

"Thought I'd give you some time off." I brush a finger down her soft cheek.

"You're not going to start treating me differently now, are you?"

One side of my mouth tilts upwards. "Are we back to that?"

"Back to what?"

"You disgruntled with me being less of an asshole to you."

She chuckles. "It's not about you being an asshole to me, it's about you still giving me as much work as you pay me to do. I don't want less work because we're sleeping together. Otherwise, I'll feel like you're paying me for sex."

"Then I'll be sure to have you working all hours of the day and night as usual."

She smiles and leans in closer to me so I can feel her breath on my skin. "Good."

Being so close, I can thoroughly study the flawlessness of her face and smooth skin. I remember the way her delicate flesh easily turns pink and wonder if her ass still has my handprint on it. Images of her cheek turning red from her father striking her abruptly creeps into my mind trying to maim this pleasant moment for me. The thought of her father still has me bloodthirsty.

"What's wrong?" she asks, staring at me with purity in her gaze.

"Nothing." I kiss her sweet lips, shaking off the gruesome memory.

"Definitely did not get this kind of service when I was here," she says after we're shown back to our private table and already served our wine by a master sommelier. Then he asked if we wanted to see the menu or if we would like to partake in a tasting menu. My natural instinct is to decide for Jane, but I am trying to impress her. When she surprises me by giving me to green light to make the decision, there's a challenging twinkle in her eye, as if testing me. I know she doesn't think I pay much attention to her because I don't make it a habit of blatantly studying her, but I do, and I know so much more about her than she'll ever realize.

"So, Kenna told me you haven't ever been in a relationship before," she says sipping her wine.

"Not since college." I wouldn't call any of them relationships, but it's the last time I dated. I don't mind being completely honest with Jane, or anyone for that matter, but I'm treading carefully because I don't think she's ready to indulge in every part of me yet. Not without trepidation. "Nothing serious. I was too busy with my studies. Already planning my future."

She smiles. "So, you were always a stiff," she teases.

"Not always."

"Oh? Tell me." She leans forward, ready to listen intently as if I'm about to tell some epic tale.

I'm not accustomed to opening myself up to anyone. Those closest to me already know about my past, or at least the gist of it. Obviously, Kenna hasn't divulged what she knows to Jane, which I appreciate. It's a past I am not proud of.

I clear my throat and straighten my utensils and plate on top of the table. "I was a little reckless in my youth." She doesn't push me to elaborate, which doesn't surprise me. Jane has always shown patience with me. As if she understands me and my needs. It gives me the encouragement that I need to continue. "I was an angry teenager and always found ways to take the animosity out on something. Or someone." I manage to make eye contact with her, expecting her to look horrified, but she's watching me with the hint of a smile to her lips. Still hanging onto my every word. "I partied a lot and got into a lot of fights. The fighting only got worse when I realized how much I loved it."

The anger sprouted from always feeling like an outcast but not knowing why. I've always felt different, strange even. The controlling urges and obsessive thoughts and tendencies. I turned to drinking, smoking, and sleeping around. Then once I got into my first physical fight—laying my fist into someone's face, it felt cathartic. Having an addictive personality, anything could become an obsession for me.

"So, what changed?"

"When I almost killed my father." Her eyes widen, but she doesn't jump to conclusions. "I had quite a few run-ins with the law, suspended from school and all. But when I sent someone to the hospital, he had had enough. We got into an argument, and he ended up having a minor heart attack."

Her face has already relaxed, and now her eyes have glossed over. "And you blamed yourself for it?"

"Of course, I did. It was me who had him constantly stressed out. Him and my mother," I state flatly as if it's fact.

"Donavon—"

"It's in the past, darling. I've since moved on. I turned that anger and remorse into motivation."

"Making sure you could set your parents up for a stress-free life and putting family first," she says quietly with a smile, and I nod once and silently beg for her to drop this. "But, Donavon. You do have to understand that stress alone cannot cause a heart attack. It can be the straw to break the camel's back, but there's more that goes into it. Like health."

I don't respond, because yes, what she's saying is somewhat true. My father's cholesterol was through the roof, and he continued to ignore it. But in the end, it was me that pushed him over the edge.

I finally remember what started this whole conversation and turn it back to her. "What about you? Any past relationships?"

She gracefully accepts the change in direction and sighs. "Ugh. Just the one." She drinks her wine. "We dated for a few years and when everything went down with my father, he was all too eager to cut ties with me and my family. Didn't want to taint his reputation." She adds an eyeroll at the end.

"What kind of reputation was that?"

She eyes me, silently asking me if I'm serious. "Well, I guess you wouldn't know because he did an excellent job at hiding our relationship." She takes a breath, and I can tell this isn't easy for her to talk about, but she's willing to be just as open with me as I was with her. "Anthony Richards is my ex."

I frown, knowing the connection instantly. "Robert Richards's son." She nods in confirmation. Robert Richards is a business associate of mine. "When was this?" I ask because to my knowledge, Anthony is closer in age to me than he is to Jane. Not that the age gap is something I can form an opinion on, but even a few years from today would put her only at nineteen years old.

"We broke up almost two years ago. Or he broke up with me," she chuckles dryly.

I quickly do the math in my head. "So, you were only seventeen when you began dating him."

"Yes, and he was twenty-eight. I know. Obviously, it wasn't appropriate."

"Your parents allowed their seventeen-year-old daughter to date a man who was almost thirty years old?"

She chokes on a laugh. "Allowed? Our parents were the ones who set us up."

"You're serious?" I clench my fists in my lap, furious with her parents all over again. It's obvious what they were trying to do with the match making.

She nods. "Yes." She drains her wine and I pour her some more. "Thank you." She suddenly looks bashful and somewhat embarrassed. "I wouldn't have dated him if I hadn't genuinely liked him." I frown, unsure where she's going with this and why she feels the need to talk about her feelings for another man. "I wasn't with him because he was wealthy. My family was no different from his at the time."

I remain reticent until it hits me. "You're afraid people will think you're only after my money, especially if they find out who you dated in the past." I fill in the blanks and her cheeks turn red. "Are you?"

Her eyes stay on mine as she shakes her head, her gaze a little sad. "No, not at all. I promise you that, Donavon."

I smile and she relaxes slightly. "Darling, you don't need to promise me anything."

"But...other people still might think so. It's kind of what people naturally assume."

"Again, you care too much about what other people think."

"I wasn't always so insecure. But what happened with my father—it took its toll on me too."

"And yet here you are."

Her smile is finally a bright one. "Here I am. Having dinner with you." She raises her glass and drinks from it. "I suppose we aren't so different. I threw myself into school, too. I knew without the financial security of my family; I needed a way to support myself. I'm just glad things have worked out so far."

I could sit here and listen to her talk for hours with her mellifluous voice and alluring smile. Her soft pink lips moving, hypnotizing me. I don't find anything she says to be insipid and the intimate setting with her comes so facilely. The reason why I'm at all fidgety is the need to touch her.

Now that I've acted on my feelings, I want more.

Dinner is over much faster than I liked, but once in the town car, I take advantage of my proximity to her. My lips are all over hers and we're both pulling at each other to eliminate any space left between us. Fuck, I don't want to say goodnight to her, but I have to. I've hardly spent any time at the club lately.

"Can you come up for a little?" she asks as soon as we arrive at her place. "You don't have to stay the night if you don't want to, but would you be able to come up for a little while?" She looks up at me with those baby blues and I can't say no. I could never tell her no. Ever. The woman already has me wrapped around her tiny finger. She has me no longer bending to my incessive rituals, which is such a freeing feeling.

"Sure, I can come up. You go on ahead though. I need to make a quick phone call."

She grins in victory and gives me a chaste kiss before energetically exiting the car. Thankfully, Garret doesn't pick up when I call him. I don't need him giving me any more shit for my absence at the club.

I leave him a brief message and tell Ron to come pick me up in the morning, because I know I won't be able to force myself to leave anytime soon.

TWENTY-ONE

Jane

Kenna is still gone when I walk inside the apartment ahead of Donavon.

I go ahead and take care of feeding Luna before heading to my room and toeing off my boots. When I hear Donavon's signature knock on the front door, I swiftly go and answer it.

He's wearing a devious grin as he kicks the door shut behind him and locking it without ever taking his eyes off me. I bite back a grin of my own as I silently coax him down the hallway and to my room.

Not a single word is spoken as we strip out of our clothes and fall back on the bed, his body covering mine. His cock is already erect, and I know I'm already wet for him. I swear there's a pulse down there as all the blood collects in that area.

He overwhelms me with kisses as his cock butts against me and slides through the slickness of my pussy. I moan and I swear I am already ready to combust. It has me pushing him back and breaking our kiss.

"I want you in my mouth," I rasp brazenly, shocking the hell out of myself.

His eyes grow dangerously dark as he sits back, and I sit up panting. My eyelids flutter when he takes my chin and uses his thumb to pry my mouth open. He stares at it and an animalistic grumble resounds from deep in his chest.

"You want a taste, baby?" I nod my head with rigor, and he chuckles. "Lie back and let me feed you my cock." My eyes widen and he begins to lean back over me, so I have no choice but to flatten myself on my back again. With one side of his mouth tilted up, he climbs up my body and I freeze, uncertain of what he has planned for me. When his knees land on either side of my shoulders, he pulls at his length that is now hovering above me. "Open wide, darling." I hesitantly open and he thumps the head of his cock on my tongue. He slaps it a few times making my pussy literally flutter in response. I want to touch myself so bad.

He stills only for a second with him resting on my tongue before gliding into my mouth. I wait for his instructions and keep my mouth wide open for him and try to breathe through my nose. The head of his cock passes the back of my tongue and bumps into the back of my throat. I have the urge to gag, but I fight it and remain calm.

"Good girl," he whispers hoarsely. "Now, close your pretty mouth and suck me."

My eyes widen and I'm all too eager to clamp my lips around him and hallow out my cheeks. When he hisses through his teeth, my eyes roll back as I bob my head and suck him all the way back to my throat, ignoring my gag reflexes every time. I concentrate on breathing, and I'm able to overcome the sensation.

The more he grunts and has to resist from thrusting his hips forward, the more my pussy throbs in unalleviated pleasure. I work him harder, selfishly trying to get him to come so I can.

He grunts loudly through his clenched teeth and retracts himself from my mouth so abruptly a string of my saliva is tethered from my mouth to his glistening cock. It dribbles down my chin and he scoots back to rub his length between my breasts. "Push those beautiful tits together, darling." I do as he says, and he hisses again as he glides himself between them. My saliva causing enough slickness to make it easy.

Watching his head disappear between them then come right at me, has me rubbing my sticky thighs together. I'm mesmerized by it and watch as it grows angry and a bead of cum drips from it, mixing with my spit.

He slips out abruptly and strokes himself. I have never been so turned on before without being touched. Watching him touch himself, I could get off with the slightest breeze.

He growls right before shooting ropes of cum across my chest. I moan, not able to tear my gaze away as he covers me. Without hesitation, I scoop some of it up with my fingers and suck them between my lips before he's even done.

"Fucking hell, Jane," he roughly whispers.

Moaning, I scoop some more up with my other fingers and reach between us to rub myself. He's stunned into silence as he watches me savor him from my fingers while I use more of him to pleasure myself with my other hand. I was already teetering so close to the edge; it takes me less than a minute to cry out and quiver.

When I finally come to and my vision comes back, he's still intently staring at me, panting as he straddles my body. There's this wild look in his gaze that has me frozen and stuck in the moment. Paralyzed.

He lifts a leg over me and scoops me up into his arms. I throw my arms around him. "Let's get you cleaned up, my dirty girl," he murmurs, causing my cheeks to burn.

I hide my bashful grin against his shoulder as he carries us to the bathroom, and we get into the shower together. Luckily, it's spacious enough for the two of us as we stand under the steaming water and caress one another. Exploring and familiarizing ourselves with the new territory we've encroached.

Twenty-Two

Jane

I never knew sex to be so intoxicating. Liberating. And honestly, I'm a little surprised I'm not entirely bowlegged walking into work Monday.

My cheeks scorch with heat thinking about the steaminess. Everything I let him do to me and everything I was willing to do in return. I couldn't even cross my legs without it throbbing. I see sex so differently now. The stamina of that man and the seduction he exudes, it's ungodly. He made me feel so comfortable in my skin and confident to express my most inner desires unabashedly.

I didn't think he would stay the whole night again, but he stayed tangled with me until the sun rose. He kissed me passionately before leaving and I laid there with the biggest smile on my face until it was almost offensively late in the day.

I haven't seen him since then, but he did call me a couple of times to check in and catch up on things we'd need to get done once back in the office.

The beginning of our relationship fast forwarded through the awkward stage and straight to the honeymoon stage. If this is a relationship. *It's something. I think...*

I go to drop my stuff off inside my office and wait to listen to messages and scroll through emails till after I take his latte to him while it's still hot. Iced lattes when it's warm, and hot when it's cold out.

He's on the phone when I enter, and he immediately smiles at me and tells whoever it is he's talking to that he'll have to call them back. I hand him his latte with a coy smile, "Good morning, Mr. Waldorf," knowing the effect it has on him.

"Jane," he responds in a husky tone sending chills down my spine. "Come here."

"We're at work right now, *Mr. Waldorf.* I told you, we need to keep it professional while we're here." He stands up, buttoning his jacket as he rounds the desk. "I'm serious, Donavon. We cannot be messing around in your office. If anyone were to—"

He cuts me off by grabbing my face and pulling me in for a kiss. Making my head spin and forget what the hell I was about to say. His soft lips pry mine apart, so he can brush his tongue against mine and I completely melt in his arms. My knees wobble and I'm putty in his hands. My pussy contracts, dampening my panties, and the desire for him is so strong it actually hurts.

I find it hard to breathe when he pulls away and I have to peel my eyelids open. "What were you saying, darling?"

"I don't know," I whisper, making him chuckle. I shake myself out of the stupor and narrow my eyes at him. "Very funny."

Spinning on my heels, he chuckles at my retreat but doesn't stop me. It wouldn't take much convincing. I close his door behind me and can't help but to smile and shake my head.

I'm shocked back into reality when Nick calls my name as he jogs to catch me as I turn into my office. "Hey."

"Hey," I reply smiling.

"You never responded to my text," he murmurs and shoves his hand inside his pockets. *Do all men do that when they're nervous?*

"Your text?" I frown and look down at my phone. "I didn't get one. At least I don't think so." I pull up my texts and realize his name is nowhere to be seen. Actually, the entire thread between us is missing.

"I'm sorry, my phone has kind of been acting up lately," I lie. "What did it say?"

He smiles sheepishly. "Something about that kiss we had."

The smile drops from my face, and I look down at my feet feeling horribly guilty. I'd completely forgotten about it. That kiss that was the catalyst to Donavon and I ending up in bed together most of the weekend.

"Oh, uh." I look Nick in the eye because he deserves it. "I'm so sorry, Nick, but I think we should stick to being friends." His smile turns into being forced. "With how much I'm always working and how I can't even commit to a date, I just don't have the time for anything right now." It's not the complete truth, but partially. Don and I agreed to keep whatever is going on between us out of work, so in order to tell him the complete truth, I'd have to out us.

He nods his head with his strained smile. "I understand. Really, I do."

"You don't hate me?"

His smile broadens. "No, I could never hate you. Only disappointed I never got a chance."

"I am sorry, but I am definitely a lost cause." If Donavon weren't in the picture, I would say never to say never, but Donavon has already ruined me for life.

He chuckles. "I hope this job is worth it."

"Me too."

"Well, I'll see you around?"

"I hope so."

I go to walk inside my office when I remember something. Turning back around, I let myself back in to Donavon's office. He doesn't even look up, but I see him smirk as he says, "Back so soon, darling?"

I prowl over to him, and he takes notice. He swivels in his chair when I round the desk and plant a hand on the surface, knowing it'll slightly irk him. He likes to pretend that it doesn't, but I've seen him slip up. Whether it's a subtle glance or an imperceptible muscle twitch.

"Donavon?"

"Yes, Jane?"

"Did you go into my phone and delete text messages from a certain *friend*?"

He feigns ignorance, tapping his chin as if thinking. "A friend?" I nod slowly. "You'll have to be more specific than that. Is this friend possibly someone you have kissed?"

I narrow my eyes at him. "Possibly."

"Then I *possibly* deleted it," he says with zero shame.

I lean in some, close enough to where my breath feathers his face, and I can see his eyes dilate. "You should know that I completely forgot about that kiss. Especially after my brutish boss fucked my brains out all weekend. Frankly, I've forgotten about every kiss before that."

I'm abruptly yanked into his lap, letting out a girlish squeak. "Then what's the problem?" he rumbles, caressing my face.

"Don," I warn and push at his chest when he goes to shut me up with a kiss.

He sighs, "Yes, I deleted it." He goes to try and kiss me again, and this time I let him.

"Donavon," I murmur against his lips and pull away. "You can't do that." I'm not surprised he did it; he's controlling and possessive. It should be a red flag. Hell, it should be a red flag on fire with smoke signals blaring, but no warning bells are going off. He's over the top, but he's honest to the point of being cruel. "No, matter the status of our relationship, you cannot go into my phone and delete things behind my back. If you have questions, ask me, and I will tell you."

I'm sitting in his lap with my legs draped over the side, and his hand is slowly creeping up my thigh pulling the fabric of my skirt along the way. "Alright. Are you going to tell him?" He kisses my neck and I'm trying to tune him out completely. Concentrating on my resistance. "So, he can stop sniffing around you?"

"Tell him what? That I'm fucking my boss? No, it's none of his business, or anyone's for that matter." He hums against my neck, and I cross my ankles to squeeze my thighs tightly together. "But I did just tell him I only want to be friends."

"You did? When?"

"Just now. When he told me he had texted me and I never responded."

I can feel the cheeky bastard grin against my neck. His facial hair tickling me. "Good."

"How did you even get into my phone?"

He's still grinning against my neck while running his lips and darting his tongue out. "I put the passcode in," he says casually.

"And how did you know my passcode?" I lift my chin to let him switch sides, his hand creeping up higher.

"I've seen you type it."

"Stalker," I murmur in a teasing tone. Knowing that I was so unaware of him watching me is more thrilling than anything.

"What does your passcode mean?"

"I can't be giving you all my secrets." I squirm and stop his hand when I feel my thigh being exposed now. "Donavon, I told you, we can't do this at work."

"Then leave," he challenges and ignores my hand on top of his. He drags it up higher...higher...higher.

With the tip of his thumb, he swipes the fabric over my pussy and I'm mush. I wilt into him, and my knees find their way apart. "Don," I whine with my eyes closed as he teases me.

His chest rumbles as he licks and nips at my neck and his thumb makes feather light touches driving me crazy. "I want the taste of you on my tongue and have the smell of you on my face to last me through the entire day," he whispers.

I have to bite back a shameless moan and I clutch onto the lapels of his suit jacket to hold myself upright. "I want that too," I whisper back.

"Then get face down on my desk, darling." He jerks his hips up to deposit me from his lap. I get to my feet with a giddy grin I try my best to hide, and I bend over his desk to lay flat. The cool air grazes the backs of my legs as he hitches my skirt higher and higher until it bunches around my hips. He's still sitting in his chair and leans in to kiss the bare skin of one cheek. His fingers trail across my upper thigh and land between them. "You're soaking yourself, Jane," he says in a teasing tone and I'm too horny to be embarrassed of it. "What the..." he mutters as he tries to find a way around the crotch of my bodysuit.

I hide my face in my hand and shake my head. "There are snaps down there." Note to self; bodysuits are not sexy for office romance. "Don, what if someone walks in?"

He slips a finger behind the fabric, his knuckle rubbing me through my panties and the fabric of my bodysuit bounces up when he undoes the crotch snaps. The air feels cold as it hits the dampness quickly growing.

I hear him pick up his desk phone. "Maggie, we'll be on an hour-long conference call. Do not let anyone disturb us." Then he slams the phone down and caresses the skin of my ass. "Did you dance ballet?"

"Most of my childhood. Why?"

"I can tell."

I look at him over my shoulder and see him stop and stare at my wet heat as he breathes over it. "My boobs were too big though."

He glances up at me and grins. "Thank God." He shoves my panties down and spreads my cheeks right before smashing his face against me. I rise up on my toes and curl them as I arduously bite down a loud moan. I'm aware enough to know that people will hear us if we're too loud. I'd be mortified if anyone did.

Squeezing my eyes shut, I push my forehead into the surface of the desk and bite my tongue. God, he's amazing with his mouth. I'd let him do this to me several times a day if he wanted to. He eats me like he's a starved man. Like I'm his favorite thing in the world to taste.

"Oh, *fuck*, Donavon," I whisper and dig my nails into the desk, needing to grab onto something. "Mmm," I moan in frustration trying to stay quiet.

He licks and eats and sucks until I'm burying my mouth into the crook of my arm to stifle my cries. His facial hair brushes against my skin, intensifying everything. Then I'm a shaky mess on top of his desk, coming all over his face.

Squeezing my ass cheeks, he stands up behind me and I hear him undoing his pants. Then his cock is slipping up and down through my folds making me shiver. "Tell me I don't need to use a condom," he rasps.

Licking my lips, I tell him, "I'm clean and I'm on birth control."

He pauses. "Good girl." Then he smacks my ass hard and shoves his way inside of me. My back bows and I hiss through my teeth. He only gives me a second to adjust, then begins pulling almost all the way and shoving brutally back in. Slamming inside of me over and over, his balls lightly tapping my clit each time.

The thought of him bare and coming inside of me has me gritting my teeth as I'm quickly climbing up to my peak. Add in the obscene sound of my wetness covering his dick and I can't hold back another second.

I bite into my arm and every single muscle in my body cramps up, paralyzing me while I float with the stars. I hear him grunting behind me when I come to, and he slides a hand under me to wrap those strong fingers of his around my neck to lift me from the desk's surface. He's literally holding me up by my throat, forcing my back to bow as he pounds into me faster.

He grunts through his nose with a jerky thrust and I feel his cock twitching inside of me, already leaking out and running down the inside of my thighs. He pumps a few more sharp thrusts before his hips finally stop.

Instead of releasing me, he uses the hold on my neck as leverage to bring me up all the way and turn my face to him. He moves his hand to my jaw, grasping me tight and staring down at me for a heated moment before searing his lips to mine.

This kiss isn't as vulgar now. It's sensual and passionate as our tongues dance together and our lips move with precision. We part slightly and both stare at each other in awe. Is sex with Donavon always like this? Or is it us?

"I have no idea how I'm going to get any work done now," he rasps, making me laugh. His smile is so broad it touches his dark eyes, making my heart completely skip a beat.

He grabs some tissues from inside his desk and wipes me between my legs, then pulls my panties into place and skillfully snaps the crotch of my bodysuit. He takes advantage of my skirt still around my waist and caresses my bottom and places a kiss on one cheek before finally pulling my skirt down to cover me.

Spinning me around to face him, he pins me to the desk and kisses me. I can taste myself on him as he strokes my tongue with his. "You taste like me," I whisper boldly. I love it when he tastes like me. Insane thoughts of claiming him with my scent conjure up inside my head. Wishing he could always taste and smell like my pussy.

Never have I been so crass nor thought I could be. But with Donavon I feel so sexually liberated, and when in the moment, I have no shame. I want certain things I've never fantasized about before. I have no idea where my brain even comes up with these things.

"I'll be tasting and smelling you all day, and it's going to drive me insane." He grinds his partly erect cock against me.

I giggle and shake my head. He's insatiable. "But seriously, Don." I play with his tie, straightening it. "We have to be professional at work. I do not want to be *that girl* fucking her boss. Even though I technically am— I just don't want anyone finding out about us."

"Stop caring about what others think." He pinches my chin and makes me look up at him.

"Don, please?"

He sighs and rests his forehead against mine. "I'll try my best, but I can't make any promises."

I grin and relish in the butterflies he gives me with every romantic syllable that parts from his tongue. "Well, good thing I have my own office."

I try slipping away, but he yanks me back to him and trails soft open-mouth kisses up my neck. "Donavon!" I laugh when his coarse facial hair prickles my skin.

Finally, he releases me and I all but run out of his office.

Twenty-Three

Jane

This week has breezed by in sweet bliss.

I've been walking around with my head in the clouds fueling off pure joy and pleasure. But today there's a dark cloud looming over my head. Our pillow talk from last night has been plaguing me ever since.

I'm more than appreciative of his blatant honesty, but some things I could do without knowing the details of. As in his past sex life. And what was more bothersome was how nonchalant he was about giving me the specifics.

I knew that I would be compared to many women, all gorgeous and affluent, but I was working on moving past that insecurity. Now, an entirely new insecurity has been born, and I'm unsure of how to get past it.

While lying in bed last night, naked and tangled up in the sheets, we talked for hours. The conversation somehow turned into talking about him and other women. *Women.* As in plural. And not over the course of time, but at one time.

I'm pretty sure it all started when I asked how he had never been in a serious relationship. And I was so sorry I asked.

He has a bit of an acquired taste when it comes to sex. At least before me—or so he says. I remained speechless as he told me how sex was always with at least two women at a time. That he would watch them *perform* for him and that would get him going. Then he would use them to finish himself off. It was never intimate or passionate, but it was certainly adventurous.

Much like he is with his everyday life, it was something he became accustomed to and eventually preferred. Anything out of his ordinary has always been strenuous for him. Including changing up his typical sex life.

That's what scares me the most. How will I be enough for him? How can sex with me compare to what he's used to? It solidifies my fears of all of this having an expiration date. He'll eventually become too restless and need to go back to the life he's mapped out for himself.

My office door opens, and the man who is occupying my thoughts enters and closes it behind him. I give him a smile and pretend to be busy with something on the screen of my laptop.

"Something wrong, darling?"

I look up at him and give him a bigger smile. "Nope. I'm good."

I can feel him just standing there, staring at me, trying to figure me out while I randomly click through his emails. "Jane."

"Hm?"

"Jane, look at me please." The authoritative undertone awakens my libido.

When I look up at his handsome face, I begin to forget what has been eating me up all morning. "Yes, Donavon?"

He gives me a crooked grin and I instantly smile back. A real smile. "Almost ready to get out of here?" I nod my head and I can tell he wants to touch me. It's beyond flattering to know that he can't keep his hands off me. His fists are clenched at his sides, his gaze traces up my body before finally meeting mine again, and he gives me another grin then leaves my office.

Donavon reluctantly stays in the car when I get out in front of my building after dinner. He said he had a lot of work he needs to catch up on so I peeled myself from his lap and bolted before he could sense the desperation.

It's Friday night and since Donavon has been easing up some with the workload on me—even though I asked him not to—I finally have some free time and I promised Bonnie she would get it.

There's a knock on the door and I practically run to it with a zealous grin. I confirm it's her through the peephole before swinging it open and she launches herself into my arms. "Ah!" I squeal and lose my footing, causing us both to fall to the floor. I start spitting and pulling her curly hair out of my mouth as we're both laughing hard. "Oh, my God!" I spit some more. "I'm eating your hair!" It only makes us laugh harder.

I hug her petite body to me tighter. I may not be a hugger, but she's like a sister to me and I hardly get to see her these days.

We peel ourselves off the floor, still giggling and she follows me into the kitchen where I was unloading the Mexican food I had delivered right before she got here.

"Let's get this fiesta going so you can start giving me all the nasty details of your sex marathon with your boss," she says with a devilish grin.

I had told Bonnie about the first night we hooked up, but I was a little reserved when it came to the details of it. Not because I'm a prude or anything, but because I wasn't ready yet. I have my doubts and insecurities and it's something I'd rather discuss with her face to face and slightly inebriated.

She peppers me with question after question and I give her every answer no matter how much my cheeks blush. Bonnie has always been an explorer in the bedroom. She's pretty much done it all. Anthony was my first, and it wasn't bad with him, but it certainly wasn't mind-blowing or kinky.

"Woo!" She fans herself with her hand. "I am getting all hot and bothered over here."

I giggle. "Stop."

"So, you think this is serious, you and him?"

I shrug my shoulders and feel a tiny damper on my mood. "I'm not sure."

"What's wrong?"

I sigh. "I don't know. He told me about some of his prior...*preferences*, and I don't see how I can fulfil his needs for long."

"What kind of preferences?"

"That's one specific you are not getting out of me." She pouts. "I'll tell you this one minor detail, but that's it." She grins and waits for the juicy stuff. "He liked to sleep with two women at once."

She laughs. "You mean a rich and obnoxiously sexy single man likes to have threesomes?" she sardonically mocks and rolls her eyes. "What man doesn't like threesomes?"

"No, it wasn't like he had a lot of them. He *only* had threesomes. As in never sleeping with only one woman at a time. Since college!"

She finally grows somber, and I see the horror in her face that I have felt since he told me. "Oh." She takes a moment to consider the bomb I've dropped. "That's...okay, wow."

I groan and cover my face, shaking my head. "I know he must sound like a total pig to you now. Saying this all out loud, I know that's what you're thinking." I drop my hands and find her watching me with a look on her face that says a lot. "Tell me what you're thinking. Please."

"Give me a second." She and I both drain our drink. "Okay. So, he had a strong taste for threesomes, but that was before you, Jane. If you're the first woman he has been privately intimate with, not to mention actually dated in over a decade, that says everything right there." She pauses. "Have you had any conversations about being exclusive?"

I shake my head. "No, but it's only been a week since this all started."

"But this isn't any man, Jane. This is Donavon Waldorf, and from what you've told me about him and the fact that he's about to be forty, this sounds like it might be kind of serious for him."

I chuckle nervously. "I wouldn't say all that. Maybe yeah, it could be more than sex to him, but I definitely wouldn't say it's *serious*."

"Is it for you?"

I peek up and stare at her for a long moment. "I'm definitely catching feelings. I mean, I caught feelings for him a while ago, but they grow more intense by the minute."

"Aww." She smiles. "You're so in love," she coos.

I begin shaking my head. "No, please don't say that. I can't think about that. If I even begin to admit that I'm in love with him, that'll be it. I will fall so hard and fast, and it'll hurt that much worse when this whole thing blows up in my face."

"Why would it blow up in your face? You're already planning on him breaking your heart?"

"I don't even know what we are, Bonnie. A week from now we might not be fucking any more. The ball is completely in his court." I told myself after my last breakup that I would only be with someone I felt equal to. Someone that I could easily have the ball in my court and not theirs.

"Then talk to him, Jane."

"Ugh, I hate feeling like that girl," I mutter.

"You don't have to ask where you guys are or anything cliché like that. Ask him, adult to adult, if you two are going to be exclusively seeing each other."

I nod my head. "Yeah, I guess I could do that. It doesn't sound that bad the way you put it."

"But I will say this. The way he flipped when you kissed that guy from work, I think you could assume he doesn't want you to hook up with other guys. So, if he doesn't want that, then I'm sure he doesn't plan on being with other women. If not, then he's an asshole and needs to go."

I laugh. "Cheers to that." I lift my glass and remember that it's empty. "Time for some more margs!"

Twenty-Four

Jane

Another sex marathon for the books.

Again, after he took me to dinner, we came back to my place and went right for my room, hardly making it there with our clothes still on. Thankfully, Kenna spends a lot of time at her boyfriend's, so we have the place to ourselves most nights he stays.

It's early Sunday morning and I'm lying in his arms half asleep with the sun beginning to come through the curtains, and I cannot wipe the smile off my face. I wouldn't be surprised if I sleep with one on my face when we're together. I could not feel more happiness than I am feeling right now.

It's hard to believe that I was ever really in love with Anthony now. Never have I felt like this in all my life. Not only happy, but content, safe, adored, desired, confident. Donavon makes me feel good about myself inside and out. The way he puts so much faith in me at work, and how much he worships my body when we're alone, makes me feel constantly desired.

The recent doubts I had have been completely obliterated. I never found the courage to ask him if he's only seeing me, but I realized I don't need to. At least not yet. I'm going to enjoy what we are right now. Whatever we are.

"Jane," he whispers my name against my bare shoulder as he holds me flush with his body from behind.

"Hm?" I answer sleepily.

"I love you," he says firmly.

Rapidly blinking my eyes open, I try to wake myself up all the way as I look back at him. *Did I hear him correctly?* "You love me?" I ask in shock. His face is impassive as he nods his head. "But...but I thought this was just like..." I scramble for the right words. "Sex," I blurt out exactly what I was thinking. I didn't mean to say it out loud.

There's a list of emotions his face goes through as he stares back at me. Impassive to disappointment to anger to hurt then back to anger. He rolls over to get out of bed and I watch in sheer panic as he snatches up his clothing and begins putting them on.

"Wait!" I throw the covers off me and jump out of bed. "What are you doing?" I run to him frantically not bothering with putting any clothes on myself. He just told me he loves me, and I pretty much told him it's only sex! What is wrong with me?! "Don, please talk to me."

He's almost completely dressed, and I know he's going to leave but I have to stop him. I throw myself between him and the closed door. "Don, wait."

He stalks towards me peeved and affronted. The only time I've seen him enraged like this was when he stormed into my parents' house. "Jane. Move," he growls, now standing over me.

I shake my head. "Not until you hear me out."

His jaw twitches on one side. "Do you understand how hard that was for me to say to you? The only people to have ever heard those words from me has been my family, and it's been very rare when I do. Falling in love with you was easy but saying it out loud was not."

"I know," I say right away, not willing to waste a second. "And I fucked it up."

He isn't hearing it though. "Move, Jane. Or I will move you myself."

"I love you too!" I rush out, being sure to say it loud enough there'll be no question he heard me correctly.

He frowns, his face still tense, his nostrils now flaring. "You do?"

I chuckle humorlessly. "God, Donavon. Seriously?" I run a hand through my unruly hair. "I was saying I thought it was only sex for *you*. I didn't mean that for me. Donavon, I am stupidly in love with you, it's just so hard to believe you feel the same way. That you could possibly be in love with me, too." I pause. "But you are," I rasp in awe.

He cages me in with his arms and the anger drains from his face. "I am."

I fist his shirt. "And I still can't believe it."

"Why not?" He angles his head down, his lips floating over mine.

"Because you're—you, and I'm just...me. You could have any woman in the world., but it's me you love."

"I feel the same, darling," he whispers with his lips brushing mine. "I didn't think a woman like you was real."

He presses his mouth to mine and kisses me slowly with the passion of a thousand lifetimes. His pants are undone, so I sneak a hand down them to rub him over his underwear causing him to deepen the kiss.

Pulling back, I slip my fingers in the waistband and pull them down as I sink to my knees. I smile up at him and he combs his fingers into my hair then grips the back of it, pulling my scalp taut and making me gasp in arousal.

I open my mouth for him, and he gradually feeds me his cock. When he reaches my throat, I know what to do. I close my lips around him and suck. I work the base of him with one hand as my head bobs and my tongue cups his shaft. He lets the quietest groan out and it entices me. Knowing that I can make a man like Donavon groan, it's empowering. I suck him down like I'm chasing my own pleasure. My eyes roll up to witness the beautiful mess above me. Hair askew and eyes wild with lust.

It pops out of my mouth when he yanks me up all the way and my legs mechanically wrap around his hips. He spins us around to slam me against the door before he viciously thrusts into me.

He eats up my gasp with his mouth and brutalizes mine with his kiss as he punishes my pussy with his barbaric fucking. The door behind me rattles and I bask in this sweet moment, pinned against the door, being ravaged.

His thrusts are erratic and raging matching my heartbeat. No rhythm, just going on the beat of love. Imperfect and rampant.

"Donavon," I moan his name and grip his cock with my inner muscles.

"I love you, Jane," he rasps against my cheek as he fills me up with his cum and I tremble around him.

I take a few breaths as he slows and pulls back slightly so I can see his face. "I love you too."

TWENTY-FIVE

Donavon

The guilt is beginning to really make its weight.

I trust Jane more than I have ever trusted anyone in my life. I've given her more access to my company than I have to my brother or even Allison when she worked for me.

And she seems to trust me. I've been so openly honest with her about almost everything, but she still has no idea about the club. I've cut my time down there so that I can be with her most nights, but it's still something I need to deal with.

I press the intercom button to Jane's office on my phone. "Jane?"

"Yes, my love?"

I instantly smile. "Would you mind getting me a coffee?"

"A coffee?"

"Yes, black please."

"Sure," she says hesitantly.

It's not at all my usual, but I've already had two lattes today and I need something stronger to help me get through the rest of the day. I'm exhausted. I was at the club till early this morning and only got about two hours of sleep and I still did a half day at the gym before coming into the office.

I used to be at the club four nights a week, now Garrett is lucky if I make it twice. And every time I do go in, I'm pained with shame and remorse. I'm aware of the fact that I do need to tell Jane about it, and the sooner the better. I absolutely detest keeping something like this from her. Anything really. But I can't lie to myself and say that I'm not terrified of her reaction. There're only two personal territories of mine I have yet shared with her. My home and the club.

The club used to be a safe space for me to release that reckless side of me that I have long since suppressed and needs to be expelled once in a while before it tries to surface on its own. But since Jane, the need to feed that part of me is less prominent. It's as if it's disappearing altogether.

Jane saunters into my office and circumvents my desk with a pretty frown on her face. She hands me the cup of coffee and cups my face with one hand. "Donavon, you look exhausted. Did you not get any sleep?"

I attempt a smile for her, but my lips only twitch. I pull on her hips to make her sit across my lap. When she rakes her fingers through my hair, I sigh in content and close my eyes. She takes that as a cue to keep doing it and massages my scalp along with it.

I'm in heaven.

"You know you can unload some more work on me," she murmurs. "It is what you pay me for."

"It is?" I murmur back. "I thought I paid you for things like this."

She snorts. "You work too hard, baby," she whispers close to my face.

I pry my heavy eyelids back and find her baby blues staring at me. I love this woman so much. Her beauty never gets old or any less shocking to me. "This makes everything better."

She smiles a little. "Are you sure you want me to come home with you for Christmas?"

I frown, the question seeming random, but she's probably been overthinking it because of the way I reacted to her being at a family dinner before. My arms wrap around her waist tighter. "Of course, I'm sure. And every family dinner after that." I give her a chaste kiss on her lips.

"Well, I won't just assume, so you'll still have to invite me every time." She grins.

"Why is that?"

She dips her chin and cocks one eyebrow. "Because I know all of this is hard for you. Letting me in your life." *Not all of it.*

My stomach knots thinking about so much more she doesn't know. Things that I cannot explain. She gets me so much and has changed the way I function and brings so much peace to my life. Though I'm unsure of how much she knows about the depths of my issues and how far they really go. I know that by keeping Jane in my life, I will have to give her more of me. Take myself out of isolation and conform to a life that is shared with someone else. She'll eventually discover the unconcealed version of myself. She may think I'm weak, or that something is undeniably wrong with me. Exactly what I've always known about myself.

No, she isn't yet ready for all of me.

I need to at least tell her about the club. I love her too much to lose her. It's possible that I could give up the club and never have to tell her about it.

"It seems a lot less complicated with you." I admit to her openly. Nothing has felt rushed or impulsive. We may have only been together for a short time, but the months before were just a build-up to what we have now.

She snorts. "I still have yet to be invited to your place. Are you hiding other women there?" Her tone is purely good-natured, absolutely no malice behind it.

"No. Just all of my illegitimate children."

She chuckles. "Gross." She drops her hands from my hair after combing it back into place then hangs her arms over my shoulders.

"Does it bother you?"

She shrugs one shoulder. "I know it's pretty much the last step for you."

"What do you mean?"

"Well, let's see. You're legitimately *dating* me, you sleep over, you trust me, you rely on me, and you love me. All things I never expected from *you* ever, let alone so quickly. So, I can be patient on this last piece. I know you need your space, Donavon. And I respect that. This is how you've been living pretty much your whole life; I can't expect you to change overnight."

I gawk at her, somehow falling in love with her all over again. It's as if she can see inside my head. So patient, kind, and understanding. "This is why I love you," I rasp.

"I thought *these* are why you love me." She thrusts her breasts forward making me chuckle.

"Those are just a bonus." I press my lips against hers and kiss her.

Her lips are instantly pliant under mine as she allows me to part them and lick into her mouth with slow, languid kisses.

God, I missed her last night. Even when I crawled into bed at two in the morning, I wished that she were there waiting for me. Even if I only got to hold her for the couple of hours that I slept.

I have to fucking tell her. When I do, I know she'll understand. Because that's Jane. She's level-headed and understanding. Then I can go ahead and move her into my place and never have to sleep without her. I want her taking over and invading my space. I want her involved in every aspect of my world.

My phone goes off and she reaches behind her to grab it off my desk. She breaks the kiss and hands me my phone, but not before glancing down at it for only a moment. When she does, something sprints across her features. I take my phone as she pushes up from my lap. "I should get back to work." She leans down to give me a quick kiss then leaves.

I sit there smiling for a moment still reveling in her scent. When I look down at the text message, my heart sinks. "*Fuck.*" I hiss. "Fuck, fuck, *fuck.*"

Garrett: Call me when you get a minute, we didn't get a chance to talk about the girls from last night.

Fuck. She hardly glanced at the screen, but all she would have to see are the words, *girls* and *last night,* and it looks fucking questionable. It looks fucking *bad.* I toss my phone down on my desk and rub my hands down my face. I am at a loss here. I'm brand new to all of this and communication isn't exactly my strong suit. Even if I went to her to explain the text, I would have to explain everything. And seeing the hint of a crestfallen face from her with what she may have seen, it has me doubting if I'll ever be able to tell her everything. I don't ever want to hurt or disappoint her. She looks at me like I'm this amazing man to her and I can't have that taken away from me.

I'm going to get rid of the club. I'll hand it all over to Garrett and never have to tell her about it, and unless she brings up the text, I won't. It will be dismissed and forgotten.

Being as it's Friday, it's one of the two nights that I dedicate to the club. Fridays and Sundays, and occasionally Tuesday or Thursday, when I can manage to part from Jane.

At dinner I couldn't help myself but to study every single facial expression and mannerism. She didn't seem upset, though she was quieter than usual. I should stay and do some damage control, but if I want to sign off on the club, I need to get the ball rolling now.

"Something wrong?" Jane asks as I'm getting ready to leave.

"No, just sorry I have to leave you, darling." I finish dressing then bend down to kiss her while she's still lying in bed. She doesn't give me much of a response when I go to deepen it. Could she be thinking about what she saw on my phone? I wouldn't blame her.

Is this what it'll be like if I were to reveal the truth about the club? No, it would be worse. I don't want that. I cannot lose her. I've become so accustomed to her in my life, in and out of work, going back to a life without her is unimaginable.

"I'll see you tomorrow," I say and kiss her again, trying to show her how much I need her so that she doesn't forget. "I love you, Jane."

"I love you too," she whispers, meeting my eyes. Giving me some kind of reassurance.

We're okay, everything is going to be okay.

TWENTY-SIX

Jane

"Are you sure you're okay?" Kenna asks me once again as she helps me pack up the large salad I made to bring to her parents' for the weekend.

Honestly? I cannot stop thinking about that text I caught a glimpse of on Donavon's phone.

Normally I wouldn't jump to conclusions, but he wasn't with me that night, and he was exhausted yesterday. What the hell am I supposed to think? I could have asked him about it. I should have. Hell, he went into my phone and deleted a message on me, so I should have rights to his phone as well, right? *Shit, when did I become that girl?* I won't. I have to trust him. If he wants to cheat on me, then so be it, his loss. But, God, it would be such a loss for me too. The thought of him with anyone else is unbearable.

Getting cheated on, no matter the reason why, it always makes the one wronged feel worse. It's a humiliating betrayal. You somehow seem to find ways to blame yourself for it. Not being good enough. Not seeing the signs. Having zero judge of character. Being clueless.

"I'm good!" Kenna is the last person I should talk to about this because it's her brother and she'll probably say something to have me thinking I'm being paranoid.

I go and grab the cheesecake I made out of the fridge and add it to the insulated bag. "You know, you really didn't have to do any of this. My mom loves doing the cooking."

"I'm the first girl Donavon has ever brought home in all his thirty-nine years of being on this earth. I want to make sure it was worth the wait."

She laughs and places the lid over the large salad bowl, sealing it shut and putting it in the bag. "My parents already know you, silly. And they love you."

"They know me as your friend and roommate. Not Donavon's girlfriend. It's different." I seal the bag up and take a deep breath as if it were a much more strenuous task. "You nervous about bringing home Tom for the first time?"

She smiles and shakes her head. "I mean, a little. But not really. I know my family will like him, and I'm pretty fond of my own family, so yeah. The only thing that would suck is if *he* didn't like *them*."

"Which is impossible. You all are pretty great."

"We sure are, aren't we?" I nod my head in agreement. "I'm going to go grab my shoes so we're ready for when they get here."

I'm not much of a Suzy Homemaker, but I desperately want his family to see me as a good girlfriend for Donavon. They're so easy to get along with, but I still want to prove to everyone that I am worthy of him.

Tom arrives a few minutes later and he can't seem to help but pace through the living room. "You nervous?"

He gives a crooked smile and flexes his hands at his sides. "A little," he chuckles.

"Well, don't be. Her family is great."

He full on smiles making his dimples pop. He's a pretty boy for sure. He's a model so of course he is. His bright green eyes, sandy blonde hair all wavy and styled nicely match his tall, lean yet muscular build. He's the complete opposite of Donavon. A baby compared to him.

Don is such a manly man. Brutish, with scruffy facial hair that casts a shadow as soon as he shaves, broad shoulders, hauntingly blue eyes, a tensity in his face and stature that makes people feel the need to submit.

I literally shiver at just the thought of him.

When Kenna finally emerges, I notice how well matched she and Tom really are. She's only an inch shorter than him with her short heels, and they look like a real-life Barbie and Ken.

I disappear down the hall to gather the rest of my things and check my phone for the thousandth time. My mother had been blowing up my phone late last night and when I finally gave in and answered, I told her she needed to call the police.

I couldn't sleep much after that. I can't keep myself from worrying, but at the end of the day, I can't keep getting involved.

So, between that and that stupid text on Donavon's phone I can't seem to let go, I'm a bit on edge and obviously tired from not getting much rest.

"Jane?" I'm shaken from my thoughts and twist around to find Donavon standing in the doorway with a concerned look on his face. "You okay?"

The smile I give him isn't at all forced. No matter what's on my mind, seeing him makes me happy. I go to him and we wrap our arms around each other. "I'm fine." I crane my neck back as he bends his to kiss me. His arms tighten around my waist as he deepens the kiss and it's so easy to forget everything when I'm in his arms and his lips are moving with mine. I said I can be patient with him, and I meant it.

"Missed you last night," he murmurs against my mouth.

"I missed you too."

"You look beautiful." He combs his fingers through my hair as he studies my face.

I stare up at him with stars in my eyes. "Thank you. And you look just as handsome as ever."

"You ready to go?" I nod and go to pull away, but he doesn't let me. "I wanted to give you this first."

He pulls something out of his pocket and holds the small box with a gold bow between us. I grin and look back up at his face. "I thought we were doing presents at your parents.'"

"We are, but I wanted to give you this one first."

I step back and he lets me, handing me the small box. I pop it open and my whole face beams when I find a pair of oval cut diamond studded earrings.

"Oh, God, Donavon. They're beautiful." I jump into his arms, arching my back and plastering my lips to his. "I love them. Thank you so much."

"You're welcome, darling. Merry Christmas." He gives my butt a little smack. "Now, get your ass moving."

Naturally, Ron is driving us and since it's four of us riding together, we're in the back of a blacked-out suburban instead of the town car.

His focus is down on his phone as he's probably sorting through emails and such. "I made you cheesecake," I say to him.

He looks down at me and smirks. "Yeah?" I nod. "Thank you, darling." He kisses me on the head and goes back to his phone.

"This is really weird to see," Kenna says from the back and I crank my neck to see her. "I mean it in a good way. It's a good weird. I've just never seen Donavon with anyone, so it'll be a shock for everyone."

Donavon chuckles to himself and ignores us, so I turn around more to talk to Kenna. He drops his arm from me and threads his fingers through mine in my lap. Having to still touch me.

The rest of the ride I talk with Kenna and Tom while Donavon stays quiet on his phone. I don't mind because I know it's so he doesn't feel the need to check on work while we're with his family. I also don't let myself wonder what he might really be doing on his phone. *Nope. I will not think about it. I will not continue to obsess over it. I trust him. I have to.*

"You alright, darling?" Don rasps in my ear when we finally pull up to his parents' home.

"I am." More than anything I'm excited by the effort that's been put into the decorations. It's one step short of the Griswold's.

My mom would do some decorations when I was a kid, but nothing like this. I'd like to think she did put in some real effort to make it a special day for me when I was little. But as I got older, the decorations and presents under the tree petered out.

We all head inside and it's the warm greeting I was hoping for from his family. More so than the last time.

"It's like he's afraid to part with you," Annie murmurs next to me in amusement as she watches her son struggle to leave my side while I hang back in the kitchen.

I feel my cheeks blush as I grin and shake my head. "He's sweet."

"I still cannot believe I get to see the day my son has brought a woman home with him. And on Christmas of all days."

I continue smiling as we work side by side rolling crescent rolls and buttering them. "Well, I am certainly honored to be the first."

"First? Honey, you will be the only, mark my words." I bite down a grin, not wanting to have my head once again fill with fairy tales. "Oh, don't get so shy on me now." She playfully bumps my hip with hers.

I release my smile. "I'm not, but we only started dating."

"Something tells me it's been a lot longer than that. You two just didn't realize it."

It's mostly true. Him and I may have only been romantic for weeks, but we've known each other substantially well for months.

"Can I ask you something?" I say quietly and glance around to make sure Allison and Kenna aren't anywhere in earshot.

"Sure, hon."

"And I hope I'm not overstepping." I pause. "Has he ever seen anyone? Like a therapist or psychiatrist?"

She too glances around to make sure we can't be overheard. "I've tried. When he was still in high school, I got him to see someone, but he came home feeling worse and refused to go back," she says sadly as if she in some way failed him.

"Maybe they just weren't right for him."

"I did try explaining that, but I'm sure you know him well enough to know how stubborn he can be."

I snort and nod my head. "Yes, I do know that. I don't think you even have to know him well to know that about him."

We both laugh. "Yes, I would agree that would be one of the first things you would learn about him." We grow quiet and I can feel her stealing glances at me. "I have to say this though. He's already smiled more since walking through that door than I've seen him in a year's time."

I smile over at her, my heart beating out my chest. "Thank you." To have his mother say that to me, it has me chastising myself for ever having an ounce of doubt with Donavon. That text means absolutely nothing. A stupid misunderstanding.

"And if you ever need to talk to me about him—for whatever reason—know that you can." The sincerity in her gaze has me choking back tears. I wish I had a mother I could run to for advice.

Kenna turns up the Christmas music in the kitchen and I tune her and her sister out as they sing obnoxiously loud and get lost inside my head. Thinking back to a conversation between Donavon and me a while ago, before we became a 'we.'

"Do you ever smile, Mr. Waldorf?"

He doesn't look at me when he replies with, "I do."

"When?"

He looks up at me without lifting his head. "When something makes me happy."

I smile to myself knowing that I in fact do make him happy. That man is actually capable of smiling, and it happens to be around me.

There's no way he could be cheating on me. He wouldn't let his guard down and put all his effort into us and tell me he loves me if he was not fully invested. Donavon only does anything at one hundred percent. He commits and does it correctly. He may be reserved and even secretive, but he is never deceitful.

After we stuffed ourselves, we went and opened presents around the twelve-foot Christmas tree. Now, we're all sitting around with our dessert and a fire going.

"This cheesecake is delicious, Jane," Dan says, and everyone mumbles their agreement.

"What's wrong, Donavon?" Allison asks him as he sits across the room with a scowl.

"He was under the impression he didn't have to share," his mother says laughing.

"You told me you made it for me," Donavon adorably mutters making us all chuckle.

"I meant that I made it with you in mind." He narrows his eyes at me playfully and I shake my head smiling.

I go back to talking with Kenna and Allison both sitting next to me on a couch. Allison and Josh are getting married in the spring, but more importantly, her bachelorette party is in Vegas and she insists I come.

"Well, that's if your brother lets me have some time off work," I tell them.

"He will. Don't you worry. It's for me so he better," Allison says. "Plus, I'm coming back to work for him soon, so I'll be there to lift some of the load off you both."

"Like Benjamin?" I lift an eyebrow.

"Benjamin still thinks he's twenty-one years old. He doesn't care about how little responsibility Don gives him. As long as he's getting paid well and can continue to party," Allison tells me.

"I can hear you, you know," Benjamin says making us laugh.

I look up to find Donavon watching me and we lock eyes. He mouths 'I love you' and I feel my cheeks heat as I tuck some hair behind my ear and mouth 'I love you too' back to him. Because I really do.

I love Donavon. I love his family. I love my job. And right now, I love my life.

TWENTY-SEVEN

Jane

The holidays have come and gone.

It's a new year and I have a feeling this will be the best year of my life.

A stack of papers in hand, I walk into Donavon's office and head right to his desk to place them down. Yes, he allows me to place them on his desk instead of me standing there waiting for him to pay attention to me and accept them.

It would sometimes irk the hell out of me when I would stand there and wait for him to acknowledge me. When I'd begin to lose my patience, I would start to mess with things on his desk until he would huff his agitation.

I tested the water with him about a week ago. I placed his latte down on his coaster and the small bag with a brownie inside right next to it like he always does. I stared down at him to study his reaction closely. He looked at the items, glanced up at me, then thanked me. As long as I place them exactly where he likes them, he seems to be okay with me doing so.

I'm not trying to change him, because I don't think there is changing him, but I also don't want to keep enabling every habit. Enabling can only worsen his tendencies.

He looks up at me smiling. "Come here, darling. I need a break."

"You need lunch."

He takes me in his lap, our arms resting comfortably around each other. "It'll have to wait, but please don't wait on me. You can go take your lunch break."

I lightly scratch my nails down his beard, admiring his handsome features and he makes a rumbling sound in the back of his throat. "You should really take some time to eat. I can bring you something."

"The only thing I'm hungry for is you," he murmurs and goes in to start sucking on my neck.

"Oh, my lord. You just had me like two hours ago." Literally two hours ago he had me on top of his desk after I sucked him off underneath it.

"And I'm hungry for some more," he mutters.

"Well, I am hungry for some actual food. So, I'm going to grab some lunch and I will grab you something too while I'm down there. And speaking of food." He lifts his head up to look at me. "Kenna is going away this weekend and I was wondering if you would maybe want to stay in to eat."

"You going to cook for me?"

I arch both eyebrows with a sardonic smirk. "Do you want me to?"

"*Can* you cook?"

"I'm sure I *can*, but I don't think you'd want me to."

He chuckles and moves my hair off my shoulder tenderly. "Take out it is. As long as you're naked the whole time."

"You're ridiculous."

"I'm infatuated."

My cheeks warm. I love it when he says stuff like that because I know he wouldn't say anything he doesn't mean. "I love you." I go to get up, but he pulls me back down.

"I almost forgot. What would you think about spending some time somewhere warm?"

"I'm listening."

He smiles and kisses my lips softly. "Somewhere near the beach," he murmurs against my lips.

"I'm *still* listening," I murmur back.

"Just say yes," he whispers.

"I wouldn't dream of saying *no*."

He presses his lips more firmly against mine and I kiss him back. Being near him things are already heated, so when we touch, it's electrifying.

"You guys need to start locking the door," Benjamin says entering the room without knocking as usual.

"You need to start knocking," Don retorts.

"We need to start locking the door," I utter under my breath to Don then kiss his cheek. "I'm going to go meet up with Madison for lunch and I'll bring you back something." I get up. "Hi, Benjamin."

He grins up at me as he takes a seat in front of Don's desk. "Good afternoon, Jane." He gives me a knowing smile that I ignore and leave the room.

Pulling out my phone I text Madison and see if she can do lunch and she immediately agrees.

We set up lunch in my office over on the coffee table placed in front of the loveseat pushed against one wall.

"So, I actually needed to talk to you about something." The tone in her voice has me pause, because it doesn't sound like this is going to be a pleasant conversation.

"What's going on?"

She's finding it difficult to meet my eye as she pushes around her food nervously. Right away I know it has to do with Donavon. I don't know why, but I know it does. "So, I just heard this—and I haven't done any fact checking, but you know Nick isn't the type to make things up or start false rumors," she prattles on.

"Just spit it out, Madison. What did you hear?"

She glances up at me, face full of pity and remorse. My heart instantly sinks to the pit of my stomach. "So, I was hanging out with Nick and he was telling me about this bachelor party he went to Friday night and..." she pauses, and I want to shake her, "and they went to this ritzy strip club and they..." she trails off again.

"Madison, please just say it. Did he see Donavon there or something?" She nods, and I take a deep breath, my appetite suddenly gone. *Okay, so he went to a strip club. No big deal, right?* But why lie about it?

"But he wasn't there as a customer." She continues and I stare at her with a puzzled frown. "Supposedly, he's the owner."

I chuckle and shake my head, knowing this whole thing is some kind of misunderstanding. "That can't be, Madison. I look over a lot of his finances and I think I would know if he owned a strip club."

"I know it sounds crazy, but Nick was very serious. He doesn't know about you two, so it's not like he would try to stir something up like this. He's not that kind of guy to do that anyways even if he did know about you and Mr. Waldorf."

"How does he know he's the owner?"

"He said he asked a girl that worked there. He asked who 'that guy' was when he saw him because he clearly was not there as a customer, and supposedly she said, 'that's Mr. W, one of the owners'."

I take another breath and lean back on the couch trying to mull this all over. Could this be true? Could he secretly own a strip club? Why so secretive about it though? Does he think I wouldn't approve of something like that?

"Are you okay?"

"Yeah." My heart is racing like crazy, anxiety gripping my gut. "Could you do me a favor? Could you text Nick and ask him what the name of the place was called?"

She nods and immediately pulls out her phone. We're both silent as we stare at her screen, impatiently waiting for him to reply. Thankfully, it doesn't take long. Her phone pings, and the screen lights up. She snatches it up to read it and I avert my gaze. Too afraid to look.

"Verity," she says. "Want to look it up?"

I rub my face with my palms and shake my head, not at all ready to deal with this yet. I'll wait till she leaves to do so. "Not right now."

"I understand. I'm sorry, Jane. But hey, maybe Nick was misinformed."

I give her a dry look. "But he said he saw him there. Regardless, he was there when he told me he was home working."

She bites her lips and nods her head. "I'm sorry," she says quietly.

We go back to pushing around our food silently. I'm embarrassed and there's this harrowing paranoia eating me up inside. It was on Friday. One of the days he never stays the night with me. Is this what he's really doing every Friday night? Was this a one-time thing? Could he really own that place? I don't know which is worse. Him lying about working and really going out to strip clubs, or lying to me about working but working at this strip club he actually owns? I don't know, but a lie is a lie no matter which way the truth leans.

Now thinking about it, he also never stays the night with me Sunday nights and he's always unusually tired Monday mornings. And every morning he wasn't with me the night before that...

"I need to get back to work. Are you sure you're okay, Jane?"

I nod. "Yeah, I'm fine." I look at her. "Thank you for telling me."

"Of course! I never want to see you hurt, but I could never keep something like this from you." She helps me clean up our containers and says she'll take the trash with her. "What are you going to do?"

I shrug. "I honestly don't know yet. I'm obviously not going to sweep it under the rug though."

"Okay. I'm here for you, you know. So, call or text me or whatever you need."

I give her a sad smile. "I know. Thank you so much, Mads."

She pulls me in for a hug and I let her, because I could use it right now.

She leaves me to my depressing thoughts, and I stare at my monitor knowing that I need to get down to the bottom of this. I really should go straight to Donavon and confront him, but what if he lies to me? What if he denies it then I find out the truth? Or in the best-case scenario, I confront him and it turns out to be all a lie and I look like a crazy person.

That text message pops up in my head again. Women. Last night. *Fuck!* I bury my face in my hands with my elbows on my desk. This cannot be happening.

My phone goes off and I see that it's Donavon calling. I hesitate to answer, but he'll only come looking for me if I don't. I can't avoid this. "Hey."

"Hey, darling. Were you still going to grab me something to eat, or should I call something in?"

I lick my licks and straighten up. "Yeah, I grabbed you something. I'll be right there."

Grabbing his bag, I leave my office and go to his. He stands up and rounds the desk to go sit down on the couch and sighs when he falls back onto it. He pinches the bridge of his nose as I stand there staring at him. I don't want to believe what I just heard. It'll ruin everything. Destroy the very image of him. Rip away that fanciful thought of happiness and fairytales.

"Jane? You alright?" He stares back up at me.

"Sorry," I mutter then place his stuff on the coffee table.

"Did you get a chance to eat?" he asks me as he unwraps his sandwich.

"Yeah." Not really.

"Will you sit with me for a few?" He looks up at me with those deep blues and I keep staring back at him for a long moment. Could this handsome man who has been nothing but wonderful to me be hiding so many secrets? Secrets that could level everything we have built together.

Swallowing around the lump lodged in my throat, I nod my head and take a seat next to him. On the couch we've had sex on countless times. Worked side-by-side on. Had meals together on.

"So, I was wondering." I turn to him and smile. "Since Kenna will be gone all weekend, I was wondering if you would want to stay tonight too?" His demeanor doesn't change as he continues eating. "I know you don't stay over on Fridays, but maybe this once?"

He finishes chewing his bite then chases it down with some water. "I would love to darling, but you know I can't."

Why not? "Okay. It was just a thought. My offer still stands where I can help you. It'd get done a lot quicker with my help."

He turns to me and playfully pinches my chin. "I'd much rather know that you are at home relaxing and getting some good sleep." Then he places his lips on mine.

"Okay," I say quietly and stand up.

"Where are you going?"

"I have stuff to do," I call over my shoulder and leave before he can say anything else or see that something is bothering me.

I open up my laptop and search the name of the club. From what I can find on it, a man named Garrett Thomas owns it. But I do know Donavon, even if not everything, and if he did own a place like that or part of it, he wouldn't put his name on it or have it so easy to find his name attached to it. It wouldn't look good for his reputation.

The only way I'm going to get my answers is if I go and check the place out for myself.

Twenty-Eight

Jane

I avoid looking up when Donavon enters my office.

"Let's get out of here, darling. I'm starving."

I glance down at my watch, which was another Christmas gift from him, and realize it's after six. "Um, I'm going to skip out on dinner tonight, if that's okay," I say as I gather my things. There's no way I could sit with him through dinner and act normal when I'm a mess inside.

"What's wrong?" He comes to me, full of concern. "You feeling okay?"

Thanks for the idea, Don. "I have a terrible headache. I just want to go home and crawl into bed."

He cups my face, making me look up at him. "I hope you aren't coming down with something." His concern is sincere and genuine giving me guilt.

"I'm sure I'm fine." I try giving him a smile. "I'll take something when I get home and get some good sleep and I'll be fine by morning."

He doesn't exactly seem convinced, but he doesn't say anything. We walk out of the office together and slip inside the back of the town car and he tells Ron to take me home first.

When we get to my building, he insists on walking me up. "Go get yourself in bed," he says as soon as we walk inside the apartment. "I'll get you some water and find you some medicine."

I nod and walk away. The last thing I want right now is for him to take care of me.

Changing out of my work clothes and into some comfy ones, I climb into bed. He comes in with a glass of water and hands me a few pills. I chase them down and set the glass on my nightstand. "You should still eat, darling." He sits on the edge of the bed looking at me solicitously.

"There's a bunch of leftovers in the fridge. I can eat something later."

He frowns at me. "I hate leaving you like this."

"Well, you have tons of work to do, right?" *Say no. Say you'll stay. Tell me you aren't keeping anything from me.*

"Unfortunately, I do." He leans in to kiss me, and I wrap my hands around his neck, so I can deepen it. If I find out something about him tonight, something that can destroy us, then this could be our last time together.

I devour him as he devours me and our clothes end up on the floor as our hands are everywhere. I push him to his back and climb on top of him. I refuse to think about the bubble that might soon burst and stare down at him with the admiration I still have for him.

Leaning down, I kiss him again as I rock my hips over his cock. "I thought your head hurt?" he murmurs but doesn't stop kissing me back.

"This makes it better."

Without breaking the kiss, I reach behind me to line his cock up and I sink down on it. I let him fill me and pause for a moment to enjoy it, then I start riding him with a pace that isn't painfully slow, but that'll make it last.

It isn't long before he flips me over to my back and begins to ravish me. His hands exploring my whole body as if he can't get enough. His mouth leaves a trail of wet kisses all over my face and neck.

He moves inside me with the same mild pace but with sharper thrusts and I wrap my arms around him tightly and squeeze my eyes shut. Trying to cherish every second of this.

"I love you, Donavon," I whisper. Because I do. No matter what, I will always love him.

"I love you too, Jane," he whispers back into the nook of my neck.

I watch him as he gets dressed, and the sinking feeling comes back. Once he's out that door, he could be out of my life. Because when the sun goes down, I'm going to that strip club and getting some answers. And I am not the kind of woman with my head in the sand.

He gives me one last kiss and asks if I need anything, then he's gone.

Turns out I do still know Donavon as well as I thought, because when I'm pulling up to the building with a sign that says Verity, he's climbing out of the back of the town car. The large man at the entrance gives him a nod of acknowledgement right before opening the door for him. Not just as if he knows him, but as if he works for him. I already have my answer, and I have enough evidence to confront him with, but I still exit the vehicle.

The same man at the entrance checks my ID and opens the door for me. I'm swallowed by the darkness and the low thumping music. My heels clack against the tiled floor until I get to the young woman at the end of the hall.

"Hey, welcome to Verity," she says with a bright smile.

"Hi." I give her a tight smile, and fish out my card.

"It's $300 for non-members." *Sheesh.* I nod my head to give her permission to run it. "Would you like to check your coat?"

"No, thank you."

She hands me my card back. "Have a nice night."

"Thanks," I murmur.

I walk through the rest of the darkness until the lights touch the floors. It isn't like any strip club I've ever seen. I grew up in the city as a rich girl, so of course I have been to strip clubs before. I have absolutely nothing against them and happen to enjoy them. I do have a problem with lying though. Huge problem.

The outrageous cover makes a lot more sense seeing this place inside. I guess it would be considered a *gentlemen's club* rather than a strip club. She did say 'non-members.'

Everything is so chic and pristine, from the stage to the chairs to the bar. It's a beautiful place.

I head to the bar and sit down without bothering to take my coat off. "Hey, sweetie. What can I get you?" The beautiful woman behind the bar greets me with an affable smile. So far every woman that works here is gorgeous.

"Hi. I would love a jack and coke. Double please." I hand her my card.

"Would you like to keep it open?"

"No, thank you."

She turns to go and make my drink, so I turn my attention to the stage and the woman dancing on it. She still has little scraps of clothing on and the way she's seductively dancing, she has everyone in the place captivated. Including me. I envy her. The serpentine way she moves her hips and rolls her body and the sultry look on her attractive face.

"Here you go, love," the bartender comes back with my drink and my check.

"Thank you." I quickly sign the receipt leaving a nice tip then pick my drink up to give my focus back to the stage so I don't miss anything.

"First time here?" the bartender asks.

I glance at her to nod. "Yes."

"That's Isabelle. She's amazing," she raises her voice over the music.

I look at her and find that she's friendly enough to pepper with some questions. "Is Mr. W here tonight?" I chance it with the name Madison said Nick heard.

"He should be," she says without skipping a beat. "But I think he's upstairs. You here for an interview or audition?"

There's a difference? Maybe an interview to work behind the bar or a cocktail waitress, or an audition to be a dancer?

"An audition," I blurt out on impulse.

"Do you have an appointment?"

I nod and sip my drink to give me more courage to continue this little ruse of mine going.

She studies me for a second, and I remain calm under her scrutiny. "If you have an appointment, then you can go give Big D over there your name and he'll let you up." She throws her head in the direction behind me.

I turn my head and look for a man that looks like his name would be *Big D*. He isn't hard to find. I assume he's the very large and stoic looking man standing at what looks like an entrance to another hallway.

I down my drink and throw her a thanks before hopping down from the barstool. As I weave in and out of the patrons, I take in their attire and realize they all look like businessmen and the elite of the city. Considering the cover, I guess it's all who could afford a place like this. Because you don't just pay the cover. You pay for drinks and for the gorgeous women to seductively dance for you and make you feel desired and wanted. It's amazing the way they can so easily lure men in with their body alone.

Knowing I need to come up with something to get past the bouncer, I take my coat off and sling it over my arm. Then I perk my breasts up some to pour out of the little dress I'm wearing and fluff up my hair.

Swaying my hips and putting up a bravado as if I'm supposed to be here, I walk right up to the bouncer. "Hi, I have an appointment with Mr. W."

He frowns, but it doesn't stop him from checking me out. His eyes lingering a little too long on my cleavage. "You sure? Because he's already in an appointment right now."

I sigh and pretend to be a little upset and anxious. "I know, I'm late. And I know how much he hates anyone being late, but I really need this job. I was supposed to be here on time but then my babysitter said she was sick, so I had to frantically find someone to—"

"I get it. I've got kids too."

I give him a thankful smile. "So, you completely understand."

"I do." He gestures down the darkened hall. "Go ahead. As long as your audition is worth it, he won't be too upset at your tardiness."

Yeah, right. Anyone that makes Donavon wait gets their head chewed off and spit out.

"Thank you, thank you, thank you," I say excitedly and scurry down the hall before he realizes what a con I am.

Every step I take into the darkness, my heart rate picks up a beat. The music in the background fades and my palms begin to sweat. I reach the doors to an elevator and look around and I spot a stairwell further down. Not having a clue what the elevator might open to, I choose the stairwell to stay inconspicuous.

So, one thing I now know for sure. Donavon owns a strip club. But why hide it from me? There could be so many reasons why he would. He might think I wouldn't approve. He might want this to be his little secret. Or he has this whole other life, one where he doesn't want me a part of or anyone to know about.

Hope for the best but prepare for the worst, right?

I stop at the top of the stairs and close my eyes. I have to do this. Ignorance is not bliss. I have to see this for myself, and he needs to explain himself to me. Either it's something we can work out, or it's something that will shatter my heart and soul into a billion pieces which will be irreparable, and I'll die from a broken heart. It's all good.

I arrive in another dark lit hallway, but I can make out the two doors along the wall in front of me. Both closed and both unmarked. Though I can faintly hear music and noise resounding off the back of one, drawing me nearer.

Closing my eyes one last time, I take a deep breath and pull the handle down and shove open the door and practically stumble inside. And just like that, my entire world comes crashing down around me.

I'm instantly sick to my stomach. I look from the two naked women heavily groping each other to the unfamiliar man sitting on the couch gawking at me to the much too familiar man sitting on the other side of the couch grinning. Though in this moment, Donavon is like a stranger to me. I may recognize his face and every feature of him, but I don't know this person.

My eyes dart back to the two women who do not skip a beat, and one slithers down the other's body, her face landing between her legs. The standing one throws a leg over her shoulder and lets her head fall back. My gaze snaps back to Donavon's and the smile he had is replaced with contrition and self-reproach. He's caught and he knows there is no explanation for this.

The crippling, inconsolable feeling has my insides contort in pain. I thought so highly of this man. I thought he was honorable and honest, but he's disgusting.

Deep down, I knew I wasn't enough. I tried to beguile myself into thinking he loved me and was fulfilled with what I could offer him. But no. He needs more. He will always need more. He will always be stuck in his ways.

With my heart in the deepest depths of my gut, I backpedal and flee the scene. My eyes are blurry with tears as I run down the stairs, tripping over my own two feet every other step. I bolt out of the hallway and through the place until I burst through the exit, and I bend over at the curb to puke my guts out.

"Miss, are you alright?" I turn to see the bouncer coming to me in concern.

I straighten up and wipe my mouth with the back of my hand and throw my coat on. "I'm fine," I choke out and stumble towards the street to hail down a cab. But my vision is impaired from the fat tears building up, I don't notice that I walked into the middle of the street until it's too late.

"Miss! Watch out!" I turn back to see the bouncer running towards me and then everything goes black.

Twenty-Nine

Donavon

"Are you even paying attention, D?" Garrett says from beside me.

I sigh in contempt and glance up at the two women auditioning in front of me, feeling like this is wrong. It's only business, but I don't think I should be involved in the auditions anymore.

I've finally decided on giving up the club altogether. This was a place where I could unleash that impudent and deviant part of myself I couldn't seem to break from. A place I could drink in excess to quell my anxieties, express my sexual desires and needs without judgement, where I could do whatever was necessary to feel...*less* abnormal.

But Jane has been filling that void inside of me, making me feel whole and not so aberrant. I was only hesitant about giving it up in the case that my execrable side may surface in our relationship, and I cannot risk losing her. I have to rid myself of this and put it with the rest of my past life.

"They look fine," I mutter and look back down at the engagement rings on my phone I've been preoccupied with this whole time. I want something custom made for Jane, but I don't even know what they typically look like. A ring with a large diamond, right?

He chuckles from beside me and shakes his head. "Alright, ladies..."

I tune him out and focus back on what's most important to me. Princess, oval, emerald, pear. Shit, how do I know what she likes when it comes to diamonds? I know what her favorite foods are, her favorite color, her favorite music, and I'm fairly sure I could pick clothes out for her that she would like. But how do I know what kind of diamond she would like? She wears silver jewelry, so I think I would get a platinum band, but what kind of diamond? And would she like it with more diamonds around it, or a solitaire diamond?

I pick my head up, staring into space like a fool as I think about proposing to her. Of making her my wife one day. Will she cry when I ask her to marry me? I'm almost positive she would say yes. I know she loves me just as much as I love her. So, I think she would say yes. How will I even do it? Should I go big with the proposal, or should I keep it simple? Now, I'm picturing her in a wedding dress. She's so gorgeous in anything she wears, I know she will be stunning in a gown that's white. Anything that's white.

The door to my office flies open, and the temptress that occupies my every waking and restful thought comes charging in. I'm too staggered to see her that I forget where the hell I am. So, when she looks at me in horror and her eyes fill up with tears, I mentally shake myself and realize I'm fucked. Not only did Jane find out, but there are two naked women in front of me putting on a tawdry show. I'm fucked. Totally fucked. And I'm too frozen with remorse to open my goddamn mouth to speak or go after her when she runs out of here.

"Everyone out," I state flatly, currently detached from any and all emotions.

"Shit, was that Jane?" Garrett murmurs beside me and hearing her name sends me into a fit of rage.

"I said out!" I roar jumping to my feet. "Everyone, get the fuck out!"

My voice reverberates off the walls and the glass of the windows as I become mad and begin to pace. Garrett knows better than to stick around and I'm sure the two women ran out of here practically pissing themselves. I'm clearly unhinged.

I might have lost the love of my life. My solace and sun. The only light that has ever been able to penetrate through my darkness. "*Fuck,*"

I bellow out causing my throat to burn. I continue burning tracks into the floors as I pace back and forth furiously. "Fuck," I say weakly and sink to the floor, my desk holding me upright by my back.

My Jane.

Those memories of being a fuck-up resurface and the memories of failing my family and myself consume me. I've failed, I've lost control, I've destroyed the one chance at happiness and total content.

Jane saw what she saw. There is no reasoning or justification for what she walked into. I oscillated between admitting the truth and disposing of it altogether, so she'll never have to know, but she found out for herself and in the worst way imaginable.

The look of disgust and disappointment in her glossy eyes will haunt me for the rest of my days. I disappointed her. Erased every high standard she held me to. Shattered her trust. I fucking hurt her.

There's a stinging in the back of my eyes and my chest feels like it's caving in. I feel like I can't breathe and that I'm going to be sick. God, everything hurts. I feel like I'm dying. I actually wish I would, because I will never recover from this. To see what life was like with her, and to try and move on in a life without her. It's unfathomable.

Her gorgeous smile flashes through my head and I can't help but think it'll remain just a memory for me. I'll never get to put that smile there again. All I'll picture is the pain in her eyes, and the crestfallen look on her face. And if she is feeling anything like I do now, I detest myself for it. I already hate myself but devastating her is the last thing I would ever want to do.

I have only myself to blame for all of this. I should have gotten rid of the club as soon as I realized my feelings for Jane and how badly I wanted her. Then how badly I needed her was a revelation that changed the course of my life forever.

God, I love her so fucking much, everything fucking hurts.

I faintly hear my phone ringing down on the floor beside me, but I can't move. It's not Jane so I don't care. No one else matters to me anymore. No one. I fucked it up. Why did I fuck it up? I could have prevented it. I could have been honest with her, or I could have gotten rid of the club.

Goddamnit.

The ringing persists and I'm tempted to defenestrate it, cutting myself off from everyone.

There's a knock on the door and I want to tell them to fuck off, but I still can't even speak. It hurts too much. The knocking persists and yet I still ignore it. The door opens. "D, it's urgent." I glance up to find Garrett and Darrel standing in the doorway. Both of them looking like they've seen a ghost or are about to. "Darrel says there was an incident out front."

"A woman ran out of the club distraught and got hit by a car," Darrel informs me.

I spring to my feet, every muscle in my body coiled tight. "What!"

"She just ran out into the street I couldn't stop her," he explains. "She's on her way to the hospital now in an ambulance."

I instantly see red and charge at Darrel. Snapping him up by his shirt, I pin him against the frame of the doorway. He might be bigger than me in size, but I am wrathful. "Why the fuck wasn't I informed the minute this happened?" I seethe.

"D," Garrett tries to interject.

"I'm sorry, boss. But I saw it all happen and went to see if she was okay and then called the ambulance and waited with her."

"Motherfucker!" I yell and release him to grab my phone.

"D, maybe you should—"

"Not now, Garrett," I snap and call Ron. "Where are you?" I ask sharply as soon as he answers.

"Just around the block, sir."

"Get here now. We need to get to the hospital. It's Jane."

I go to storm out when Garrett lays a firm hand on my shoulder stopping me. I seethe and I'm ready to rip his arm off. "Call me if you need anything. Anything at all," he says with such sincerity.

Luckily, he removes it himself and I continue towards the exit. Ron pulls around the corner and heads in my direction, but I'm too overwrought to wait and I meet him halfway. "I don't care how many laws you have to break; get me to that hospital as soon as you can."

"You got it, sir." He steps on the gas.

I bury my face in my hands and pray that Jane is alright. What if she fucking dies hating me? What if she dies? What the hell would I do? How the fuck did everything go from rapturous to ending up in ruins? *Me.* That's how. I will never forgive myself if something happens to her. I will never forgive myself. Never.

We pull up to the hospital at the Emergency wing in record timing and I jump out. "I'm looking for Jane Donahue. She should have just arrived in an ambulance," I say as soon as I hit the front desk.

The woman's fingers fly across the keyboard. "Yes, I see that she has. It shows here that she is getting a CT scan right now, so it will be a little while until anyone can see her."

I slam my fist down making her and several other people jump. "Where is she?"

"Sir, you need to calm down."

Fuck this.

I charge past the desk and down the widened hall, ignoring anyone who protests and threatens to call security. I don't give one fuck. I need to get to Jane. I need to see that she's alright.

"Jane!" I bellow her name because I don't know what else to do. I'm frantic and terrified. "Jane!" I somehow manage to project my voice even louder, calling out all the nurses on the floor.

A woman comes from behind me and tries to stand in my path. "Sir, if you would please—"

"I need to find Jane Donahue. My wife. She was in an accident," I rush out.

"I understand, but if you would please come back to the waiting room—"

She's trying to make me leave without any resolution. "Jane!" I step around her and she follows me.

"Sir! I'm trying to explain that if she was just admitted, she might not be in a room yet. If you can please calm down, I can go find out where she is and when you can see her." I stop and glare down at her. "They will call for security if you do not calm down. I am trying to help, but you need to let me."

Her words finally knock some sense into me. If they call security, it will only enrage me and the cops will have to be called. None of that will help me getting to Jane.

"Then get me some goddamn answers," I hiss.

She nods her head and scampers off. I don't follow her, afraid to move my feet. It feels like an eternity until she comes back as I'm lost inside my own head with the most dreadful thoughts and emotions.

"Sir, Ms. Donahue is getting a CT scan right now. She hit her head pretty hard on the ground and although there wasn't any external bleeding, she still lost consciousness before the ambulance had arrived."

"So, she's okay."

"Yes, sir. She seems to be."

The instant relief that washes over me has me swaying on my feet slightly. "Can I see her?"

"As soon as she's done with her scans, they'll take her to a room, and I will have you informed right away."

"Right away," I demand.

She nods. "Yes, I promise you. Not a moment later."

I take the stairs two at a time to the next floor and head for the reception on the floor the patient nurse said she would most likely be admitted to. I give them Jane's name insisting to be informed as soon as they have a room number for me. My feet begin pacing in front of the desk and if she wants to get rid of me, then she'll tell me where to find Jane the second she can.

Something draws my attention from down the hall, and I catch a gurney being rolled down and I see that angelic face light up when she sees me. I run to her, almost pummeling one of the nurses over.

Jane chuckles weakly. "Hey."

"Jane," I rasp her name, and take her hand in mine feeling like I can take a breath. "Are you alright? Where are you hurt?" I start examining her body as they continue to roll her down the hall and we turn into a room.

"I'm okay. A little banged up. I got hit by a car," she mutters the last part as if embarrassed. "I don't remember it, but that's what they said when they were getting me in the ambulance."

I frown and study her more closely. Other than seeming a little tired, she seems to be in good spirits. As in she isn't angry with me. Or angry at all.

"The doctor will be in shortly to talk with you," one of the nurses says as they transfer her into the hospital bed and begin hooking her up to monitors. She says she'll give her an IV for dehydration to be safe. All the while my hand never stops squeezing hers.

"I'm okay, Don," Jane says to me with a sleepy smile. "Just a minor concussion and some bruises, but I'm fine."

"I'd like to hear it from a doctor," I mutter.

The nurse reassures me that the doctor will be in to talk with us shortly before finally leaving us alone. I kiss her hand clasped in mine and close my eyes. The amount of guilt cramping my stomach and the penance constricting in my chest is almost too much to bear.

"I'm so thankful you're okay."

"I am."

I look up at her and find her still lazily smiling at me. "How are you feeling? Are you in any pain right now?"

She shakes her head. "No, they already gave me something strong because I'm feeling a little loopy." She grins and my lips twitch. "It's weird though." Her smile falters. "Where I got hit by the car, I don't know what I was doing there. Considering you weren't there when I came to, I assume I wasn't with you?"

I swallow hard. This is it. Confirmation that she doesn't remember coming to my private business. Doesn't remember my deception. The part of me she couldn't possibly love if she knew.

I open my mouth to say something when the doctor knocks before entering the room.

The doctor says her scans look normal, but it can be tricky with head injuries, so she needs to be closely monitored overnight and for a few days afterwards when she goes home. When Jane mentions not having recollection of the events leading up to the accident and as far as the past two days, he says retrograde amnesia is common. Also, that her memories could come back, or they may not.

After I harass the doctor with several more questions he leaves us, and Jane wraps her arms around my arm hugging it. "You're so sweet. I love you." She yawns and closes her eyes.

I kiss the top of her head and breathe her in. "I love you, too."

"I'm sleepy."

"Rest your eyes, darling."

"Don't leave me," she whispers and my heart tremors in my chest, close to shattering.

"I'll be right here."

Her breathing evens out in seconds as she succumbs to sleep. I stare down at her beautiful face and know that I have a decision to make. I could confess to her the whole truth and risk losing her. Or I could do things right this time around and pray that her memories never come back.

Thirty

Jane

"This is ridiculous, Donavon. I do not need a week off work. It was just a concussion and some scrapes and bruises," I say from my bed, all tucked in, in the middle of the day like an invalid. "And I do not need to still be in bed. The doctor said to take it easy for a few weeks, not to be on bed rest."

Donavon brought me home Saturday and hasn't left my side since. Nor has he let me get out of bed unless it was to go to the bathroom or bathe. Which he insists on doing with me. And it's been three days now. He's brought his laptop and clothing to stay this whole time.

"You're my patient now, and I say you need a week of rest and relaxation and maybe you can come back to work next week."

I look over at him lying in bed next to me with his laptop open in shock. "I will not stay in this bed another day, Donavon. And I will be back at work next week, so help me God," I say in warning.

The corner of his mouth twitches and he finally looks over at me. "How about we compromise?" He shuts his laptop and sets it over to the side. Then he peels back the covers and climbs on top of me.

"Compromise how?"

He lowers his head to kiss my neck. "You stay in bed the rest of the week, and I'll let you come back to work on Monday," he murmurs. Between his breath and his facial hair against my neck, my skin sizzles with goosebumps.

"And if I don't stay in bed?" I wrap my arms around his broad shoulders and my thighs squeeze his hips. "And how is this a compromise?"

"Because if you don't, you don't come back to work till the following Monday."

"You can't survive two whole weeks without me," I tease, although it isn't a joke.

"I'll manage. Especially with Allison and Benjamin there to pick up the slack."

"Something you should be letting them do regardless," I say dryly.

He picks up his head and stares down at me intimately. "There's only one person I relinquish any control to."

I push back some of his hair and run my nails through the sides of it. "You really trust me that much?"

His Adam's apple bobs in his throat. "I do. With my life."

"You know you can trust your siblings too."

"In time I might be able to. It's a slow process, but you've managed to show me that I am capable of it."

I give him a slow grin then pull him down on me to kiss him hard. Arching my back into him, I moan into his mouth. I can feel his erection through his pants, and I know how wet he's going to find me.

"Get this fucking thing off," he mutters as he pulls at my t-shirt. I sit up and pull my shirt up and over my head as he shoves down his sweats and underwear. His cock springs out and I lick my lips in anticipation. I love every single ounce of this man. He is so perfect. My very own Adonis.

He covers my body with his and starts peppering my neck and chest with kisses as he nudges me with his cock. Teasing me. I love exploring my sexuality with Donavon. But what I love the most is any position where I can feel the weight of him on top of me and where he takes complete power and fucks me, usually with a hand around my neck that gradually constricts until my vision is fuzzy. *Nothing like gasping for air and having an orgasm simultaneously.*

He slides his cock inside me and begins moving and I get so lost in him. "I love you, Jane. I was afraid I lost you," he rasps.

I smile at his dramatics. "I know, baby," I whisper and arch my back into him. "I'm okay though." My nails dig into the skin of his back, and he growls like he does before he's about to go apeshit on me.

Sitting back, he pulls my butt into his lap as my upper body is still horizontal and uses the grip on my hips to drive into me good and hard. His face is all intense as he rams me against him causing a lusty slapping sound from my ass. "You can't leave me, Jane."

"I won't. I promise. I'm not going anywhere," I whine as I feel myself so close to shattering.

He leans back down a little and takes my neck in his hand and squeezes. Using it to hold me in place as he fucks me. Forcing our pleasure to its peak in unison.

I moan and try thrusting my hips back at him, but I am at his mercy. Under his hands, under his body. I'm his.

The first orgasm crashes through me so abruptly I practically see stars. Don doesn't even pause or skip a beat. He covers my body with his again and sears his lips to mine. I can barely kiss him back, feeling exhausted from that soul shattering orgasm. But he fucks me until he pulls another orgasm out of me before he comes, grunting as his cock twitches.

He lays on top of me panting and holding his weight up with his forearms. "Mmm," I moan with a big grin on my face. My limbs are wrapped around him like an octopus. "On second thought, I won't mind staying in bed for the rest of the week." He chuckles against me. "As long as I get some of this every day—make that multiple times a day—and we have a deal."

"Then we have a deal," he murmurs.

THIRTY-ONE

Jane

Today is my birthday and I can't help but to think about everything good in life as I sit here doing my hair and make-up, getting ready for my date with Donavon. The most amazing boyfriend in the world. The most amazing man.

My phone starts going off and I look down at the screen to see that it's my mom calling. I'm always hesitant to answer when she calls, it usually mean she's fighting with my father.

She could be calling to wish me a happy birthday, but it's unlikely. She's forgotten my birthday more often than not. Too self-absorbed with the problems she continues to live with.

I take too long to decide whether or not to pick up, and she's sent to voicemail. I go back to finishing up my makeup and my phone starts going off again. Sighing, I pick it up to get whatever this is over with.

"Hello?"

"Jane. Wow, you actually answered for once." I grip the phone, already close to hanging up on her. Her snarky tone is uncalled for, and I don't appreciate it.

"I'm sorry. I've been pretty busy with work." *Plus, I don't want to deal with their messy shit anymore. I'm perfectly happy with them outside of my bubble.*

"Well, you could still pick up once in a while. I am still your mother."

"Yes, I know that." She did give birth to me exactly twenty-three years ago.

"Well, I wanted to call you and wish you a happy birthday and see when we could take you out to lunch or something."

"Oh, uh, thank you." *This is...unusual.*

"How about tomorrow?"

"Oh, I can't tomorrow."

"Why the hell not?"

"Because I have plans."

"You can't give your parents a couple hours of your time to take you out for your birthday?" I chew on my lip and remain quiet. "Jane, I do love you. And I miss you. I feel like it's been months since I've seen you. You couldn't even make it over for Christmas. Can't I at least see you for lunch for your birthday?"

I sigh, knowing she's already won. She always knows how to guilt me into anything. "Okay, we can do lunch tomorrow."

"Oh, good. We'll take you to your favorite restaurant in the city. You still love that place right?"

"Yes."

"Great. Give me a call with the time tomorrow, Jane."

Of course, she's leaving it up to me to make the reservations. "Okay."

"Love you, honey."

I make a tight smile. "Bye."

"Who was that?" My head whips around to find Donavon standing there, leaning in the doorway, looking like a billion bucks. He's wearing a dark gray suit with a cream-colored dress shirt underneath. Sans the tie. This man makes suits look like everyday clothing and somehow make sweats look classy.

I stand up grinning and let him draw me in like a magnet. We snap together, our arms automatically circling around each other. "You are so sexy I could cry." He grins and chuckles lowly in his broad chest as I beam up at him as if he's some god or something.

He picks me up by the backs of my thighs and goes over to my bed and sits down with me in his lap. He stares at me quietly, scanning my face with this sentimental look in his eyes. "Why are you looking at me like that?" I almost whisper.

"I really love you, Jane. I hope you know that."

My heart rate increases because it feels like there's some meaning behind his words. Like a sad one. "I do. And I love you too." I tighten my arms around his neck, bringing our faces closer. Then he does the oddest thing. He buries his face in the nook of my neck and hugs me. He squeezes my body into his closely and we stay there like that for a couple minutes. Not a sound or movement. He's given me hugs, but nothing like this.

We both pull back, and I look at him closely. "Are you okay?"

He gives me a small smile and combs his fingers down my hair, stroking it. "I am. Happy birthday, darling."

"Thank you." I kiss his lips softly.

"How much longer until you're ready?"

"Give me like, ten minutes."

"Take as long as you need."

I climb off his lap and head back to my vanity before I disappear inside my closet. I admire the dress that Kenna gave to me this morning as a birthday present. It's short, off-white, and shimmery. The sleeves are long and billowy, and the rest of the dress is tight and stops mid-thigh.

"Is that what you're wearing?"

I look at the dress and then at him standing in the doorway. "I might. It was a birthday gift from Kenna."

"You should wear it. It's pretty."

"It'll be okay for wherever we're going?"

He nods. I know nothing about his plans, only that we're staying overnight somewhere in the city.

I notice over his shoulder something on my bed that wasn't there before, and my eyes widen. "Are those presents, Mr. Waldorf?" I ask coyly.

"Why don't you come and see?" His voice dips low coming out all rough and gravelly, and I bite my lip as I look up at him, ready to unwrap *him* as my present.

He moves to the side, and I try to keep it in my pants in the meantime. Laying my dress flat on the bed, I eye Donavon over my shoulder, and he has this youthful smile on his face. He stuffs his hands in his pockets, and I turn to sit on the bed.

There's nothing in the world that could be better than having him as the most precious gift.

I start with the biggest box and work from there. Each gift is better than the last. I'm very familiar with the brands of each and know that they aren't items just anyone can walk into a store and purchase. You have to not only be a rich someone, but someone of importance.

I didn't own either of these bags, but my mother did. They were sold off along with any expensive material item I had—bags, jewelry, shoes. Every time I came home between breaks from college, more of my things were gone.

The last box holds a pair of red bottom heels with strassed nude-colored mesh. I gush and jump off the bed to leap into his arms. He chuckles into my hair as I squeeze him tight. "Don, these are incredible. Thank you so much."

"Of course, darling." We simultaneously pull back to press our lips together. His arms constrict around me as I arch my body into him. "You can finish thanking me later," he rasps, the timbre in his voice has me rubbing my bare thighs together. I pout before smashing my mouth against his again. He chuckles, trying to break the kiss gently. "Get your beautiful ass ready. We have a big night ahead of us."

Thirty-Two

Donavon

Jane comes out looking like a dream and figment of my naughtiest imagination.

The physical remnants of the accident have long since healed, but the enormity of guilt continues to burn inside of me like acid. She still does not remember that day and the memories from the two days prior are still a little fuzzy to her. No memory of leaving work with a headache or skipping dinner or showing up at the club uncovering the only secret that could ruin us.

I let her come to me even though I want to run to her and confess everything. Purge myself of this plight that could possibly kill me. As much as I want to confess, the risk of losing her is too great a gamble for me to risk.

Her slender arms go around my neck and she gleams up at me. Her eyes shining and her cheeks pink with heat. "This is already the best birthday I've ever had, Donavon." She presses her lips to mine and rasps, "I love you." She delves her tongue into my mouth and my hands move to her plump bottom. I give it a good squeeze making her moan into my mouth and her tight little body rubs against mine.

I've had a fucking hard-on since I walked through the door, but we're on a time crunch here.

"Let's go, darling," I grumble reluctantly against her pliant lips.

We climb in the back of the town car and take off. "You never told me who you were on the phone with," I murmur, feeling slightly insecure, which is an unwonted feeling for me. We're together entirely too much for her to keep anything hidden from me. It must be my own omissions plaguing me.

"Oh," she looks down shyly, "It was my mom." The mere mention of her already leaves a horrible taste in my mouth. "She wanted to wish me a happy birthday." She looks up holding my eyes. "She and my father want to take me out to lunch tomorrow."

I cannot believe what I'm hearing. "No," I clip out.

Her eyes grow round. "No? Um, excuse me, but you cannot refuse to let me see my parents. I know you don't understand my relationship with them—"

"You're damn right I don't understand it. Your father physically abuses you and your mother stands back to watch," I seethe. The hostility is instant where her parents are concerned.

"It wasn't something that happened all the time! He was drunk and decided to pick a fight with my mom, and it escalated," she says defensively. "It's not like he's going to go smacking me around in the middle of a restaurant. And I'm not going to see *him*. I'm going to see my mother because she is still my mother. She misses me."

I soften for her when she puts her vulnerability in the spotlight for me. "Jane..." I say calmly. "You do not need people like them in your life."

"People like them?" she rears back as if I've offended her. "They are my parents. The people who brought me into this world and raised me and provided for me. My dad may be wasted effort, but my mother still loves me."

"Jane, darling. I know what I saw. Your mother hardly even flinched when your father raised his hand to you. That is not a mother's love."

"It's the only way she knows how," she says meekly with her eyes bubbling up with tears. "She wasn't always so callous and...uncaring. I do have good memories with her. A time when we were close like mother and daughter."

A tear manages to escape, and I cannot endure it. This is her special night and here I am making her upset to the point of crying. "Okay, darling." I kiss her forehead and murmur, "You can go to lunch with your parents tomorrow." I pull back and cup her face in my hands, wiping the lonely tear with my thumb. "But I am coming with you." She opens her mouth most likely to protest. "It's the only way, Jane. I promise to behave and keep my comments at a minimum, although I would love to kill your father." She gives me look of warning with the sliver of a smile to her lips. "You can't blame me for possessing the desire to protect you. Jane, when I saw your father strike you, I saw red. Never in my life have I ever been so irate. I wouldn't tolerate any man hitting any woman if I could help it, but the fact that it was you…" I swallow down the rock in my throat and let it sink into my chest. Thinking about it gets me worked up and the itch to fight is thrusted to the fore of my brain. "I wanted to kill him, Jane," I say in a pinched tone.

Her body wilts against me. "You cared about me that much back then?"

"From the beginning," I admit. But what I don't clarify is what the beginning was. The moment she caught my eye, she was a permanent fixture in my head. Her physical beauty hooked me, then her brilliant personality sank me. She walked into my office that first time, and I never wanted her to leave.

The change she created in me was instant, yet I was slow to realize. Changes I thought were impossible. At first, it scared the fuck out of me. Then it was freeing. It was as if she were unshackling me from the restraints I've been bound to my entire life. Liberating me from the prison my mind has created and kept me in.

Her lips connect with mine and we kiss until we arrive at our destination. Which happens to be one of my hotels.

"Wow," she gasps when we walk inside. "I forgot that this is one of yours." Her head rolls around to absorb it all. "It's gorgeous. It reminds me of the way my office was decorated."

I watch her and marvel at her keenness. "I used the same designer. Let me take your coat, darling."

She slips it off and lets me take it from her. "Are we making a quick stop at our room before dinner?" she grins up at me seductively, her eyes full of suggestion. I'd love nothing more than to take her right up and sink myself deep inside of her over and over until she can no longer walk, but what I have planned cannot wait.

"Something like that."

She narrows her eyes suspiciously at me. "You're being a little too cryptic for my liking."

I stifle a laugh as we finally get to the ballroom and as soon as we walk through the door, everyone shouts, "Surprise!" causing Jane to gasp and stumble back.

I'm right there to steady her and I press my lips against her tiny ear. "Happy birthday, baby," I murmur.

She twists her face to gawk at me through teary eyes. "You did this for me?" I nod once. Her smile radiates from within and it's every bit worth it to see this smile. To be the one to put it there. I hate the crowds, I hate the spotlight, and I know she isn't a fan either, but I know having those closest to her and those closest to us would be important for a night like tonight. "You wonderful man," she gushes and throws herself into me.

I don't have time to respond as she's quickly swept away by her guests, and I'm more than happy to stand back and bask in her joy. "So, son." My dad comes up to me. "You nervous?"

I shake my head. "No."

My father laughs. "Boy, sometimes I honestly don't know where you came from."

It's true. My family is outgoing and carefree where I'm more reserved and a bit arrogant. Calm on the surface, but they have no idea how tremulous I am on the inside. Only my mother has slim awareness. She once tried to help me by seeking out professional help, but not even a professional could fix me.

Kenna heads my way with a smirk. "I hear you spoiled her."

"Of course, I did." I've wanted to for so long, and I plan to for the rest of our lives.

As the night drifts away, I continue to stalk my woman with my eyes as she mingles politely with her infectious smile and contagious laughter. I adore the way she gracefully walks and the girlish way she sips her drink. She's my most recent and profound compulsion.

"So, where are her parents? I was hoping to meet them," my mother asks and everyone standing close enough looks my way. Kenna, her boyfriend Tom, and both my parents.

"They couldn't make it," I say as I sip on my glass of whiskey to help calm the nerves abruptly rising.

Drinking has remained my only real vice for the past decade. A habit of mine I'd like to think I hid well. It was the only way I could get any sleep, aside from when I would succumb to insomnia and keel over, sleeping like the dead.

Then came Jane. Now, drinking is a rarity and I've never felt healthier or stronger. Both mentally and physically. Insomnia still torments me, but with my mind constantly on Jane, it curbs the trivial thoughts that keep me up at night.

"Shouldn't you have maybe planned this on a night they could have?" Kenna asks, and I look directly at her in forewarning. I'm not sure how much Kenna knows about her unhealthy relationship with her parents.

"This is her surprise birthday party. Why would I plan it on a day that isn't her birthday?"

"Yeah, but it's more than her surprise birthday party. I'm just saying she might have wanted them to be here," Kenna pushes and it only pushes *me*.

"Drop it, Kenna," I snap a little too defensively and everyone gets quiet. I walk away with irritation from the minor interrogation.

"Hey, where's Garrett?" Benjamin says when he comes up next to me at the bar and I have to pray to anyone who'll listen to give me a sliver of patience.

"He couldn't make it." I give him the same dismissive answer.

Garrett is my best mate, and the only real one that doesn't share the same blood. It didn't feel good to tell him about tonight and inform him that he was not invited, but I was afraid his presence might trigger Jane's memories. I'm still in an internal battle with myself over whether to tell her or to continue to omit the truth. If I were to confess, it would have to be the absolute truth. The club, and the exploitation of her retrograde amnesia.

"Afraid he'll let the cat out of the bag?" he muses. It's not his fault the unbeknownst jabs my temperance, making me want to shove my fist through his face for making light of all of this. Even if he doesn't know the entirety of it.

"We're not talking about it," I growl. He's the only other person who knows about what happened that night. "Besides, I'm signing it over to Garrett. I'm done with it."

"You know, you could always let me buy you out."

It isn't a bad idea. Benjamin wanted in when I let him in on my little secret, but I wasn't looking to make the club a family business. I didn't want my name on it and I damn sure did not want his.

"We'll talk." I take the last sip of drink for the night. "But right now, I have more important things to focus on."

THIRTY-THREE

Jane

"You better hide those shoes from me next time I come over," Bonnie warns.

I grin down at them. "Like your hobbit feet could fit these," I tease her.

Everyone laughs but when my eyes land on Madison, she's again forcing her smile. I don't know what's going on or if I did something to her, but she's been this way towards me for a couple weeks. Skittish and awkward. I'll have to find some time to talk with her privately. Maybe have lunch at work one day this week. I hope it has nothing to do with me being with Donavon. She was one of the first people I told and had been encouraging before it even started.

A pair of large, warm hands encircle my waist and my eyes automatically flutter shut. "How are you, darling?" Donavon rumbles in my ear giving me goosebumps down the entire right side of my body.

I tilt my head back to look up at him. "I'm good. How are you holding up?" I murmur, knowing he must hate this. It means that much more to me that he would willingly place himself in an uncomfortable position.

Suddenly I feel everyone growing awfully quiet and all eyes are on us. The music playing in the background even fizzles out to a low volume, making the room feel eerily quiet and somehow smaller. Donavon steps around to the front of me but never drops his hands, which are the only things grounding me with the unwanted attention on us.

He takes a deep breath in and leans in to speak lowly in my ear, for only us to hear. "Jane, from the moment you walked into my life, you've brought me peace. A peace I have never known. You unearthed that contentment inside of me and destroyed that containment I've been stuck inside." My breath rushes out of my lungs, and I shake against him, fisting the fabric at his biceps. "I've been a prisoner to myself, and you were the one to set me free. I haven't been living, only surviving. But with you, I have never felt so alive." I squeeze my eyes shut as my breath continues to studder. "There is no life without your love, Jane. No life without being able to love you in return." I suck back the tears and hold onto every single syllable coming out of his mouth. "I will never stop loving you, and if you'll let me, I will spend every day showing you."

I'm lightheaded when I feel him trying to drop to one knee. My eyes snap open and I hold onto him tighter, looking at him in panic. His face drops a little then he realizes I don't want him to let go. I don't need him on one knee for me. The tears escape as I give him a reassuring smile.

"Marry me, Jane," he says quietly, but loud enough for those close to us to hear since the room is now deathly silent. His face becomes one big blur when he slides one arm all the way around my waist to help support me as he uses his other hand to pull out the dark blue box to hold between us. He pops it open and I only glance at it, then immediately go back to his handsome face.

I feel like I could faint, but I will not mess this up like I did when he first told me he loved me. That was hard for him, and I left him hanging. Now he's declaring his love and commitment to me in a room full of people.

"Yes." I throw myself into him and inhale his kisses. I'm only thankful for the cheering in the background because it reminds me that we aren't alone and stops me from climbing him like a tree.

"Donavon," I breathe. "How did I get so lucky?" I whisper as I close my eyes and rest my forehead against his chin. Just savoring the moment. I feel like Cinderella right now. From riches to rags and back to riches. I look back up into his deep blue eyes. "You are the most wonderful man."

"Only with you," he whispers back. "Did you want me to hold this all night for you?" he muses, and it doesn't register right away.

Then I gasp and look down at the ring in the box he's still presenting to me. I cover my mouth and giggle. "I'm so sorry." He plucks the ring out of the box, and I study it as he slides it onto my ring finger. The band is platinum with diamonds wrapped around it and the center diamond is oval shaped and huge. I don't know if I want to walk the streets of New York wearing this, but I could never take it off. I grin up at him, feeling like I could float away. "I love it."

"You sure? We can always go and pick out another one," he murmurs.

I drag my nails down one side of his beard. "I wouldn't want any other ring besides the one you propose to me with, Donavon." I mean it wholeheartedly. It's about the meaning and its representation. Paper ring, gumball machine ring, a piece of twine. It symbolizes his love for me, and I wouldn't dare to ever replace it.

Though I'm ready to finally be alone so we can celebrate this moment together, I won't push him to call it a night until he's ready. I know he's completely drained his social interaction capacity for the day, so I'll happily entertain our guests.

My parents' absence hasn't gone unnoticed. I'm not upset with Donavon for not extending the invitation to them, I only wish they were the type of parents to be missed. My father would only get drunk and make a scene at some point. Then I'd be worried sick when my mom would have to take him home and I'd be anxious to hear from her until the next morning. And I know Donavon wouldn't be able to hold his tongue very long, especially when it comes to me and my safety.

"I see why you got me this dress now," I say to Kenna with a smirk.

"You're welcome." She grins proudly.

"Did you pick these shoes out for him too?" I gesture to my feet.

She shakes her head. "Nope. That just happened to be an amazing coincidence."

"Do you know how long he's had this planned?" I ask as my eyes seek out my husband-to-be. His eyes are already on me as he converses with his father and brother.

"I don't know how long he had the initial proposal planned, but he contacted us all about two weeks ago saying there was this mandatory party for us to attend."

I scan the room, so happy with the small gathering. I frown when I find someone missing, realizing I haven't seen them in about an hour now. "Do you know where Madison went?"

"She said bye a little while ago. You were talking to my parents, so she didn't want to interrupt," Kenna explains.

So weird. She's hardly spoken to me all night and wouldn't even make eye contact. I can't let it bother me. It'll have to wait till Monday when I can talk to her in person.

Right now, I'm reveling in this rapturous cloud Don has placed me on.

My eyes wander back to my wonderful man. His dark gaze turns to me on instinct, and he eyes me over the glass that he sips from. *I still cannot believe he's mine.* He's like a living daydream, and I'm the one he's walking to right now.

"Darling," he rumbles in my ear as his arms wrap around me to hold me close. "I'm not sure how much longer I can keep my distance from you."

I reach up to nip at his earlobe and I feel his fingers flex on me. "I need you," I rasp and let my lips graze along the shell of his ear. "I want you to claim every single inch of me tonight. All of me. I'm yours."

He growls and squeezes my body, encasing me with his large one. "You sure you know what you're asking for?"

I pull back so I can look him in the eye and nod my head.

"Then say goodnight," he quips and takes me by the hand to traipse me around the room to give our short goodbyes.

I'm a little tipsy when we get up to our suite, and I've been so hot for him for hours I don't even bother to look around what I'm sure is a gorgeous room. Once that door is closed, I'm on him. "I'm all yours, Donavon," I say in between messy kisses and groping as he backs me further into the space.

He groans which is such a rarity for this man. He's not the groaning type. The grunting and growling yes, but not groaning. And I shudder when he grinds his erection into me through his slacks. "Promise?"

"Yes," I hiss as he sucks on my neck, rubbing the skin raw with his facial hair.

I'm abruptly spun around, his erection now pressed into my ass, and he rolls his hips as he clues me in on where he wants to be. And I am very much willing to give exactly that to him.

I hook an arm back around his neck and arch my back so that my ass rubs against his erection. He sucks in some air through his teeth and holds me by my hips, digging his fingers into the bones there. "Whatever you want." I turn my head up to look at him and what a beautiful sight. I love seeing him so dazed. "I trust you." Something weird flashes across his face, but he quickly masks it and covers my mouth with his.

He makes quick work of my clothing then tells me to lie face down and ass up on the bed. I don't even hesitate. I crawl onto the large bed on top of the fluffy comforter and present my ass and my throbbing core to him. Excited to give everything to him and yet again experience something new sexually.

"Jane," he groans my name, "you are glistening, darling." I go to sit up some because I want him so bad right now. I want to straddle him and ride him all night long. But he has other plans. The bed dips behind me and he shoves me back down roughly by the back of my neck, firmly holding me there. "You asked for this, remember?" he gravels out in my ear, tone full of threat. I love when he unleashes himself and all chivalry goes out the window.

I clench in anticipation as he releases his hand from my neck and glides it down my spine. Then he gives my ass a good and hard smack, making me jolt forward and bite down on my lip. He kneads the area then does it to the other cheek.

Spreading me nice and wide for him, he starts feasting on me without much warning. Licking and tonguing me hole-to-hole, grunting and growling so that it sends vibrations through me hitting me hardest in the core. His tongue laves up through every nook and cranny.

His thumbs peel open the tender flesh around my clitoris to flap his tongue with a quickened pace and it's exactly what it takes for me to cry out and see stars as I come all over his face. "You have the tastiest cunt, baby. I could never get enough."

I feel him move around behind me then he's slipping inside of me with his cock. I'm so wet it gave no resistance. He glides his long cock in and out of me and I feel his thumb rubbing at my tight hole, spreading my juices and massaging the tight rim of muscles.

He uses pressure with his thumb to gain access and I clench up purely on instinct. "Let me in, darling." His husky voice makes my eyes flutter shut. I will myself to relax and let him press his thumb all the way in until it bottoms out. It's an odd feeling. My body wants to fight it, but I'm no less curious. I want him to show me the vulgar thoughts he has in his dirty mind for me and let him fulfil every single one. "Touch yourself."

I reach a hand down and find my clit. I begin to play with myself, and it has me easing my muscles. He slips his thumb out and I can tell he's replacing it with one of his long fingers. It's still just as unyielding, but I don't allow myself to tense up again. He pumps his finger in and out as he fucks me, and I touch myself. Then he adds a second digit, and oh, my fucking God. I am so full. How will his massive cock fit inside without ripping me?

It's all so intense I can hardly see straight anymore. But an amazing intensity.

He slips his cock out of me and starts rubbing it in the crease. It slides easily coated with my juices. "Keep touching yourself, darling."

I whimper as I keep rubbing my pussy and I feel the head of his huge cock start to press into that tiny hole. I want to clench up again or squirm on instinct, but I hold still and relax for him. I want him to have all the pleasure. I want him to know that I trust him. With my body as well as my heart. I am at his mercy and his to exploit.

He exhales loudly as he presses in past his head and pumps slowly in and out. It's a bizarre sensation. It doesn't necessarily hurt, at least not yet. It just feels different. A little uncomfortable and foreign. But not horrible.

I keep massaging my clit as he spreads my cheeks and pushes further in. Giving it several pumps for me to slowly adjust. "Put two fingers in your pussy, baby." His voice comes out strained and rough. Like he's already coming apart. I press two fingers inside my pussy and gasp. "You feel me in your ass?" I can feel his cock pumping in and out of me through the thin wall there that separates both channels. He groans as he slowly pushes further in. All the way until his balls touch my knuckles that thrust inside my pussy. He releases a heavy breath as he stills. I automatically still my fingers too. "You okay, darling?"

He moves my hair out of my face and looks at me. He breathes heavily with half-lidded eyes and his hair all out of place. God, he's stunning. I nod my head for him but I'm feeling too much to say anything right now.

He stares at me as he pulls out slightly and slides back in. I gasp at the crazy new sensation and my fingers start pumping again. He begins to plunge into me with more aggression and my hand stumbles trying to keep pace.

The intensity of his movements grows with every thrust until he's pounding into me brutally. The discomfort now nonexistent. Only pleasure remains. The most otherworldly pleasure there is.

My face is buried in my hair and the sheets as he fucks me so hard it takes my breath away. My hand falls from my pussy as I have to fist the sheets.

"I'm going to turn us, Jane. I want to see you," he rasps and pulls out some, but not all the way. My muscles are already jelly as I make the weak attempt to help him roll me over to my back.

He looks down at me with this animalistic glare and hoists my legs up having me hold them in place. He's gentle with the way he begins fucking me again, but once he sees the lustful look on my face, he pounds into me.

From this new angle it feels even more different. Tighter I think, yet my muscles feel less rigid. He reaches down and plays with my pussy and my mouth falls wide open to the euphoric sensations. He impales me with two fingers, and I can feel all my muscles coil so tight I feel like my bones are going to shatter. Then I come.

I come so hard I yell and contort my body and spasm as I release so much liquid, it comes out of me in quick spurts. Drenching us both.

I can't even see anymore but I hear him grunting and then his cock twitches inside of me. His lips are suddenly on mine as his thrusts slow while he's releasing his warm cum, filling me up to the point where I'm already leaking out and he hasn't even pulled out yet.

I hardly remember what happened next. I'm pretty sure I passed out. I just remember hissing a little when he finally pulled out of me.

Then he's cleaning me up with something soft and wet. Then nothing. I pass out in complete and utter bliss.

Thirty-Four

Jane

"You promise to behave?" I'm only half serious when I ask Donavon this. Again.

"I promise to be on my personal best behavior," he confirms cheekily as he strokes the side of my face.

I narrow my eyes at him and fight back a smile. "Your personal best?" He only shrugs one shoulder unabashedly. "Mhm," I mutter and look out the window of the back of the town car as we get closer to the restaurant where we're meeting my parents.

"How's your head feeling, darling?"

"Better." I woke up with a killer hangover. After a couple orgasms, I felt good as new.

"Is there a special reason why we're going to this restaurant?"

"It used to be my favorite place," I say quietly and occupy my hands with pretending to straighten his tie.

"Used to be?" he tilts my chin up to make me look at him.

"It was when I was a kid, and they would take me to eat here every year. It was no longer my favorite place, but I let them think so. I guess it helped fill that maudlin void they've left inside of me. They think they're doing something nice for me." I shrug again, wanting to end this conversation. "And it makes me feel like they are too."

"I'm sorry you don't have the parents you deserve."

I smile and snake my arms around his waist. "I have you, which is more than I deserve."

He shakes his head. "You are much more deserving of anyone you choose."

We pull up to the restaurant and I take a deep breath before heading inside with my fiancé gripping my hand tightly in his. No surprise that we're the first to arrive and we both order a stiff drink while we wait for them.

My parents finally arrive and I look to Donavon, silently begging him once again to be amicable with them. I stand up as my mother heads our way with a phony smile on her overly botoxed face. They might not have the money they used to, but there are things they are both unwilling to let go of and accept that they are luxuries they can no longer afford.

"Jane, honey," she says, grabbing my shoulders and kissing me on each cheek.

"Hi, Mom," I reply with a tight grin.

She looks me up and down and makes an attempt to budge her eyebrows upwards. "You've put on a little weight," she says smiling as if she's paying me a compliment rather than making a blatant dig to my confidence.

"Hi, Dad," I choose to ignore her lame attempt at hurting my feelings, or trying to somehow make herself feel better, and greet my father with a hug.

"Hi, Jane. Happy birthday," he murmurs with a timid smile.

I turn to make sure Donavon is standing up to properly greet them, and thankfully he is. He isn't jumping at the chance, but idly waiting by to appease me. "This is Donavon," I gesture to him then turn back to face them, "my fiancé."

They both look a little shocked, then my mother is the first to feign enthusiasm as she smiles and claps her hands together. "Engaged? Wow!" She goes into hug Donavon, and I internally cringe. He hates physical affection as much as I do. Other than each other's that is. Then she turns to me. "Congratulations, my baby." She hugs me tight, and I let her. My father is silent as she looks at him. "Isn't that great, dear? Jane is engaged."

"To Donavon Waldorf. I heard." He looks to me with a tight smile. "Congratulations, Jane." Then looks directly at Donavon and nods his head and offers his hand to him. I'm prepared to elbow Don in the side, but I'm pleasantly surprised when he accepts the handshake on his own. "Congratulations."

Donavon doesn't verbally respond, only gives him a firm dip of his chin then we all take our seats. He already scooted my chair closer to him and he slings an arm protectively around the back of my chair.

It's mainly my mom and me carrying on conversation. Both Don and my father visibly acting like they'd rather be anywhere else. Though Don sits there confidently sipping on the same drink, whereas my father's eyes keep jumping elsewhere as he downs one after another. It's obvious he's intimidated by my fiancé. Everyone is.

"Let me see this again," my mom says reaching for my hand with the engagement ring. "It's simply gorgeous."

"Jane sure knows how to pick 'em," my father says dryly, and I can feel Don stiffen next to me.

As always, my mother doesn't rush to my aid or make any effort to defend me. She grows quiet and tries to change the subject. "So, how's work?"

"Work is good. I still love my job." I smile over at Don and his lips twitch.

My father scoffs. "I'm sure you do," he snidely remarks under his breath, not even having the guts to look at either one of us.

It doesn't go unnoticed and I can almost hear every muscle in Donavon's body coil tightly as he leans forward, inserting his dominance. He places his elbows on the table, looking at my father in challenge. Daring him to elaborate. Giving him one good and final reason to pummel him like he so badly wishes to.

My mom turns a deaf ear to him as usual and starts talking to me more about herself. What she's been up to and how she spends most of her time now that she is no longer a part of the inner circle of the city's socialites.

Lunch was brief and luckily for my father, and for my sake, my father gets to live another day.

Thirty-Five

Donavon

The guilt heavily plagues me. Boiling inside and consuming me, like a geyser ready to explode.

All I can think about is all the deception I'm very much responsible for. I never meant to deceive Jane. Never meant to keep things from her. But I never planned for Jane to begin with. She was never supposed to walk into my life and turn everything I ever knew on its head.

The guilt of keeping the club from her has always been there, even if only faintly. But I didn't see the harm in it. Especially because I was getting rid of it for her.

But the pure and earnest way she looked at me and said that she trusted me, it's been eating me up inside. The penitence I'm now encumbered with is crushing.

I've never been a liar. Never had a reason to. Never had anything to lose. Now I have *everything* to lose.

Jane can sense there is something off with me, and I don't know how much longer I can fake it before I break and confess everything. All to see the disappointment and hurt on her face. Hurting her is something I never wanted to do.

In time, the guilt should fade, and all of this can be put behind us.

My heart pulls me to Jane's office, and she smiles up at me as I walk in. She's on the phone, so I close the door behind me and have a seat on the couch to wait for her. I watch as she so naturally conducts her business and then politely excuses herself off the phone.

"Hey, baby." She smiles over at me and my chest aches. Her engagement ring shines as the sunlight from the window hits it. I can't believe she's wearing my ring. She said yes. And I could easily lose her forever. "You okay?"

I swallow the lump in my throat and nod. Then I look at her desk and notice a picture frame I hadn't seen before. I get up and go to it. Picking it up, I see that it's a picture of us from Christmas at my parents' house. We're sitting next to each other at the large dining table. Her head is on my shoulder facing forward laughing at something and my face is buried in the top of her hair. Someone managed to capture my most favorite thing in the entire world. Jane's smile. I can't lose this. I love her so fucking much.

I can't go back to the crippling anxiety and compulsiveness that I've fought with my whole life. To remain alone and miserable, only waking up every day with the drive to succeed and to take care of my family financially. Because there's no replacing Jane. There isn't anyone out there that can come close to comparison. Jane was it for me. My one chance at happiness.

"It was a gift from Allison. I finally got around to opening them without you."

"They were your birthday gifts. My attendance was never necessary."

"They were engagement gifts, and you know it."

"What if someone sees this?" I place the framed picture back in its place.

"We're engaged now. Meaning eventually, we'll be married. It's not something we can hide from everyone anymore. Especially when quite a few people from work were invited to our engagement party."

I eye her with a smirk. "It was your birthday party, and I just so happened to propose to you."

She gives me a cheeky smirk of her own. "It was both and you know it."

I smile and shove my hands in my pockets. "You hungry?"

She sighs and leans forward. "I could definitely eat."

"Let's go to lunch somewhere. I need to get out of the office for a little while."

She arches her eyebrows with a frown. "Really?" I nod and she continues frowning when she stands up and comes to me. "You sure you're okay?" Her melodic voice is full of concern, and I feel like I'm about to burst with contrition.

I fake a chuckle for her and gently remove her hands from my face when she cups it. The motion only seems to raise more concern. "Because I want to take you out to lunch, something must be wrong?" I tease.

She gives me half a smile. "No. Not because of that. You look like something is bothering you." She pauses. "You've been this way all week," she murmurs and looks down at her feet. "Are you having...doubts?" she peeks up at me and there's a fracture cracking my heart down the center. "It is a bit rushed and—"

I immediately take her in my arms and shake my head. "No, never." I somehow feel even more sickened in grief seeing her blame herself for my poor mood. Giving her doubt and insecurities about us when it couldn't be further from reality. "It has nothing to do with us," I swallow that truth revealing lump in my throat. "I'm only tired and would like to take a break and for you to join me."

Her smile is hesitant, but she accepts it. "Okay, I'll grab my stuff and we can go."

She goes to pull away and I yank her into me to kiss her with such deep passion it'll have both of our heads spinning. Sliding my fingers over her cheek and into her hair, I tenderly move my lips with hers and stroke her tongue with mine. I hold her and kiss her with all the arborous sentiment I can possibly summon, but it's like she can see my internal suffering so I part from her before she can bring it up again.

We're seated at a nearby restaurant and I sit here staring at her as she pulls her phone out. The woman loves working almost as much as I do. Can't ever sit still without thinking of all the things she can be doing.

"I still think you should rethink buying out Winston Industries." She leaves half a pause. "The amount of work and time it'd take to have it up to your standards and begin making any kind of profit isn't really worth it. Certainly not worth the headache," she continues with her focus still on her phone.

"Okay," I say robotically on a sigh.

Her gaze snaps up to me. "Okay?" she questions me as if she might not have heard me correctly.

"Yes, I agree. We can forget about that deal."

"Donavon, are you sure you're alright?"

I can't say I blame her for her suspicions. It's in my nature to be contentious, always ready to argue. Even when I'm wrong, I will manipulate any situation to make me seem like I'm in the right. And money is always worth the headache for me. But I do not need more headache right now.

"I said I'm fine. Just tired," I say a little too grumpily.

She studies me for a long moment then picks her phone up again. "Then maybe you should stop working so late," she mutters, and that guilt gnaws at me again. She thinks that when I'm working late I'm in my home office.

"Could you put your phone down please?" I say and rest my elbows on the table as I rub my face with my hands. This is it. I need to come clean, and I need to do it now. I can't do it anymore, and it's only unfair to her. Especially because she's getting mixed signals from me and worried it's her and not me. She'll forgive me. She has to. She has to understand.

"Don—" she starts but she's cut off.

"Donavon." My heart plummets when I hear the familiar voice of my best friend.

I look up to find Garrett sauntering over to us and I'm like a deer caught in the headlights. I give him a look of panic and warning, telling his ass to turn around—but it's too late. Jane twists in her seat and Garrett stops in his tracks.

To not seem so suspicious, I step in. "Garrett," I stand and redirect her attention, "how are you?" He closes the distance, and we shake hands.

"Good. What a surprise seeing you here."

Jane stands up and smiles. "Garrett, this is my fiancée, Jane."

She tilts her head to one side and narrows her eyes. "Haven't we met before?"

Oh, fuck. Oh, fuck. Please, God. No.

Garrett chuckles a little. "I don't think so. I, uh, know Donavon from college and we haven't seen each other in a while." He looks over at me and starts to say something, but I can't tear my eyes away from Jane.

I watch her closely as if I'm about to witness a car crash in slow motion. I can see the wheels turning and I know the moment everything collides. The room grows quiet as her gaze snaps to mine. She looks at me in complete horror and I'm pretty sure my heart stops. It's the same look she had before she fled from my office at Verity. My stomach turns as she jolts backwards, her chair scraping the hard floors, causing people to stare.

"You," she starts in a caustic tone. Her face already red with anger and her fists clenching at her sides. "You!" she shouts this time. "You lying, cheating bastard!" Her beautiful eyes fill with fat tears. "I cannot believe you," she almost whispers, her tone reeking of disappointment. "I can't believe you!" Her voice cracks, and she snatches up her phone and her bag. She shakes her head at me in absolute revulsion before bolting. Leaving a trail of smoke behind and my heart flayed.

I tune everything and everyone out as I stand here staring at the space Jane was just occupying. I'm caught inside this despairing trance, feeling like I'm dying inside. Already feeling the loss of her.

I was given the chance to right all my wrongs. To do everything over and everything right. And I failed. I lost. I fucking mutilated it.

No. Fuck that. I don't lose. I never have and I don't plan on starting now. I've fucked up more times than I care to remember, but I have always made up for it. And this isn't even something that could be broken. Tainted and tampered? Yes. But not destroyed. She has every right to be mad, to be hurt, but it is not over for us.

She can have an hour to cool off, but she will listen to what I have to say and accept my apology. If she needs some space while she comes to accept it, she can have it. But we are not over.

Not like this.

Not ever.

THIRTY-SIX

Jane

I'm literally tremoring in fury, bile burning the back of my throat.

My memories slammed into me like a brick wall. Having lunch with Madison and her telling me about Don's secret club, faking a headache, making love to Don, then going to find the truth for myself. The images so clear now. It has me wanting to puke all over again.

I stumble the entire way home, as scolding hot tears hinder my vision. A sob has been bubbling up, but I suppress it and refuse to let go until I'm finally safe inside my apartment. Not until I've put enough distance between myself and that lying motherfucker.

I hate him. I hate him so much.

This is why he hasn't invited me over to his place. Because he has so much to hide from me. He was such an amazing actor.

I slam my apartment door shut and run for my room. "Whoa there," Kenna says popping out of her bedroom and I jump to a halt from being startled. "Oh, my God. What happened? Are you okay?"

The moment she asks, I fall apart. My knees quake as the sob finally escapes me and I almost collapse, but Kenna is there to catch me. "Jane," she gasps. "What's going on?"

I push away from her and stagger into my bedroom, wailing and hyperventilating. My heart has crumbled into a million pieces and now lays dormant at the pit of my stomach. My legs buckle and I crash onto my bed to curl up into a tiny ball of vulnerability and angst.

It all hurts so badly, I wish I were dead. It's an unbearable pain. "I hate him," I cry. "I hate him!"

I can feel her sit on my bed. "What did he do?" she asks quietly then places a gentle hand on my back, making soothing circles. I sob so hard I can't form any more words. "Sshh. It's okay. Take a deep breath," she coaches me, but she's wrong. It's not okay. Nothing is okay.

The trust I had in him was absolute. I honestly thought he was a good man. A wonderful one. But he's the worst. I hate him. God, I hate him. I wish I had never met him. I wish I never got a job at that company.

The ineffable sorrow morphs back into anger, and I'm able to stop the tears from coming. Taking a few deep breaths, I say, "Your brother is a sick bastard." Then I go on to tell her everything. From the way he mistreated me when I was still an intern, to the way he continued to abuse his power, to the club he secretly owns, to the lies he told me to have me believe he was up late working when he was going to his club to enjoy watching private shows in his office, to exploiting my memory loss and using it to his advantage.

By the time I'm done spilling my guts, Kenna is speechless as she stares at me in horror. Completely gob smacked. "I...I..." She licks her lips and tries again. "I am so sorry, Jane. I honestly don't know what to say."

"Please don't say anything. He's your brother and has only been good to you, and I hate that this casts a shadow on all of that. But I caught him with two women in his office. The office in his secret strip club. He may not have been touching them, but I do not and will not believe for even a second that he wasn't planning to. You should've seen the look on his face as he watched them. He was *enjoying* himself!"

"I'm so sorry," she says quietly. "What can I do? What do you need?"

I shake my head. "I just want to be left alone for a while. If that's okay."

She nods her head and stands up. "I have to go out of town for a few days. That's why I'm home. I'm packing and then we leave on the red-eye tonight." She chews on her bottom lip. "I could—"

I shake my head. "I'll be fine, Kenna. I promise." She looks like she wants to say more, but she doesn't.

As soon as the door clicks shut, the tears begin again, and I sob into my pillow. I give into the pain, hoping that I can expel it all at once. Just get it all out and hopefully I'll begin to feel less like death.

Heartbreak is a real thing that comes with physical pain. My stomach feels like it's caving in on itself and there's this massive weight crushing my chest in. My eyes burn and I know they're already puffy and my throat aches from sobbing so hard. But it's my heart that hurts the most. The pain in it is the only sign that it still beats.

My sobs turn into hiccups as I blankly stare out of bloodshot eyes. I have no idea how long it's been, but when I hear a loud and firm knock on the front door, I shoot up and I'm instantly fraught with ire. *How dare he...*

I hear Kenna open the door and they immediately start arguing. Donavon's voice getting louder as he draws in closer to my bedroom door. "I need to see her!" I hear him bellow over her.

"She wants to be left alone!" Kenna shouts back.

The doorknob begins to rattle, and he pounds loudly on my door. "Jane! Let me in!" I swing my legs off the bed and shake with anger as I stand firmly to my feet. The audacity of this man.

"Donavon!" Kenna shouts again as he bangs some more on the door.

"Jane, open this door or I'm breaking it down!"

"Donavon, stop! She needs some time!" Kenna tries again, but it's no use. He's completely unhinged!

"Kenna, I swear to fucking God, stay out of this," he sneers, and I see red. It's exactly why I do not open that door. Who knows what I will do? "Jane! Last chance to open this door, or it's coming down in pieces!"

"Fuck you!" I scream until my lungs give out. "How dare you come here and demand anything from me! And do not speak to Kenna like that!" I roar like a crazy person. He pounds his fists again growling idle threats in between and Kenna is still trying to talk some sense into him as I start pacing my room like a caged lioness. I have never felt so goddamn out of my mind before. Like I am actually losing my sanity. I want to burst into flames and take everything out in my vicinity.

There are no more warnings before he literally crashes through my door in one aggressive thrust with his entire body. He looks just as enraged as I do, and it isn't right. He does not have the right to be angry right now.

"We are going to talk about this," he says lowly with a menacing timbre.

My eyes widen as much as they are capable of with all the swelling around them. "There's nothing to talk about, you fucking psycho! I remember everything! *Everything*! You're a fucking liar! End of story!" I project with maximum effort causing my insides to burn.

"I know I should have told you about *Verity*," he says calmly, cautiously taking steps towards me.

I jump to the defense. "That's what you're starting with?! The fact that you own a strip club?! That is far from the top of the list!" I grab the lamp off my nightstand in a haste and throw it at him. The chord being attached to the outlet in the wall completely throws my aim off and smashes against the wall. He stands there as I begin to cry hysterically. "You cheating asshole! I knew you were too good to be true! I knew you couldn't do it!"

"I didn't cheat on you," he says evenly, like the practiced liar that he is.

"Bullshit!" I screech, and pick something else up to throw at him. A shoe, and it wizzes by his head as he ducks this time.

"I didn't touch those women, and I was not going to."

"Watching them carpet munch each other is just as bad!" His lips twitch and I swear to God I black out for a moment in rage. I roar and find the next nearest thing to crank it over my head with both arms and launch it. He easily dodges it. "Do you find this funny?!"

He opens his mouth to say something then closes it as his lips twitch again. "I'm sorry, darling. I'm trying to get past the carpet munching thing."

I am so past the point of anger, the tears cease and my body sags in defeat. Everything is beginning to shut down. The amusement leaves his face, but it's too late. Nothing about this is salvageable. "Just leave, Donavon. There is absolutely nothing more to talk about. We're done." I stand there and look at him with disappointment. Then I shake my head and avert my gaze. "I can't even look at you right now."

I know he cannot stand to lose, and it's ingrained for him to stay and to fight, but this is one fight he will not win. This hurts me more than it can possibly hurt him because I was the one blind to all this. I was the one walking around with rose colored lenses, lost behind a veneer of bliss.

To my surprise, he turns and leaves without saying another word.

I release my breath and squeeze my eyes shut until I hear the front door slam shut. I open my eyes to find Kenna in the doorway. "Jesus, I'm so sorry, Kenna. You shouldn't have seen that." I sniffle and wipe at my face. "I'll clean everything up and have the door fixed."

She walks in with wide eyes shaking her head. "No, please don't apologize, Jane. I'm only worried about you." She pauses and we both stand there awkwardly. "How about I draw you a nice bath in my tub? You can relax there for a while and drink a bottle of champagne. Or even a bottle of vodka," she muses trying to make me smile, but I can't even fathom the point in time where I can easily smile again.

"You don't have to do that." The rawness in my throat has my voice coming out hoarse.

"I know I don't have to, but I want to, Jane. You're my best friend." She closes the gap and takes me in her arms, opening the flood gates all over again.

"It hurts, Kenna. It hurts so bad." I choke the words out through snot and tears. "Why did he have to do this? Be so wonderful to me, just to break my heart."

"I don't know," she says softly. "I really don't."

I'm like a zombie as Kenna lures me to her bathroom to get me into her large, jetted tub for a hot bath. She pours in a bunch of stuff that I'm sure would smell good if I could experience anything but sorrow right now.

I sink down into the hot water, and she comes back with a bottle of champagne and a flute. Really, she should have just brought a straw.

She perches herself on the side of the tub. "Have you eaten anything today?" I shake my head. "What are you in the mood for?"

Death.

"Nothing."

"How about some greasy pizza?" I shrug my shoulder and drink from the bottle. Then there's a knock at the front door and she looks at me in worry, but there's no need. It's not him. *It's not his knock.* "I'll be right back," she murmurs.

I slouch further into the water and close my eyes. Giving into the numbness that has begun to take over. It doesn't hurt so bad now, and I couldn't cry anymore even if I wanted to. My mind drifts off into nothing-ness as if I'm floating away into an abyss.

I hear Kenna quietly enter the bathroom again. "I guess he already called for someone to replace the door. I'm gonna go order us some pizza and give you some time alone. Can I get you anything else?"

I look up at Kenna, so incredibly thankful for her. "I'm fine. You've done more than enough. Thank you."

She nods her head and gives me a somber look. "We'll get through this, kay?" I nod back.

I'm left alone with my thoughts once more and I lay there motionless, only moving when I bring the bottle to my lips and work it down my throat. Not only is my heart broken, but my life is in ruins. My job, where I live, it all has to go. I don't even know if I could stay in this city any longer. I couldn't bear to accidentally run into him. This is the kind of pain that no amount of time can heal.

Once my bladder feels like it's about to burst and my skin is pruned all over, I decide to call the quits and drain the water. I sluggishly wrap a towel around myself and drag my feet back to my bedroom. The remnants of the door and lamp have been swept away like nothing ever happened. But it did.

It's already dark out and I have no idea where time went. It felt like only an hour ago I was happy, but it's been several hours of despair.

Kenna tries to distract me with trashy reality shows and binging on pizza and booze. But it does little to the pain that comes in waves, knotting up my stomach.

I continue to drink long after Kenna leaves and I'm able to pass out. But only for a couple hours. I wake before the sun is all the way up and I get myself ready for work. Still slightly drunk and sleep deprived. But hellbent on removing my existence from his company and his life.

THIRTY-SEVEN

Donavon

I overslept.

Last night, I had to drink myself into a stupor to keep myself from going back to Jane or driving myself mad through all hours of the night. This is how it'll be without her.

Sleep was a rarity for me before Jane, then sleep came easily when I was within arm's reach of her. Now, it'll be impossible without the aid of some form of illicit substance.

I glance down at the cracked screen of my phone and my heart drops when there's no word from her. Not that I expected it, but there was foolish hope inside of me. Pulling up the tracking app on my phone, I sit up when I see that she's already at the office. That foolish hope of mine expands, giving me the energy to get my ass moving.

I make it to work less than an hour later, and Jane is still here. I thought she would try to clear out her office and quit, but maybe she's deciding not to call this all off after all. The door is closed to her office, so I retrace my steps and head into my office first. I'll give us both a minute before I charge in there and try to talk to her again.

I sit down behind my desk and sigh as I rub my hands down my face. I shouldn't have reacted the way I did yesterday when I showed up at her place. I should have gently tried coaxing her to open up and not demand it, then force my way inside. She'll eventually see that destructive side of me, but that wasn't the time to be giving her my true form.

She's angry, and she has all the reason to be. But when she tried locking me out, I lost it. My temperance was obliterated, and I reacted solely on emotional instinct. Then she accused me of cheating. Lying? Yes, I lied by omission. Deceit? Yes, I misled her into thinking I was working from home some nights when I was working at Verity. But never once was I unfaithful to her. Never had I even been remotely tempted. I have not touched another woman since I admitted to myself that I had feelings for Jane.

I rub at the ache in my temples from the hangover I'm stuck with. My tolerance for alcohol has depleted and I'm feeling the effects of it. I take several large gulps of the water I brought in with me and I prepare myself for another showdown with Jane.

My mind must be warped when I go to stand and I notice something shiny placed on the center of my desk that I didn't catch right away. I snatch it up and fist it as I head out the door to Jane's office.

She's prudent in leaving her door unlocked this time as I barge in and shut the door behind me with hostility. She pays me no mind as she packs a box with her belongings. She isn't wearing her usual work attire, dressed down in jeans and a hoodie.

"Why aren't you wearing your ring?" I hold it up, getting angrier by the moment.

She still doesn't even look at me. "Why the hell would I wear that thing?" she growls as she continues to work.

"Because I asked you to marry me, and you said yes."

She finally glares up at me, fire in her bloodshot eyes and ready for another fight. Her eyes are slightly puffy likely from crying, and it guts me. "Yes. Under false pretenses."

"What are you doing?"

"Packing my shit up. What does it look like?" she sasses with venom on her tongue.

I clench my fists and stalk towards the desk that separates us. "I understand that you are angry—"

Her head snaps up with wide eyes. "Donavon!" Her voice comes out shrill. "You think I'm just mad at you?! Holy hell." She slaps a hand across her forehead. "You are on a whole other level of crazy. Donavon. This isn't some fight or some premarital squabble. We are over. Broken up. Done. Finished." The word crazy is certainly a trigger for me, but I can sidestep that for now. She must sense the uneasiness her words may have caused me, and she softens. "Donavon. You lied to me. You hid things from me. *Big* things!"

My hand furls around the ring harder, the metal and diamonds cutting into my skin. "We are not over," I say with vitriol through clenched teeth. "You are not quitting, and you will put this ring back on." I lean over the desk and hold the ring up in her face. "You can be mad and take a break from work, but you are not quitting, and you are not to take this ring off."

She literally shakes and then she absolutely snaps. She uses her arms to sweep everything off her desk including the box she was filling with a high-pitched shriek and rounds the desk fuming. "I am quitting, and I will not touch that ring. I'm also moving out of your sister's apartment and out of this city. Completely out of your life. You will never see me again." The calm resolve in her voice was the most heartbreaking thing I've ever experienced.

We're toe to toe when I glance down and see the framed picture of us staring up at me, shattered. I was hanging on by a tiny thread, and it breaks.

I have her body pinned to the surface of her desk and my hand around her pretty little neck, giving her no chance of escape. "You are not going anywhere," I hiss and gnash my teeth.

"Yes, I am," she says, still so calm. "I'm removing myself from every part of your life and you'll be left to suffer alone."

I press my body into hers, my erection throbbing and my hand around her neck constricting. She narrows her pink eyes, throwing daggers at me. "Of course, you're turned on. You're *sick*." She tries thrashing her body, but it only has her rubbing herself on my hardened cock.

I curl my lips up into a sinister smile and use my free hand to run it down her body. I make it down to the waist of her jeans and tease her with my fingers slipping under the hem. She pants in rage, her eyes bursting of fury. Popping the button open, she grunts and growls as I dip my hand inside to aggressively cup her pussy over her damp panties. "Then I guess you're just as fucked up as I am," I taunt her and wiggle my fingers. "So, here's how this is going to go. You quit, and I'll fire every single person here that you might consider a friend." Her eyes widen and I know she's eager to spit her invective at me. "I'll put every one of them out on their asses. No reference—nothing."

"You wouldn't do that. It could ruin your company and your reputation."

"I could shut my company down right now and walk away still a very rich man."

"You're bluffing. You're obsessed with your job," she spits. "And just as worried about your reputation, you wouldn't have hidden your name from Verity's ownership otherwise."

I lean forward more and move my fingers over her panties again making her inhale sharply through her flared nostrils and squirm. "I've found a new obsession," I say in a low voice and her pupils dilate.

"You wouldn't know what to do without this place. It means everything to you."

"You mean more to me than anything." Her face drops some and she doesn't say anything. She doesn't need to because I've won. At least this round. "And feel free to move out of my sister's apartment. But the only place you'll be going to is mine."

She scoffs. "As in move in with you?" I nod slowly. "You've never even allowed me over to your place."

I look between her eyes and her moving lips. She's such a beauty. Especially when I ruffle her feathers and get her temper going, she's sexy as fuck. "I think it's time that I make an exception for my fiancée."

"I am not your fiancée." She's scathing mad as she shows her teeth.

Reluctantly, I withdraw my hand from the front of her pants and pick up the ring. "It's part of the stipulations," I say as I shove the ring back into its place on her finger. Where it belongs and will remain.

"You can't make me marry you."

I stroke her cheek. "You have no idea what I am capable of, darling," I rasp with a grin.

"I'm quickly learning," she whispers, and the rage turns into sadness as tears bubble up in her worn eyes.

Why can't she see how remorseful I am? That I know I fucked up and I was only terrified of losing her if I told her about Verity and the events leading up to the accident. I'm done with it, and I will never keep anything from her ever again. I will flay myself for her, let her see every raw secret of mine from the very depths of my soul.

"Why me, Donavon? You could have anyone out there to jerk around. To have wear your ring... Why do you want me?" Her chin wobbles as she speaks softly, the vulnerability leaking from her eyes.

I pet her hair back gently and frown at her. "Because I love you, Jane." How doesn't she know this?

She stares at me for a moment then shakes her head. "This isn't love, Donavon. This is possession."

My eyebrows knit and my body stiffens. "It's both."

"It can't be both."

"Sure, it can. I can be in love with you," I glance at her hair as I glide my fingers down it, "possessive of you," I brush my fingers across her cheekbone, "and obsessed with you," I say as my fingertips graze across the seam of her perfect mouth. "It's not like any of them cancel each other out." I give her a lop-sided grin, but she's unresponsive to it. Understandably still agitated with me.

Closing the small gap of space, I place a soft kiss to her cheek, tasting the salt of her tears. Then I stand up and release her as she lays there, staring up at me in shock. Her body sprawled out on her desk has my cock aching for her and I have to leave before I really do something unforgivable.

I yank at the lapels to my jacket and straighten my tie. "Now, clean this mess up. And feel free to take the rest of the day off."

Bending down, I pick up the broken picture frame and leave her office.

Thirty-Eight

Jane

I never realized how quickly a dream of a man could turn into such a nightmarish villain.

I'm still reeling from what just conspired here in my office. Donavon is actually blackmailing me to stay here. Using my friendship with some of the interns to exploit and use to his advantage.

On top of his anxiety and OCD, apparently, he's delusional if he thinks I will eventually get over this. I will never—and I mean *never*—forgive him. He didn't make a mistake, he was pulling a wool over my head and deceiving me the whole time. What he did is totally unjustifiable. There is no excuse and he could never make up for this.

He's a very stubborn man, but he has no idea how deep my resolution actually goes. I possess the ability to forgive, but only when I want to. I can certainly be just as immutable as he.

So, what do I do now? I'm being forced to work next to a man that has hurt me beyond repair. He used my retrograde amnesia to brush something huge under the rug and pretend like it never happened. He rushed to the hospital like he had a right to be there with me after what I had just witnessed. Like he was my perfect, loving boyfriend who was so worried about me. Like he was my protector. Not the vile human being he truly is.

The way he took care of me that entire week after the accident and every single day since—it wasn't out of pure love. It was out of guilt. He felt like the accident was his fault and he wasn't going to tell me what was essentially knocked out of my head. Now, I see everything he's done from a different perspective.

God, what I saw. Those women... And the look on Don's face. He was smiling. He was *happy* with himself and bared no shame. I cannot un-see any of that. I could get past the part about owning a place like that. He probably assumed I wouldn't have been okay with it. I'd have been angry for the secrecy, but it would have been something we could've worked out. It's his duplicity we cannot work on.

Why, Don? Why?

Bringing my knees up, I bury my face in them and cry. I don't want to feel like this. I thought I felt heartache before when my ex completely abandoned me in the toughest time of my life, but that was nothing compared to this. I was sad, I cried, but I didn't feel this amount of pain.

I wish I had never met Donavon. I'd rather never had experienced the love I had for him than feel the pure agony he's burdened me with. I can't be deserving of this. I may be far from perfect, but haven't I already endured enough emotional stress and abuse already? He puts my parents down for their cruelty towards me, but what exactly puts him above them? I loved him so much more than I have ever loved my own parents or anyone in my life.

I feel like such a fool. I was so easily beguiled. Of course, this was all a hoax. Men like Donavon portrayed himself do not exist, and women like me do not get so lucky to ensnare them.

There's a soft knock on the door. I pick my head up sniffling and wipe my face with the sleeves of my hoodie. "Yes?" I call out and continue facing out the large window behind my desk.

"Jane? Do you mind if I come in?" Allison's voice rings out softly. "Sure."

I hear the door gently click shut then a couple moments later she's standing beside me. "Hey, how are you?"

I have no idea what she knows and I'm too tired to pretend like nothing is going on. But telling by the amount of pity in her voice, she already knows something. "I'm okay."

She leans her hips against the desk. "Kenna asked me to come check on you."

"She told you?" I ask softly, without any bitterness in my tone.

"She only told me that our asshole brother did something pretty fucked up and that I should come check on you. She didn't tell me what."

I appreciate Kenna's respect for my privacy. I feel embarrassed enough, no need to let everyone in on the joke.

"Can I get you anything?"

I shake my head. "No. Thank you."

"Have you eaten?"

Funny, everyone keeps asking me that. Doesn't everyone know that when your heart is broken you don't give a shit about food? Why does everyone want me to have some? I shake my head. I ate a piece of pizza last night and had some breakfast yesterday morning. Maybe if I stop eating altogether I can just wither away and no longer suffer.

"Let me bring you something. You should really eat."

"I'm really not hungry, Allison."

She stands up and comes to stand in front of me, then crouches down. "I don't know what happened between you and Donavon. Kenna said what he did was horrible, and I'll take her word for it. But what you and him have is so real and rare. I'm not saying to forgive him because I don't even know what he did, but I'm saying that maybe you should give it some time. You know, to think things over. To cool down and take some time to ponder. See things a little more clearly."

I finally look at her. She looks a lot like Donavon. They all look alike, but no one has Donavon's deep blue eyes.

I give her a nod and a polite smile. She's only trying to help. "I could do that."

She smiles back and stands up. "I'll go grab you something to eat."

I humor her and let her leave without protest. Then I spin around in my chair to see the mess that I've made. Taking a deep breath, I get to my feet and begin cleaning.

Allison comes back with my favorite salad from the café a block over. I'm sure Donavon told her about it since she would have no other way of knowing.

I sit there and pick at my salad while she tries to make conversation, not at all put off by my poor attitude. She must sense it's time for her to leave and gives me a hug before saying goodbye.

I go back to staring out the window, not having the energy to get myself up to leave yet. I've never known such sorrow before. I hate that he did this. I hate him for doing this.

I hear the door softly open then click shut. I know it's him even though it's not the way he usually enters the room—with confidence and authority. He appears out of my periphery. "Jane," he says my name so tenderly I almost check to make sure it's really him. "Can we please talk? I want to fix this."

The anger again begins to stew, but I keep a lid on it. "You can't fix this, Donavon." I wish he could. God, do I wish he could.

"Anything can be fixed if it's worth it." He isn't his conceited self when he says this. There's lucid doubt in his tone.

I look up at him and he looks almost as miserable as I do. *Almost.* "Could you please give me a week, Donavon? If I'm stuck here having to work with you, then will you please give me a week without having to talk? About us. Strictly professional for one week."

"I can do that," he responds quickly then looks down. "I'll give you your space for a week. But then I want to have an actual discussion about us. No screaming, no fighting."

"Give me a week and then we can talk calmly and rationally." *If he doesn't piss me off before then.* "And I want tomorrow off."

I need time to purge the stupid lingering maudlin feelings. To expel them into exile, and wallow. I need a fortitude built stronger than ever.

He looks at me and holds my stare, then nods his head. "Okay. I just want to say one thing." He moves in front of me and squats down. "I love you *so* much." I watch the lump in his throat bob. "I am willing to do whatever it takes to make this right." I open my mouth to argue but he doesn't let me as he continues. "Because I know I can. You're mine, Jane. And I won't stop until I make everything...right again." He swallows. "I'll give you your week of peace." His eyes bounce around my face before he stands up and leaves before I can say anything.

Does he not realize that he has yet to take ownership of what he did? To sincerely apologize for everything? He's defended himself and proclaimed he'd restore what we once had. He thinks he can *fix* things, but does he even understand how he broke it?

Gathering my stuff, I leave for the day, wishing I could be walking away forever. As soon as I get home, I grab the bottle of whiskey and crawl into bed with my laptop then pull up a streaming app and play a movie. Something with zero romance. Zero humor. Only violence and gore.

Kenna and I text back and forth for a while. I give her minimal insight on how my day went with Donavon, purposely excluding the part where he blackmailed me into staying at the company and pretending to be his fiancée. Instead, I give her the farce of being brave and refusing to let him ruin my career and my life entirely.

I slowly sip on the whiskey, letting it burn all the way down and leave my head fuzzy. I'm not trying to get trashed because that could lead to bad decisions, but I drink enough to help alleviate some of the pain.

A few hours later, I pick up my phone to find Bonnie calling me. *Shit, Bonnie.* I have to tell her. And I have to tell her everything. We don't keep anything from each other, and if anyone can help me through this, it's her.

"Hey, Bonbon."

"Open up."

I sit up in my bed. "What?"

"Come let us in."

"You're here?" I get up and start heading for the front door. "And who's us?" I pause in my steps with apprehension.

"Madison and I."

I squeeze my eyes shut for a moment. Fuck, this is just great. It's not that I don't want to see Madison, it's that I'm not ready to face everyone right now. But Madison isn't everyone, she's one of my closest friends. "I'll be right there."

As soon as I open the door, Bonnie flies in and Madison hesitantly trails behind her. I close the door and Bonnie spins around and places a big tote bag down on the dining table and peels her coat off.

"Okay, first things first." She looks at me and opens her arms.

I run into them and immediately break down. This girl is literally the sister I never had. We don't need to share blood to be as thick as thieves. "How'd you know?" I ask through my tears.

"Kenna called me and told me you could use us right now. Something about Donavon being an asshole," she says the same thing Allison said as she strokes my hair.

Kenna may not be here right now, yet she's making sure I am taken care of and doing what she can from afar. I don't know what I would do without the women in my life.

I pull away and wipe at my tears. "We come with gifts. And by gifts, I mean snacks and booze," Bonnie says.

"I remember everything," I say as I stop Madison and wrap her in a fierce hug. "Is that why you've been so distant lately?" I ask holding her at arm's length, and she nods.

"I'm sorry," she says, and with a heavy sigh I wrap her in my arms again. There's more for us to discuss, but Bonnie begins barking out orders.

"Alright, Mads, you're on snack duty, let's get set up in the bed-room. Jane likes to be in bed when she's depressed."

I snort and smile bashfully. "We don't have to get in my bed. We can hang out on the couch."

"Nonsense. Go get your skinny ass back in bed and we'll be right in. Then you can spill your guts. Giving us every dirty detail," Bonnie demands and I salute her before turning back to my bedroom.

Once we're all piled in my bed, I word-vomit everything, divulging every little detail from beginning to end. I tell them more than what I told Kenna because at the end of the day, Donavon is Kenna's brother, and no matter what, I would never do or say anything to cause a rift between them.

"Holy shit," Bonnie says once I'm done.

"He cannot do that!" Madison exclaims.

"He can do that, Mads," I say.

"Well, fuck that. I can find another job," Madison replies with.

"It's not just you, Madison. It would be a bunch of other people, and it wouldn't be fair to them. I can't live with that." Neither of them have a response because there is none. "Madison...why didn't you tell me?" I ask the question that has been hanging between us like a festering cloud.

She groans and slaps her hands over her face, shaking her head. "How do you tell someone about something like that?" She drops her hands and gives me a dry look. "Like, 'Hey, that day you lost your memory, you found out that your boyfriend has some secret sex club and you got hit by a car fleeing from it. Oh, and I know this because I'm the one that told you.' And I had no idea if he told you at some point either. It was...a shitty situation." She leaves a gap of silence. "I also heard that it can be super stressful on someone with amnesia to try and force memories back into their head. Like, it might hurt them to make them try and remember things they have forgotten."

"I've heard that too," Bonnie adds quietly.

"I get it, Madison. I can't say I would know what to do in your situation."

"Are you upset with me?"

"No." I shake my head with a sad smile. "Not at all. If anything, I feel horrible about the position you were forced into."

"Please don't."

"How about neither of you feel sorry and both of you agree that all this shit sucks," Bonnies says making us both chuckle.

"It certainly does suck," I admit.

"So, what now?" Bonnie asks.

I shrug my shoulders. "Right now, we drink," I say holding up my glass to clink against theirs.

I have a long weekend ahead of me, so I'm going to enjoy this time I have with these two because once they leave, the misery will overtake me.

THIRTY-NINE

Donavon

I've spent the last week moving entirely on autopilot.

No matter how much it killed me, I gave Jane the space she requested. It's been an ongoing joke that I could never go back to work without her after having her to rely on for so long, but it's no exaggeration. It's a habit to pick up the phone to call her for my every need. Though she anticipated most. She isn't only irreplaceable as my intended mate, but also as my right-hand at work.

She's shown up to work every day this week so far, but she's hardly done much while here. If her intentions are to make me fire her, she'll be sorely disappointed.

The only interactions I've had with her have been strictly professional, and only when absolutely necessary. Though I may have brought her coffee and lunch, I would deliver it wordlessly and then leave.

Her week is up tomorrow and I'm watching every second tick by, eagerly awaiting that moment. It isn't in me to show this much patience, and I don't think I could ever do it again. First thing tomorrow, we will talk. We'll put this to rest where it will rot away until there is nothing left of it.

My work phone beeps, and I pick it up. "Mr. Waldorf. Your ten o'clock interview is here," Maggie says over the line.

"Send her in," I murmur then hang up.

Even with Allison working here, I still can't keep up without Jane fully functioning, so I decided it's time for an assistant. Only until Jane decides to stop being so petulant.

Less than a minute later, there's a knock on the door and I give them permission to enter.

I look up to see an attractive woman putting a little extra sway in her hips as she approaches me. "Hi, Mr. Waldorf. I'm Amanda." She smiles and reaches her hand out over my desk for a handshake.

I glance at it then gesture for her to have a seat, declining the formal greeting. She tries to brush off the affront and sits down. She crosses her legs and I have a feeling 'the talk' will come a day sooner than planned. This woman doesn't compare to Jane, but I think it may get a rise out of her. It may or may not have been my intentions when accepting the few interviews that I did.

I'm desperate for her attention and to find out what her reaction will be. I'm terrified that I'm really losing her. If this woman doesn't have any effect on her, I'll know that I have.

"Tell me about your last job," I say, not looking forward to hearing anything this woman has to say. She's only a means to an end.

I tune her out as she babbles on, trying to give me a sultry smile and bat her eyelashes as if it would move me in any way. But I'm immune to the charms of every other woman than Jane. I couldn't be seduced even if I were completely impaired.

Ashley or Bethany or whatever-her-name-is continues on as I sit here and think of the most grandiose gesture I could make to show Jane how committed I am to us. It's obvious that it needs to involve her coming to my home. But it needs to be more than that.

"Alright, Emily," I cut her off midsentence.

"It's Amanda, sir." Her smile is still suggestive, not at all insulted that I couldn't remember her name.

"Yes, I will give you a call if I decide to go with you."

"I certainly hope so, Mr. Waldorf. I think I could be a good fit for you."

I nod once and already have my focus elsewhere. "You can see your way out."

"Thank you so much for your time and I hope to hear from you soon." She stands up and waits a moment as if I'll stand with her and walk her out. She finally gets the hint and takes her leave.

I sigh and rub at my head. No way in hell am I hiring her. Even if it were for a temporary position. I glance at the chair she had occupied and growl when I see that she's left her coat. I glower at it as if it'll make it disappear and erase the faint memory of her because I am quickly regretting it now.

No, this was the worst idea I have ever had.

I pick up my phone and call for some backup. "Hello, jerk," Kenna answers.

"Hello, dear sister. I need a favor."

She scoffs. "You need a favor? Seriously?"

"Please, Kenna," I state flatly.

"What makes you think I'll do anything for you?"

"Because you're my sister and you love me."

"And you're also the man who broke my best friend's heart."

"And I'm trying to fix it."

She sighs and pauses for a moment. "Fine. What do you want?"

"I need you to give me a list of necessities for Jane."

"What kind of necessities?"

"As in what she would need to be comfortable at my place."

"I'm not sure I follow."

I grind my teeth. "I would like for Jane to stay at my place, possibly live there, so I need to know what she would need to do so."

"Like, move in with you?" she asks in shock and I'm close to hanging up on her and figuring it out on my own.

"Yes, Kenna. So, are you going to help me or not?"

"Am I missing something here? Did you guys make up, as in today? Because last time I talked to Jane, which happened to be last night, you two were still broken up."

I grip my phone and refrain from shattering the screen again. "We were never broken up."

"Um, I was there, Don. And I've been here with her ever since it went down. Listening to her cry herself to sleep most nights and walking around here like a zombie."

I rub at the ache in my chest on instinct. "We're going through a rough patch right now, but she is still my fiancée and I still plan to marry her. So, are you going to help me with this or not?" I demand, losing my patience.

"You know, this situation really sucks for me. What you did was really messed up and I don't think I could forgive Tom if he ever did something like that to me. But at the same time, I've never seen you like this with any other woman before. I'm rooting for you, Don, but you have to make some real effort here to even stand a chance."

"That is why I am calling you," I growl through clenched teeth.

Kenna ends up helping me out, and I have an ongoing list of things to buy for Jane. Everything from toiletries to clothing. I also have come up with quite a few ideas of my own.

It's nearing lunchtime and I plan on getting some food from Jane's favorite Mexican place close by. Just as I'm picking up the phone to have Maggie put in the order for me, there's a knock at the door. "Come in," I call out.

The woman that was here for the interview, Ava or Lisa, comes in and closes the door behind her with a smile. "I'm so sorry, Mr. Waldorf, but I believe I left my jacket."

I glance at said jacket and want to throw it at her so she can hurry the fuck up and get out. I should just tell her she's not getting the job. *No one is.*

I ignore her as she takes her time to retrieve her jacket and lets out a little giggle that gets under my skin. "So sorry about that." She pauses and I keep my gaze glued to the screen on my desk. "Is there anything I can do for you?"

I only look up at her to frown, wondering how she could be so goddamn daft. I open my mouth to ask her exactly that when Jane walks in. Her head is down as she's focused on the papers in her hands. There's this unfamiliar panic rising within me, and I can't do anything to stop the situation I've regretfully put myself in.

"Here are—" Jane says and then comes to a halt when she glances up and notices the random woman standing in front of my desk.

"Do you need something else?" I ask the pest still invading my space.

"Oh, no." She lifts her jacket up. "I look forward to hearing from you."

"Leave," I finally snap at her.

She's flustered from my discourtesy and left speechless as she almost runs out of my office. But my eyes are on Jane as she watches the woman leave, then her eyes snap to mine, and they are lit up.

"Who was that?" she rushes out.

"A candidate for my assistant position." I mean to go on and tell her that I changed my mind about hiring anyone, but she's too quick to jump down my throat.

Her arms drop to her sides as her eyes turn to saucers. "You hired someone else to do my job? *Her*?"

"Not yet, but you haven't exactly been doing everything like you used to, so yes. I need another assistant."

"And that's who you hired?" she deadpans.

She's looking at me with hurt-filled eyes and not angry ones I was hoping for. I didn't want to further hurt her, only to get a rise out of her. "I haven't hired her, and I don't think I will."

Her beautiful eyes glisten with unshed tears as she stares at me like I just killed a puppy right in front of her. *What have I done?* Without saying anything, she throws the papers on the floor shaking her head. She storms out leaving the door open then a moment later, she slams the door shut to her office.

Fucking hell. What the fuck is wrong with me? I'm supposed to be fixing this. Not making her cry more. I fucked up. Again. Everything I have been doing has been a complete failure. I can't go back to being that man. That man that fails and fucks up. I cannot be that again. I have worked so hard for perfection and success. This is not me.

Making the short trek to her office, I feel as if I'm walking the line. I enter without knocking and close the door gently behind me. She's lying on her quaint couch with her back to me, but I can hear the sniffling.

I go to her and get down on my knees. "Jane. Please talk to me." She cries softly and refuses to answer. "I'm not hiring her. In fact, I'm not going to hire anyone." Still nothing. I didn't think any of this through. I thought she would either blow-up at me or not care. I didn't think about her crying like this. I've seen her cry, but those were angry tears. This is different. These are tears of pain. Pain I once again inflicted. "Jane, darling. Please tell me what upset you so much." I pause, trying to breathe through this. "Give me something, darling. You're killing me."

I wish she would yell or throw something at me. Her silence is antagonizing, stirring up my temper. Her reticence and tears are a lethal combination, like bleach and vinegar.

I rise to my feet. "You can take the rest of the day off." My voice is too harsh coming out. I know I need to be gentle with her, but I can only give in so much before I start demanding what I want. "Go home and get some rest. I'll see you tomorrow."

Knowing there's nothing more I can do, I leave.

This might be my doing that was the catalyst to all of this, but she holds all the power to forgive me. To let us move on and get back to being happy. We do not need to continue to live in pain like this. She's tormenting us both by being stubborn.

I sit down at my desk and look at the picture of us I replaced the frame to. The one she had on her desk a week ago and broke it in her little tantrum. I know she's seen it, but she's made no comment.

My phone rings and I pick it up when I see who's calling. "Hello?"

"Don, you've been avoiding me like the clap." I snort. "How's everything with you and Jane?"

"Not good," I mutter. "She fucking hates me right now."

"I am so sorry about that. I really had no idea it was her and—"

"I know, I know." He's already apologized profusely for his part in this disaster.

"So, are we doing this or what?" He's referring to me signing my share of the ownership over to Benjamin.

"Yeah, I'll get started on that as soon as I can. I've been a little preoccupied lately. How's everything going over there?"

"Things are good as usual. Benjamin has been coming by more often to help me out with some of the paperwork."

I chuckle, "You really need to learn how to do that shit on your own."

"Why? Now I'll have your brother."

I smile, shaking my head. "I guess you do. I'll be by soon to start getting things in motion."

"You sure you're ready to part with the club?" he asks in all sincerity.

Garrett has always been a good friend and confidant. We had this dream together in college and gradually brought our vision to life only a couple of years later. He was content with what the club brought in, but I needed more. I used what I made to build an entire empire. Starting with buying out failing businesses and getting them up and running bigger and more successful than ever. I made all the right moves and was quickly on my way to the success I have now.

The club is no longer that haven for my inner demons to reveal themselves. No longer my refuge. It's something that could have taken Jane from me. It's what hurt her, and I want nothing to do with it anymore.

"I am," I say firmly.

He's quiet for a moment. "Then you better not give up on her."

"You're encouraging me to fight for a monogamous relationship?" Like me, Garrett has never done relationships. But unlike me, he's always enjoyed dating. Never holding onto one woman at a time and known to leave a trail of broken hearts along the way. At least before Jane, I made it very clear with the women I slept with that it was only sex, though there being more than one woman in my bed, there wasn't much confusion.

"Hey, I hope I find what you have."

"You do?" This is news to me.

"Hell yeah, Don. I don't go through women because I'm an asshole. I just haven't found the one to make me want more yet."

I'm the asshole here. I've been seeing him from the wrong perspective all these years. The only real and true friend I've had. How do I not understand him after all this time?

"I'm not giving up."

"Good for you."

"I'll talk to you later, Garrett." I hang up and lean back in my chair staring at the picture.

Now what?

Forty

Jane

As soon as I saw the attractive woman in Donavon's office, it gave me flashbacks of the naked ones I discovered at Verity.

Bile instantly rose in my throat, and I wanted to die. The wounds hadn't even begun to heal, and it was like ripping them open and pouring salt in them. The pain was not only fresh but it somehow worsened.

He acts as if this is all killing him, but he's the one that did this to us. To me. Then he went and did it again. Was that his plan? To hurt me more? To drive a dagger straight through my broken heart? Was he trying to show me that I'm replaceable?

If he did this to toy with me like this is all some big game, he's beyond cruel. I do not deserve his mistreatment. And I will not take it from him.

Wiping away my snot and tears, I gather my belongings and go home for the day. Kenna isn't home from work yet, so I head right into my room and change out of my work clothes before crawling into bed. Exhausted from the stress and all the crying, I fall asleep pretty easily.

I wake up later to the sound of Kenna greeting Luna. Rubbing the sleep from my eyes, I throw my bed head up into a messy bun and slip into my slippers.

"Hey," she says when she sees me coming out from the hall.

"Hey." I give her a half smile. "How was work?"

"It was good." She takes in my appearance. "You okay?"

I shrug my shoulders and pad into the kitchen to make myself some tea. "I'm alright."

"Did something happen today?" she asks following me around but keeping a safe distance.

"Donavon is an asshole. That's all." She doesn't say anything to that. "Want some tea?"

"No, thank you." She watches me in silence while I fill up the kettle and place it on the burner. "He's not like us, you know." I look at her. "He doesn't...think like we do. Like normal people do. I know it's no excuse for what he did, but I almost think he's not even sure what he did wrong. Like he didn't know any better."

"Kenna. He's a grown ass man. He knew damn well what he did was wrong. That's exactly why he hid it from me."

"I know," she groans. "It's hard to explain."

"I know what you mean, Kenna. I really do." I understand more than anyone can. "But he's a smart man. He understands where he went wrong."

"You're right," she sighs and sits down at the breakfast bar. "It's just that he's changed so much since you. In a good way. He was still brooding and over-protective and controlling, but he was happy. He laughed and smiled with ease instead of always looking like it was forced. I had no idea he would ever want to settle down and actually start living with someone." She takes a breath. "I guess what I'm trying to say is, if it's worth it, you should let him fight for you."

"And if it's not?"

"It is, Jane. It wouldn't hurt so terribly if it weren't. And I'm not saying this because he's my brother and you're my best friend and I love you both to death. I'm saying this because I have never seen either of you so happy before. You deserve that immeasurable, infinite happiness."

"He did make me happy, but he also violated my trust. What kind of a relationship would we have without it?"

Even if she had an answer, she doesn't get to voice it because Donavon's signature knock sounds at the door. Kenna goes to check the peephole and looks at me in question. I know she'll tell him to go away if I asked her to, but instead I give her a subtle nod, silently telling her to open the door.

They don't exchange any words as he comes in and Kenna mutters something about making herself scarce and disappears into her bedroom. I lean back against the counter and wait as Donavon makes his way inside the kitchen. He leans against the counters across from me, shoving his hands inside his pockets and crossing one ankle over the other.

He looks sheepish and remorseful before he speaks. "I'm not hiring her."

"Why am I still working for you, Donavon? I'm not doing my job, we're not together anymore." The weight of the ring on my finger is a heavy burden.

His jaw ticks and I know he wants to argue that point. "How else would I be able to see you every day? To make sure you aren't going to disappear on me? I know you won't invite me to stay the night, I don't think you would agree to come and stay at my place." He pauses as I stare back at him in wonderment. "I'm terrified that you'll run away," he says quietly with the most vulnerability I have ever seen on him.

"You're forcing me to work for you so that you can see me and make sure I don't leave?" He nods once and I shake my head. "Is this just a game to you?"

"Nothing about this is a game."

"This is all a game!" I raise my voice. "Your manipulation, and secrets, and using that woman today to mess with me! It's all one big game!"

He stands up straight. "I do all of this because I love you."

"No, you don't."

"I would never tell you I did if I didn't mean it whole-heartedly."

I study him for a second. "Fine. Let's say that you do love me. But Donavon, I can't be with you, and I definitely cannot marry you."

"Why not?"

"Because I don't trust you, that's why. All credence is gone. I decided to put complete faith in you from the beginning even though I knew you didn't do relationships and you make it impossible to let anyone in. But I chose to trust you, and look where it got me," I say exasperated.

"I did not cheat on you, Jane. If that's what you are worried about—don't. I did not touch those women or any other woman while we've been together."

"Watching two naked women go down on each other in the privacy of your office is just as bad. How don't you see that?" I ask in frustration. "It's like if you walked in on me masturbating in front of another man."

I can see his fists clenching inside his pockets and his teeth clench making his temples twitch. "That's not the same."

"Well, I guess the same would be me watching two guys suck each other off, but that's just not my cup of tea."

"It wasn't for my entertainment, Jane. It was strictly business."

"Business," I deadpan. "So, is it a strip club or a sex club?"

"It's an exclusive gentlemen's club, but there are private rooms for people who pay top-dollar for that kind of entertainment. Those women were auditioning," he states so carelessly.

"So, that's something you do all the time?!" I exclaim with wide eyes.

"It's not very often, but yes. When we have women who want to audition for private party entertainers, I have to be there to make sure they are worth the money they will be paid."

I am stunned. Floored. "Oh, my God! And you still think this is okay?! Do you even hear yourself?!"

"It's strictly business. I swear. I do not touch them."

"Did you use to?"

He doesn't answer right away, and he doesn't need to. I have my answer and it makes my stomach turn. "Sometimes I would entertain them if they were attractive enough and obviously willing." I clutch my stomach, ready to puke. "But I have not touched a single woman since you, Jane. Since before you and I were even together. I would never do that to you."

"Holy hell," I whisper feeling faint. I look at him right in the eyes and shake my head in bafflement. "You really don't get it, do you?" He doesn't respond. "Don, I saw the way you were watching those women. You had a fucking smile on your face, so don't tell me you weren't enjoying yourself. It might be for business, but it was also for your pleasure."

"Jane." He takes a step forward. "I wasn't even paying attention. I was sitting there looking at engagement rings on my phone. Maybe my eyes were in their direction, but I was looking right through them, thinking about *you*."

I internally laugh. It's like when a guy cheats and he says they were thinking about you the entire time. "Please, leave." I direct my eyes down at the floor because I can't keep looking at him.

He surprisingly doesn't fight me. After a moment of standing there in tense silence, he walks away and leaves the apartment.

"How'd it go?" Kenna asks as she reenters the room. I suspect she heard everything.

I shake my head and sip my tea. "He just doesn't get it. He still doesn't see how that was as bad as cheating. And he admitted that it was something that has happened before. As if it were completely normal."

"If he did, would it make a difference?" I wait for her to elaborate. "Like if he genuinely realized that it was just as bad as physically cheating, would that make you reconsider giving him another chance?"

Good question. "It would be a start," I murmur.

"Then make him realize."

"How would I do that?"

She shrugs. "Maybe give him a taste of his own medicine."

FORTY-ONE

Jane

Make him realize. Give him a taste of his own medicine.

Kenna's words of advice play on loop in my head for almost two whole days.

How the hell would I go about doing that? I'm not petty enough to actually cheat on him or use some poor guy in my scheme of revenge. I couldn't do that to anyone because it would probably ruin their life. So, what can I do to make him feel exactly how I did when I walked in on him? Make him realize how much he hurt me.

Donavon got Kenna and Allison to try and talk me into family dinner tomorrow. No way in hell would I go to sit in front of his parents and wear my ring, pretending like Donavon and I are still together. I couldn't lie to their faces like that. But they should be aware of what an asshole their son is if they don't already.

Kenna admitted that their parents have no idea we broke up because Donavon claims that we haven't. He's out of his goddamn mind.

Now, it's Friday and I'm drinking myself into another narcosis state. Kenna's at Tom's for the night and I wouldn't subject anyone to my despondency. So, here I am. Sitting alone in my apartment, getting drunk. While I'm sure Donavon is at his special sex club watching women get naked and fuck each other.

The man has still yet to say, "I'm sorry". He thinks this is all about him owning a strip club and not telling me about it. Dumbass. Men are dumb. So dumb. They have no common sense, and when it comes to women, they are dumb as shit. Fucking clueless. Dumb pigs.

I take another swig of whiskey, which I hate drinking straight, but it gets me drunk a lot quicker. And the drunker I get, the more hatred I feel for Donavon. He's so cruel. A monster.

Me: You are a monster and I hate you.

It takes me a few times to actually type this because I'm pretty damn drunk now.

Me: Are you at your sex club now? It is Friday. Of course, you are. Probably watching women fork. Did I mention that I hate you?

He would tell me he would be working all night...Liar.

Cheating Bastard Boss: I'm only here to help Benjamin with the transition.

Cheating Bastard Boss: I won't be here much longer. Can I come see you after?

"Hah!" I burst out. What a joke! Though the thought of seeing him gives me butterflies and the decision between saying yes or no is a struggle when it should be an automatic *no*. The alcohol is obviously having the opposite effect I intended it for. Wait, what transition?

Me: No. Just wanted to let you know that you are a monster and I hate you. If it weren't for you blackmailing me, I would never see you again. Goodnight asshole.

He texts me something back, but I ignore it. I have plans tonight. Plans to turn the tables on Donavon and give him a taste of his own medicine. Thanks to his own sister's advice, I finally know what I can do to get him back.

I put on my most scandalous panties and then the sexiest dress that I own. It's cold out, but who cares? I can wear a coat.

I am dressed for revenge.

FORTY-TWO

Donavon

"You okay, Don?" Benjamin asks from the chair in front of my desk.

I sigh and put my phone down. Jane stopped responding to my texts. "Just shit with Jane," I admit to him.

He shakes his head. "Told you. You should've told her about it."

"I don't even think that's what she's mad about. She's more pissed about me watching the women audition for the private parties."

Benjamin busts out laughing. "Yeah! No shit, sherlock! You know me. I don't have the best track record when it comes to relationships, but even I know that would piss any female off."

"It was business, nothing more. Hell, I stopped enjoying it since the moment she walked into my life."

"That shit doesn't matter. You don't watch naked women like that no matter what. Shits not cool." Great. *Now* he's telling me this. Where was this sound advice from him before?

My desk phone rings, and I pick it up. "Yeah."

"Hey, boss. Your fiancée is here. I told Big D to go ahead and let her up," Darrel who is the security at the front says.

"What?" I snap.

"Should I have not let her in?" he asks unsure now.

"When did she get here?"

"She just walked in."

"Goddamnit," I grumble and hang up to phone Big D.

"Yeah," he answers after the first ring.

"My fiancée is here. The one you foolishly let up weeks ago. Find her and escort her upstairs to me," I quip.

"Yes, sir."

"What's going on?" Benjamin asks as I stand to my feet, livid as all hell.

"Jane's here."

"Here? As in inside the club?"

"Yeah, apparently."

I sigh and face the windows overlooking the place. Her texts from not too long ago were a little out of character for her. I think maybe she was drinking, and showing up here, I can confirm that's what kind of state she'll be in when I get a hold of her ass.

It's been a few minutes too long without word of her location or update on her whereabouts. I call Big D again. "Do you have her?"

"Not yet. I have every guy on it though."

"How the fuck haven't you found her? She just walked in!"

"I know, sir. I'm on it. She couldn't have gone far."

"I want her up here in my office in the next three minutes or you're fucking gone." I hang up and growl. Should have fired him after his epic failure from weeks ago when he so easily bought Jane's story and let her come right up without consulting with me or Garrett first.

"Want me to go take a look around?" my brother asks.

"I actually would," I murmur.

"No problem."

I'm too preoccupied with surveilling the room below me to show him any gratitude as he leaves. I can faintly hear the announcer mumble in the background in between sets and I'm basically tuning him out until I hear, "Now, welcome to the stage, Don's Little Darling."

My heated gaze turns to molten lava as it snaps to the stage. She wouldn't. She couldn't. This isn't a fucking amateur night at some hole-in-the-wall strip club. These women are professionals. Some of them fly in from all around the country to headline here for our preeminent clientele. You can't just bat your eyelashes at security and our DJ to be able to step foot on our stage.

A melancholic song begins, and to my horror, Jane walks out onto the stage in a pathetic excuse for a dress and the red sole heels I gifted her for her birthday. I don't need to see anymore to understand her intentions. I run out of my office and fly down the stairs, taking three at a time.

I can see her elevated above the patrons and onlookers and my throat constricts when she begins to let her dress fall from her shoulders. I can't make it to her fast enough. She's here to prove a point and piss me off—and it's working.

Whoever let her up on that stage is fucking *dead*. And Jane is going to get the spanking she will never forget. Her ass will be red for days. I am done tiptoeing around her feelings. This shit stops now. She is mine and it's time to remind her of that.

I almost stumble over people as I don't dare take my eyes off her and I want to scream when she lets her dress fall and everyone gets a good glimpse at her perfect breasts right before Garrett jumps up on the stage to throw his jacket around her.

I'm at the stage as soon as he scoops her up and he disposes of her right into my arms. "Woo!" A giggle bubbles out of her. I lock my jaw, too irate to say a word to her. "But my shoes, Don," she whines, whiskey oozing out of her pores.

"Shut the fuck up, Jane," I say through my teeth and whip around everyone.

She giggles again and I want to fucking gag her. She whines some more about her shoes, but I have to ignore her, or I will explode. I carry her all the way up to my office and Benjamin is there, looking like he's getting his coat to leave.

"Hi, Benny!" Jane says smiling over at him.

"Out," I snap at him.

"I'm going, I'm going." He puts his hands up in surrender with a little smirk on his face. "Bye, Jane."

"Aww, you're leaving?" she pouts.

Shut the fuck up, Jane. Please, just shut the fuck up.

The door closes behind Benjamin, and I toss Jane down on the couch and begin pacing the room. I'm furious with her right now. "I'm sorry, Donavon. Was me taking my clothes off in front of other men painful to see?" she coos.

Shut the fuck up, Jane. I fist my hair so I don't throttle her.

"I just thought that you know, since I'm your fiancée, I should be somewhat involved with your precious strip club." I continue pacing, wishing she would just shut the fuck up before I really lose it. "If you don't want me on stage then maybe I could bartend. Or be a cocktail waitress." She pauses. "Oh! I know! I could audition for private parties," she says with a taunting tone.

I come to a halt and snap my head in her direction. She's sitting there with her long legs crossed and swimming in Garrett's jacket. Stalking over to her, I slam my hands on either side of her head landing on the back of the couch while she looks up at me unperturbed with a little smirk on her beautiful face. "Don't you ever do that again," I growl, fuming.

"Well, that's not entirely fair, Don. You get to have your little fun behind my back, it's only fair that I have some fun too. I can totally see myself falling in love with stripping." She grins. "It was exhilarating. I can only imagine what it's like to perform for *private parties.* Girl-on-girl." She bites her bottom lip. Imagining her with another woman does not at all appeal to me. What would be the point? I would only be watching her. She's all I want to see. All I want to touch. The only woman that can make all the blood rush to my cock with a single glance.

"You want to audition to be a private party girl?" She shrugs her shoulder calling my bluff. "Alright." I stand up and go to lean back against the front of my desk. "Go ahead. Here's your chance." I even pull my phone out and play something over the Bluetooth speakers in my office.

She gives me a seductive smile and rises to the occasion. Standing up on her long legs, she opens up the suit jacket and lets it fall to the ground. Her glorious tits shining like a fucking beacon to my entire body. She doesn't make a move to remove her black panties. Instead, she turns around and bends over, planting her hands on the couch to showcase her perfect ass.

I'm already salivating, and my cock is already pulsating in my pants, so when she reaches a delicate hand between her legs and pulls the fabric of her panties aside, I have to fist my cock and stifle a groan. It's been so fucking long since I've had her, and her pussy is fucking glistening for me. All I want to do is fuck the stubbornness out of us both and hear her tell me she loves me and that I'm still her wonderful man.

When she looks at me over her shoulder, her eye lids flutter when she sees me fisting my cock through my pants. She watches me as she begins to play with her wet cunt, and it's more than I can take.

Pushing off my desk, I stalk toward her. My hands itch to touch her. *Anywhere.* "I thought you said you don't touch them," she says breathily.

"You are not *them*, darling. You are mine," I loosen my suddenly tight tie, "and if you want the job, you got it. As my very own personal entertainment." I reach her and run a hand across the soft skin of her ass.

Her breath hitches. "Then I respectfully decline." She straightens up still looking at me over her shoulder. Then she turns and heads for the door, wobbling slightly.

"What the fuck do you think you're doing?" I snap.

She stops at the door and shrugs. "My clothes are out there. It's not like anyone would notice me walking around like this, since I won't be the only naked woman in the place."

Bullshit. Everyone would notice. She is impossible not to look at. "I'll have your clothes collected and brought up." I go to her and all but shove her back to the couch.

"But my shoes," she bitches about them again and plops down pouting. "I hate that they're from you, but I love them."

I take my suit jacket off the back of my desk chair, and I drape it around her bare body. "I'll make sure you get your shoes back." I head back over to my desk to sit down feeling this massive weight on my shoulders and chest.

"But what if someone stole them?" she continues as she lays down and uses my jacket as a blanket.

"Then I'll buy you a new pair."

"But I don't want a new pair. I want those," she complains causing my mouth to tilt at one corner.

"So, you do care that they're from me?"

"I don't want to," she murmurs, closing her eyes.

"Then I'll make sure to track them down for you."

She makes a girlish humming noise and settles into the couch more. I watch her as she quickly falls asleep looking peaceful. I watch her for a while then I call down to one of my guys to make sure her stuff is retrieved. He says they already are but didn't want to disrupt me. I have them brought up and wait outside of the door so that she isn't disturbed in any way. I'm still reeling from the petulant stunt she pulled.

I go to stand over her serene form and admire seeing her in this state. Her hands are tucked under her soft cheek like a pillow, her engagement ring sparkling. I want to remain angry with her, but in some way, this feels like some kind of break through for us. If she no longer cared, and truly wanted things to end between us, she wouldn't have done what she did tonight. She'll soon be my wife, and we'll sooner move the fuck on from this.

Toeing my shoes off and removing my tie, I climb over her and settle in behind her, holding her back to my front. Having her back in my arms, it doesn't take long for me to find rest.

I don't think I've been asleep long when I wake up to Jane pushing her ass into my erection that will not go away. I groan a little and find her hip bone with my hand. "Jane," I rasp with my eyes closed.

I assume she didn't mean to, but she can't do that again or I will pounce on her. I am so hard up for her it's insane. I'm about to relax again when she pushes her ass into me again. This time, I know it was intentional. The way she rolled her hips and the way her breathing picks up.

My eyes pop open and I lie there very still. Afraid to make any sudden movements. She presses her ass into me again and she lifts an arm up to cup the back of my head.

I'm instant to react. I throw the jacket off her and to the floor then bring my lips to her neck and begin kissing her. Sucking and licking like a crazed animal about to have his first meal.

She moans and undulates her body again and again. Taking my hand that's gripping her hip, I slide it across her stomach and up to cup one of her breasts. I give it a nice squeeze and then roll her nipple between two fingers. God, I fucking love her breasts.

She continues rolling her hips and I take the arm that's pinned between us and slip it under her to grope her other breast so I can remove my other hand to journey down the flatness of her stomach. She doesn't stop me, so I don't hesitate.

My fingers make their way inside her panties to slip through her wetness and she whines, arching her back more. "Jane," I rasp against her neck then latch my mouth on it. Making sure to mark her so she can't possibly forget when she sobers up.

She moans in response and rides my fingers. She must be as horny as I am. Feeling sexually deprived. I massage her clit as she bucks her hips and pants. It doesn't take long for her to cry out and flood her panties.

I'm too fucking ravenous to get inside of her. I tear her panties off and undo my pants to pull my cock out in record timing. Hooking one arm under her knee, I crank her leg up and rub myself against her cunt to cover my cock in her slick juices.

I point my cock in the right direction and thrust inside of her. Her hand is still at the back of my head and I watch her beautiful face as I move inside of her. "Kiss me, Jane."

Her eyes only open to two slits as she turns to look at me. When I lean in, I'm surprised when she actually does kiss me back. And with just as much enthusiasm. Her fingers brush against my cock as I slide in and out of her and I break from the kiss to watch her touch herself.

"Fuck, Jane. I miss you."

"Wait, Don," she says without pausing her fingers. "We need a condom."

I snap my eyes up to her. *The fuck?* "I'm not putting on a fucking condom." I pant.

"I'm not on birth control anymore. I missed it a bunch after being in the hospital, then again after we broke up."

Ignoring her concerns, I continue moving inside of her. "I'm not wearing a fucking condom," I repeat.

"I don't know where the fuck your dick has been," she moans, close to coming, not at all fighting me off of her despite her words.

"No where. I've been with no one but you," I seethe, rising to her bait.

"Fine," she pants. "Then pull out."

"Why?" I keep fucking her.

Her eyes widen. "Are you serious?" I don't respond and start kissing her neck which I know she loves. "Wait, Don."

"No." I don't want to fucking wait. I've waited long enough.

"I swear to God, Don. If you don't pull out—"

I sear my lips to hers, shutting her the hell up and she sets off like fireworks. Twitching and quivering. Strangling my cock.

I fuck her straight through her orgasm making it roll into another one. This time I'm ready to come with her. "If you get pregnant, then so be it." It'll be a great excuse to hurry up and get married sooner rather than later.

I don't let her respond as I kiss her again. She can't talk anyways because her pussy begins to grip my cock like a fist, triggering my own climax. I don't pull out. I meant it when I said I wouldn't. She can get mad all she wants. She's mine.

After I shoot every ounce of cum I can inside of her, then and only then do I pull out. She doesn't say a word, and neither do I. She keeps her back to me, and I spoon her again as we both fall back asleep.

I hate these walls that she's tried building up between us. She was never so guarded and stubborn like this before. How can she sit here and act like she doesn't love me anymore? I don't think there's a single thing she could ever do that would make me stop loving her. Nothing.

Forty-Three

Jane

I wake up in Donavon's arms. "What are you doing?" I rasp out.

"Ssh. Just go back to sleep, darling. We're going home," Don says, and I nuzzle into his chest and close my eyes once again. Feeling already at home.

"Did you find my shoes?" I mutter.

I feel his chuckle against my body. "I did. They're safe and sound."

"That's good," I whisper and drift back off to sleep still feeling the effects of the whiskey and the sleep deprivation.

Next thing I know, he's carrying me through a place that's foreign to me. "Where are we?" I frown looking around the warm space.

"Home."

"Wait, stop. Put me down." I squirm in his arms.

He sighs before gently placing me on my feet. I scan the room and find it spectacular. An industrial loft with windows making up half the vaulted ceilings all the way down to the floor. Brick walls and neutral colors. It's definitely a bachelor pad, but it has incredible bones and architecture. The only real décor scattered throughout are all the indoor plants.

"Let me show you around," he murmurs.

I follow silently behind him, hugging his suit jacket around me. As soon as you enter, you find the lavish kitchen overlooking the open living area with tons of natural lighting. There's a half-bath on the first floor as well as a laundry room and his home office. Then he leads me up the iron spiral staircase that takes you up to the loft area where the bedroom is located. Everything is masculine yet tasteful.

The bathroom attached to the bedroom is gorgeous, but I'm distracted by all the feminine products neatly displayed on the counter. I feel that panic that has my heart racing and that lump in my throat making it difficult to swallow.

I don't understand. Whose things are they?

"Kenna helped me out by putting together a list for me with all the brands you like and everything you would need to stay here." I turn and frown at him as he hangs back sheepishly in the doorway. My hands shake and his head tilts to one side as he frowns back at me. "What's wrong?"

I twist my head back to inspect the feminine products and toiletries and it takes a moment for it all to click. Every item I see is something you would find in my bathroom at home. The same brand and scent. They're...mine.

I swallow and release the breath I was holding, feeling silly for jumping to conclusions like this. Yes, I do have some trust issues still to work through with Donavon, but to think he would have some other woman staying at his house, it's a little extreme.

I close my eyes and shake my head with a soft chuckle. "Nothing's wrong."

In fact, everything is feeling right again. All the pieces falling back into their rightful place.

"There're even some clothes in the closet for you. Again, Kenna helped me with sizing and what to buy," he says quietly.

I finally turn to face him. "When did you do all this?"

He rubs at the back of his neck nervously. "Monday?"

"I don't know what to say."

He cautiously diminishes the distance between us. "Say that there's still an *us*," he rasps, and I can tell he desperately wants to touch me. I'm desperate for his touch, too.

I lift my left hand up. "I thought that was *part of the stipulations*," I mock.

He gives me half a smirk and steps in even closer so that I have to crane my neck back. "Say that you want there to still be an us."

Sighing, I step back to give myself some much-needed space. "I don't know, Donavon. I'm not sure I can ever trust you again."

"I'm done with the club. I'm signing my share over to Benjamin and I will never step foot in that place again."

"It's not about the strip club, Don. It's the secrecy. The lies. The fact that you would watch women please themselves in your office and called it business as if that makes it all perfectly okay. And how you took advantage of my memory loss."

"And I understand that now," he rushes out. "I understand how wrong that was. All of it."

"I can't seem to get those images out of my head. I don't think you truly understand how badly you hurt me. How messed up it made me."

He's finished being patient and with his self-restraint as he steps up to me again and this time, he slides his hands onto my cheeks. "I do, Jane. Hurting you hurt me. Hiding things from you—it was constantly eating me up inside. I was sick to my stomach and consumed with guilt. I could never do that to you again. Never. And last night seeing you up on that stage, exposing yourself to everyone in that room, I have never felt rage so intense. I hate myself for hurting you, but I swear to you, I have not touched another woman since you, darling. Have not even had the tiniest sliver of temptation to."

Staring up into his deep blue eyes, I can already feel my walls crumbling. I believe him. I do. All I've needed was for him to understand what he did wrong and to take accountability. I didn't even know that's what I needed until right now. But he has still yet said the words 'I'm sorry'. I know that he is, but can't he allow himself to be vulnerable for one moment with me? *For* me?

"I wish I could forget everything and go back to the way things were, but I'm terrified. I'm so afraid of you breaking my heart again. I'm afraid you'll one day realize that I'm not enough for you." He starts shaking his head with fear in his eyes. "What if down the road, you find that you need more? Are you going to one day ask me to have a threesome, because I can tell you right now, I am not willing to share. Ever."

His hands press more firmly on either side of my face and his body fuses with mine. "I would never ask that of you. The thought of another man touching you is pure agony. You are more than enough for me, Jane. That's why I want to marry you." His face inches closer and my walls are shaking. "I want a family with you." My chin trembles. *Oh, God.* "I want you in my space every minute of every day. I want my space to become *our* space." His lips hover just over mine. "I want you around all the time. You and only you. From now until forever," he murmurs. "I love you so much, Jane. I'm sorry. *So fucking sorry.*"

I'm somehow able to see him through my watery eyes. "That's the first time you've actually apologized," I whisper.

His fingertips thread into the back of my hair as my head falls back. "I'm sorry for that as well. I really am. Vulnerability isn't exactly a strength of mine, but for you, I will hand you my pride, my heart, and my soul over on a silver platter. You can have it all, Jane."

I gawk up at him and my lips crack into a smile. The walls crumble to pieces and my heart once again beats, making me feel human. Then his lips come crashing down on mine and I don't object to it.

We devour each other with such hunger and angst. I want to crawl inside of him and never come out. I don't know how I held onto this resentment for so long. Only hours ago I was adamant about never forgiving him, then in a single moment, everything changed.

"Wait." I break from the kiss and we're both breathing hard. I look up at his handsome face. "Could I have a minute?"

His lips are glistening from mine and there's the hint of a smile on them. "Sure, darling." He kisses me softly on my cheek.

He closes the door gently, and I turn to the mirror. Taking a deep breath, I lean against the counter and find my hands shaking. Kenna said that if it's worth it, I should let Donavon fight for me. But there was that tiny doubt that he wouldn't. That he would get bored and move on. That he would remember why he never wanted a relationship before. But he never stopped. He had fought for me. And I let him because, yes, we're worth it.

The bathroom is almost a contrast to the rest of the condo. It has the same neutral tones, but there's a gorgeous clawfoot tub with a skylight over it, the lavish enclosed shower has its own skylight as well. It's like a beautiful sauna compared to an otherwise industrial space.

I relieve my bladder then head over to the sink to wash up. There's a new looking toothbrush similar to mine at home and the kind of toothpaste I like and assume they're mine. After I brush my teeth, I take a good look at myself in the mirror. "Holy Hell," I whisper and start running my fingers through my hair to tame it. It's a total mess, but not as bad as my face. I have freaking racoon eyes.

I slap my hands over my face groaning. He must really love me if he said all that to my face when it looks like this.

Digging through the cabinet underneath, I find makeup remover and the face cream I like to use. There're even hair ties so I can twist my unruly hair up into a knot on top of my head. I scrub my face clean and feel a little less like a mess. I'm still in only his suit jacket and I bring the lapels up to my nose and take a deep breath in. I love the way he smells. I've missed his spicy, manly scent so much.

Exiting the bathroom, I find Donavon sitting on the edge of the bed. He stands up and offers me a glass of water. I take it and practically chug the whole thing. He chuckles as I bring the glass back down. "Thank you," I gasp. "I needed that."

He grabs at the back of his neck with a boyish smile. "I've never seen you drunk like that."

My cheeks feel hot, and I set the glass down on the nightstand. "I haven't been drunk like that since my twenty-first birthday." Something on his nightstand has me do a double take stopping me. I pick up the picture frame and study the picture of us I haven't seen before.

"It was from our engagement party." I forgot there was a photographer there. "All of them are," he says.

I turn to him. "All of them?" I look around and spot a couple more pictures of the two of us on display. Another one on his other nightstand and one on the wall between some simple art he has up.

"I just got them back a couple days ago. You want to see them?"

I give him a slow smile. "Later." I drop his jacket to unveil my body and go to him. His gaze darkens as he drinks me in.

He sits down on the edge of the bed, and I climb into his lap as our lips come together. My hands rake through his hair as I rub against his hard cock through his pants, and he roams my back side with his rough hands.

His lips move from mine and drag down my neck and chest until he reaches my breasts. The man loves my breasts. He takes a nipple in his mouth, and I drop my head back to moan. Then I'm being abruptly flipped to my back.

He wastes no time traipsing down my body to come face-to-face with my throbbing core. No buildup, no teasing. He delves right in, stealing the air from my lungs and making every part of my body coil tightly.

His hands grip each thigh, prying them wide open. My hands fist his soft, dark hair and pull. "Oh, God," I rasp, and he replies with a grumble, vibrating my flesh.

"I'm going to do this every day for the rest of my life," he proclaims.

Fuck, yes.

It should be embarrassing how much I twitch and convulse this time, but I remain shameless. My eyes practically roll to the back of my head, and I black out for a bit. As soon as my vision comes back, he's covering my body with his warm one. I must've been out for longer than I thought because he had time to remove his clothing.

The look in his eyes is something I haven't even seen from him. It says volumes. He doesn't need to tell me, but he does anyways.

"I love you, Jane."

I swallow hard and study him some more. I know he does, but there's the tiniest piece of me still guarded.

He doesn't wait for me to respond, and I let him make love to me. And I don't ask him to pull out this time.

Forty-Four

Donavon

I'm lost inside a dream-like trip as I prepare lunch for Jane and I. Fraught with ethereal visions and thoughts of our present and future together.

There's the slight chance that she was only having a weak moment from the alcohol she binged on. She could wake up angry with me all over again, and I'll have to be that haughty, possessive asshole again. If I have to keep her here as if she were a prisoner, then so be it. I hope it doesn't come to that, but her spanking is long overdue. Her refusal to stay would only cement that unpaid punishment.

Sleep never came for me early this morning. Not as if it's unusual, but remarkably so it had nothing to do with the fact that there was another person sleeping in my bed which is still unmade. Nothing to do with so many things already out of place. Nothing to do with the lack of privacy and someone else's things cluttering up my bathroom. It had everything to do with the certain sleeping beauty saturating my sheets with her palatable fragrance.

Not only did my home not burst into flames with the intrusion, but I'm...okay. I'm comfortable. Content. Possibly more so than I have ever felt inside my own home. As if she was the missing piece to it. Instead of it being where I can hole up and shut the world out, it's now the private haven for Jane and me.

I spent quite a few hours in bed admiring every inch of her perfection like a fucking creep. I'm not at all ashamed of it. I shamelessly watched her sleep, studied her every pore and every strand of her latte-color hair that she tied on top of her head.

I must have been much deeper in thought than I realized as two arms encircle my waist from behind. I automatically smile knowing she's not back to being inexorable. "Mmm, something smells good." She drags her lips sensually across my back. "I didn't know you cooked."

I switch off the burner and I pull her in front of me to prop her up on the countertop. She's grinning as I wedge myself between her thighs and cage her in with my arms. "I don't cook often, but I do like to from time to time. I prefer take-out though."

Her arms drape over my shoulders as our faces drift closer. "Me too," she rasps.

I eye her body up that happens to be clad in one of my dress shirts. "I told you that you do have clothes here, didn't I? Not that I mind this," I mutter as I'm trying to not let my tongue hang out of my mouth.

"I know, I saw them. But I wanted to wear something of yours instead."

"So, I've been thinking."

"Mmm," she hums and slides her hands down to my bare torso, "tell me what you were thinking," she purrs and rubs my chest.

"You." I lean in and kiss her neck, making sure to rub my facial hair against her skin to make her squirm. "Me." I do the same to her other side but rub my beard against her a little more, causing her to squeal in delight. "On a beach."

"Mmm," she moans, "I like the sound of that."

"I know we talked about getting out of the cold and spending some time somewhere warm," I say into her neck as I drag my lips up and down, flicking my tongue out over the mark I left on her last night. "But let's go somewhere. Now. Get away for a few days."

"Now?" she says all breathy as she drops her head to the side to bare her neck for me.

"Yes, now. We could both use a little vacation."

"And what about work?"

"I think it's time for me to start trusting Allison and Benjamin more. They'll have to handle things in our absence."

"We can still take work with us."

I bring my lips up to her face. Her pupils are dilated and her eyelids are heavy when I look at her. "No work," I whisper.

Her eyes widen just slightly. "No work? Who are you?"

I grin and rub my nose gently against hers. "I'm your fiancé and a man who has been deprived for too long."

"Oh, poor you," she sasses dryly.

I lean in to bite her neck. She wiggles and pushes at my chest laughing in reaction. My arms coil around her body and I continue to ravish her with my teeth, lips, and tongue. "I have still yet to punish you for last night," I murmur into her skin.

"Punish me?" she exclaims. "That was payback, Donavon. Payback you more than deserved."

"You exposed yourself to a room full of men." My jaw locks with tension thinking about it.

"And you had naked women in your office. We're even."

I fist her ass and growl, yanking her against me so her legs clench around my hips. "We're not even yet."

"How so?"

I pull back with a dark look on my face. "Once I put you over my knee, then we'll be even."

Her jaw goes slack as I release her and tend to our food before it gets cold. She's speechless as she watches me plate our food and head over to the table. Her mouth is still agape as her head swivels around to follow me with her eyes.

"Come, darling. Let's eat."

She hops down and comes around the island. "I'm sorry, but did you just threaten to spank me?" Her voice hitches in outrage.

"No threat, darling." I gesture for her to take the seat beside me.

She falls into the chair. "Donavon."

"Yes, Jane?"

She narrows her eyes at me. There's so much on the tip of her tongue, but she's reluctant to provoke me. Thinking if she dismisses it, I'll forget all about it. But the picture of her ass brightening under my hand, it's all I can think about until it happens.

She clears her throat and tries to compose herself. "So, a mini vacay," she says as casually as she's capable of and begins to pick at her food.

"Yes."

"Okay, but let's leave tomorrow."

"Why not today?"

"Because I want to spend the entire day and night secluded in your home. Really test this whole thing out. Leave messes and possibly discover some more of your secrets," she muses.

"Do your worst, darling," I taunt back.

She twists her lips holding back a smile as she studies me. Probably waiting for my panic to abruptly set in.

We fall into a companionable silence as we eat. She tells me how good it is, and every time she moans around another bite, my cock jumps inside my pants.

She doesn't finish her whole plate but once she sees that I've cleared mine she stands up to collect them. I don't let her get far though. The plates can wait.

She chuckles as I pull her into my lap, and she lets the plates clatter to the table. Her open thighs grip my hips as her hot cunt blankets my erection. "I want you to do whatever you need to do to this place to make you feel at home," I say in earnest. Her arms loop around my neck and she lets her breath hit my face. "Or we can look for a new place."

Her eyes dart around my head. "I don't know. I actually really like it here. It could use a bit of a feminine touch, but it's amazing."

I play it cool when she passively agrees to move in with me. It's not like I would let her leave anyways. But it's nice to have her here willingly. Though I also wouldn't mind a little scuffle and being forced to tie her to my bed until she agreed.

"We might *need* to look for a new place. One with another bedroom."

Her perfectly arched eyebrows twitch. "Why? It's only us. Unless you're open to having guests stay here and we need a guest room."

Definitely not.

I follow my own hand with my eyes as I rub my palm across her lower belly, thinking about the possibility of a child growing in there. "Yes, it's only us." I glance up at her. "For now."

She cocks her head with an unamused sigh. "Don, we really should be careful. I want to focus on us living together first, then getting married, and then we can think about kids."

"It might be too late though. You could already be pregnant."

"I guess we'll have to wait and see, but until I get back on birth control, we need to use condoms."

I almost rear back with animosity. "I'm not going to wear a fucking condom with you," I fume. We stopped using condoms a long time ago, I'm not going back. If we get pregnant, then so be it.

"Then you have to pull out until I'm back on birth control. I can call first thing Monday and get a refill; it'll just be a couple weeks"

I stare at her for a moment and my instincts tell me to argue until I get my way, but I'll play along. For now. "Okay, fine." Only when she reminds me to.

She smiles and my eyes glance down at her mouth. "Thank you." She smiles even bigger, hypnotizing me. "I kind of like this more agreeable man."

"Don't get used to it, darling."

She bites back a huge grin. "Don's little darling." My entire demeaner drops and she throws her head back in a roaring laughter. She promptly sobers up and gasps. "I cannot believe I showed my boobs on stage." She slaps a hand over her mouth when a giggle bubbles up. When she realizes I won't be joining her in hilarity and she senses my uneasiness, her arms loop back around my neck and tighten. "Oh, come on. It's kind of funny, and you deserved that little payback."

"In no way was it funny."

She gulps back another chortle. "I'm sorry."

"No, you're not. And that's exactly why I'm going to turn your ass red." Now when she gulps, it has no humor in it. "But it'll have to wait. I have something to show you, now that it's light out."

FORTY-FIVE

Jane

I'm morbidly curious when Don has me put a coat on and the pair of slippers he has for me here, when he didn't have me put any pants on.

Taking me by the hand, he leads me over to the wall of windows and I'm fascinated to find that one of the glass panels is a portal to a terrace. He steps through first then easily lifts me over the ledge.

The view is incredible to no surprise, and it's much more spacious than it looks. "Wow, I didn't even realize you had a terrace." The edge draws me in and I get a closer look at the scenic view of the park and the prettiest side of the city. I turn my head wondering why Donavon is not joining me, prepared to tease him by asking if he's afraid of heights when I take notice of the greenhouse he's standing near.

There's an arrogant smirk as he watches the way my face lights up and I'm magnetized to it. Compelled like a moth to a flame.

He opens the door for me, and I feel like I'm drifting on air as I enter through the gateway to the secret garden. My mouth hangs open in astoundment as I roll my wide gaze around the enclosure. It's like a tiny forest. Then directly in the center is a quaint bistro style table and chairs with a chandelier hanging over them.

"There's a heating system in here as well," he murmurs from somewhere behind me. I hear a couple clicks then fairy lights suddenly light up along with the chandelier and I spin around to face Donavon. I'm incapable of words or movement. "This can easily come down during the summer, then put back up again for the winter every year."

I chomp down on my bottom lip and begin to explore. Each plant is labeled and I can tell well taken care of. Some I recognize and some I don't. I'll have to read up on how to care for the unfamiliar ones, but I'm certainly happy to do so.

I circle around and land at the center. I smile at Donavon and lean back against the table. I'm suddenly very aware of how warm it is in here, especially with his coat on. I wouldn't care even if I weren't, I was already planning on getting rid of it.

I slowly pull down the zipper and his gaze is instantly ablaze and his feet are moving forward with confident strides. He slips his hands in the coat and pushes it off my shoulders, letting it fall behind me. His body grows closer, and I'm prepared to perch myself on the table. But he takes a seat in one of the chairs, his knees spread wide.

"I think it's time for your spanking, darling."

Blood rushes to the apex of my thighs and I tense in exhilaration. He gives me a good spanking when fucking me from behind, but has never put me over his knee and spank me in *punishment.*

The threatening look gives me the feeling that if I were to refuse, he'll force me across his knee. Why does that make my nipples insanely hard?

His chin dips. "Come, darling."

I'm hesitant, but then I remind myself that he has never disappointed me intimately, so I put one foot in front of the other until I'm standing directly in front of him. His large hands engulf my hips to pivot me and lay my body across both thighs of his. Already I'm imbued with the feeling of vulnerability and being exposed in this position.

His rough hands tenderly pet my bottom, sliding all around my soft skin. "If you ever expose yourself to another man again," he gravely grumbles before *whack!* The first smack has me biting my lip and cringing, "or even threaten to, I'll have you tied to my bed for days."

Oh, God. Why does that sound heavenly?

He chuckles lowly as if he can hear my inner thoughts. Then he smacks me in the same area with just as much force. "Dirty girl. You'd like that, wouldn't you?" He smacks me two more times back to back in blunt force. "You answer me when I ask you a question," he demands.

"Yes," I hiss.

"Yes, what?" he snaps.

"Yes, sir." The answer is automatic.

"That's my good girl," he murmurs and kneads the tender area then squeezes it harshly causing me to grit my teeth and make my toes curl.

His hand brushes across my ass, switching to the other cheek. Before I can take a breath, he lands a resounding blow to that untainted cheek and I gasp, my thighs now becoming sticky as they involuntarily rub together. "This is all mine."

Whack!

Yesssss...

"Mine," he growls and smacks the same cheek again and then again. The more my flesh stings the hotter my core becomes.

Sex is always adventurous and exhilarating with Donavon. But this is again new for us. I had no idea it could get any more intense.

He fists my newly tender cheek roughly and I hiss through my teeth in wanton pain. I know my skin will remain ruddy till tomorrow.

His grip loosens and he rubs the delicate globes of my bottom gently. "You took your spanking like a good girl." His hands continue to slide all over the sensitive flesh, creeping dangerously close to my seams. My hips jolt upwards on instinct, desperate for him to touch me where I'm really aching.

Another chuckle releases from deep inside his chest. "Okay, darling." I moan when his fingers slide in between my legs. "Is this what you want?"

"Yes," I whine and move my hips, begging for stimulation.

I can hear the grin on his face when he says, "You're already a mess, baby."

He thrusts two fingers deep inside of me all the way to his knuckles taking the air from me and stills. He twists and turns them then pulls out to slam back in. Every thrust quicker than the last until he's fucking me with his fingers.

Those fingers curl inside me and his palm slaps violently against my sore cheeks. He growls and jerks me against him slamming his palm against me over and over. Grunting and growling each time, trying to fuck me with his fingers harder. Then he adds speed to the pressure and there's this unexpected and unfamiliar build-up starting from my fingertips sizzling its way through my body and boils around in my core. I whimper and clench and every muscle binds up until I combust into tiny clusters and the sound of water slapping has me convulsing. My pussy ejects liquid covering his hand and everything between us. My thighs, his thighs...

His fingers retract from me and he pushes me up to my feet as I slightly sway on them. Wetness drips down my legs and I gaze at the wet spots on his pants. "I made a mess," I rasp weakly.

He gets to his own feet, backing me up with a devilish grin. "Good girl." Then he whips his cock out and thrusts me up onto the tabletop. When his hands grip my thighs, wetness coats them and smears as he moves them to my ass to jolt my body forward and he's pillaging his way inside of me.

My fingers slip under the hem of his shirt to graze the skin at his sides, and I grin when his skin pebbles. He grins back down at me and threads his fingers through the unruly hair that escaped from my messy bun.

He bends his head down to kiss me and his hips rock into me. My knees hitch up on reaction and I start grabbing at him to get closer. Our mouths fuse together as he fucks me right there in the middle of my little greenhouse with fairy lights twinkling above our heads. The smell of sex and greenery swirl around us.

His fingers flex on my sore ass as he uses the grip to hold me in place so I don't go flying off the table. But I feel like I'm flying regardless. I don't know how, but he pulls another orgasm from me and I feel like he's right behind me.

"Remember to pull out, baby," I whisper.

"No need, darling."

His cock abruptly abandons me and he jerks me off the table to spin me around and shove my upper body down over the table's surface. He's not at all subtly when he spreads my globes wide and slides his length up and down my drenched creases.

I hide my delight in biting down on my hand. We've only done this a few times, and every time, I enjoy it more.

I'm completely relaxed when he rubs up and down my spine. Then he lines the fat head of his cock up with that tight hole and begins to press in. My mouth pops open and my head cranes back in unhindered pleasure. He grunts as I moan when he pushes forward, burying himself further.

He bottoms out and only lets me take one breath before he pulls back and rams in to the hilt. His pelvis makes contact every barbaric thrust, bluntly hitting me over and over. I cry out and hiss through my clenched teeth. I don't even need to touch myself this time for the peak of my pleasure to capsize and have me shaking.

His growl and painful grip on my hips sends me into an aftershock and he empties himself inside of me. My vision going dark and my senses depleting until he freezes behind me.

He slides out of me and spins me around to give me a crushing kiss to the mouth. We're breathing hard and holding onto each other and trying to catch our breath.

When we finally part, we look down between us at the crude, beautiful mess we made. It's a shame we'll have to wash it off.

After we christen his shower, we do the same on the couch and end up staying there. Donavon lights the fireplace and we cuddle up under some blankets.

"Bonnie gave me my first plant," I say quietly as he strokes my hair and bare shoulder poking out of the blanket. "When we first moved in together for college. She thought it could be something I could care take of and might help cheer me up. That's when everything really started happening, but it hadn't hit the press yet." I know I don't need to specify what everything means. He knows I'm referring to my father and all his scandals and crimes. "She was right." I snort, smiling as I reminisce. "It was a healthy distraction. But it didn't quell my anxiety. No matter how many plants I had to nurture. I've always struggled with anxiety, but it was always manageable. I saw a therapist for it, but medicine for it didn't become necessary until everything came crashing down at once." His hand stops, but I don't. He needs to hear this. He needs to know that mental health is not something to hide, ignore, or be ashamed of.

"My father hit the news, Anthony broke up with me, then I was getting followed around and harassed by the press. Everyone in college would stare and whisper, my friends began dropping like flies." His arm around me tightens. I turn and kiss his bare chest, closing my eyes and finding comfort in his scent. "It became harder and harder for me to leave my apartment. Bonnie was a saint. She made sure I got out of bed every morning and didn't fail any of my classes. I was avoiding my therapist, and Bonnie urged me to see her again. That I couldn't keep going on like that. Long story short," I sigh, "she got me on some medication for my anxiety and I was able to get my shit together. I was able to put all my focus into school and became determined to take charge over my life. To make it so I didn't need my parents for anything anymore."

"But your mother still needs you."

He's totally missing the point here.

I pick my head up and I crawl on top of his body to rest my chin on my hands folded on his chest. "Don. I know how strenuous mental illness can be." His face has no change in it, but he can be a master of disguise. "I know what it's like to struggle with anxiety and depression with and without medication and therapy for it." I'm prepared for him to shut down, or even get agitated with me, but he still gives me nothing. I'm not sure if he's restraining himself, or if he's genuinely listening to me. "Having a mental health issue is nothing to be..."

"Embarrassed of?" he finishes for me.

I nod my head. "I need you to know that with me, you can be your absolute true self. There's never any need to hide anything or pretend doesn't exist. One of my most favorite attributes with you, is your blunt honesty." I pause. "That's why it hurt so bad to find out you were keeping things from me. You've always been so honest. Not just with me, but in general. Honest to the point of being heartless." He starts stroking my cheek tenderly. "Donavon, I know that you struggle with anxiety, and probably some OCD as well. I've known it since before I became your executive assistant. Way before we became romantic. And before I fell in love with you. You don't have to suffer in silence."

"I'm not suffering," he says evenly.

"Okay," I say quietly, already feeling like this was a total failure. "But please let me say this, and then I promise to drop it." He waits, his hand still moving. "I believe you when you say that you are fine with me being here and us moving forward, but it might not feel that way for long. Your need for space, your revulsion to socialize, your compulsive habits, your perfectionism, your insomnia..." I take a breath. "They're all symptoms of anxiety and OCD. Which they are due to a chemical imbalance. Something that is out of your control and can be consuming and even crippling at times. Right now, you may feel fine, but it's not something that can be cured overnight."

"Ever since you came into my life, Jane, it's allayed those internal struggles. You've freed me of it."

I give him a little smile and cannot express how much that means to me. "But I don't want to be the only reason you feel better. I can't be your only remedy."

His hands go to my sides to slide my body up his so that our faces are lined up. "You mean you don't want me to be dependent on you. And it's much too late for that. I've been dependent on your for so long now, I wouldn't be able to survive without you."

"Donavon..."

"Hush, darling." He slams our lips together stealing my words along with my next breath.

Forty-Six

Donavon

We're in the back of the town car and back to reality.

We might not be on an island anymore, but I still feel like I'm living in paradise. There's hardly a moment I have to be apart from Jane. I know it may be premature of me to make such concrete claims, considering we have only been officially living together for a couple of weeks, but I know that without a doubt, the aversion of having to share space with someone does not include Jane. Never has, and it never will.

She was wrong about being my remedy. She's the exception. Completely exempt from that uncontrollable quirk of mine. But the quirk is still there as far as everyone else is concerned.

Our mini vacation was exactly what we needed to get our relationship where it should be. Stronger than ever. I took her to a private resort secluded on an island located in the British Virgin Islands. When she wouldn't fuck me on the beach, I dismissed the entire staff and ordered the chef to remain in his quarters unless we request him. I rented out the entire resort for a reason.

Jane sighs when her phone goes off again and she silences it. I know by the discomfort in her posture that it's her mother calling. And when she calls back-to-back like this, it isn't with a positive purpose.

Jane looks out the window and chews on her bottom lip. "She's just going to keep calling," she mutters, reading my mind.

"Then answer it."

She looks over at me. "You know she'll beg me to come."

"Then tell her to call the cops or stop calling you for good."

"I can't do that, Donavon. She's still my mother and obviously has the worst way of showing it, but she does care about me."

My hands ball into tight fists when I turn to face her. We shouldn't still be having the same argument. I wish I could shake some sense into her when it comes to her unfit parents. "She is no mother," I say in a harsh tone. "My mother would take a thousand beatings before she'd let anyone touch any of her children. That's a mother's love. Yours is no mother and cannot love you like she should. You are better off removing her from your life entirely."

There's no warning before the tears bubble over and stream down her elegant face. "Shit, darling," I hiss under my breath and tuck her into my side. She willingly curls up in my embrace and sniffles. "I apologize for seeming insensitive, but I cannot permit their mistreatment of you any longer. I will never allow harm to come to you—family or not. Do you understand me?" She nods her head against my chest and brings her arms all the way around my torso. I hook a finger under her to chin to give me her glossy eyes. She wasn't born with a hard exterior, she was forced to construct one through the harsh conditions of her home life. But her interior is still fragile, and that's what I love most about her. She can be strong when she needs to be, but she also knows how to be tender and nurturing.

I bring my lips down to hers. "I love you, baby," I whisper.

"I love you too."

The rest of the night I cater to her every need, and we both stay away from the subject of her family. Knowing how much it means to Jane, I will allow her to have her mother partially in her life, but her father is cut out. When we had gone to lunch with them for her birthday, I stole the first chance I had in pulling him aside and warning him that if he ever lays a hand on her again, I will murder him. Absolutely no one will miss him either.

The next morning, we breeze through the routine we've established. I wake up around four in the morning and go to the gym in my building. By the time I come back, she's just getting in the shower, and I join her. After I've worked her body over, we get ready for actual work. I'm dressed and ready before her, so I head down to the kitchen to make us some breakfast. When she joins me, she makes me a latte and herself a coffee.

Heading into work today, we both know we still have a demanding week ahead of us. We're taking a long vacation to Bora Bora where my family will eventually join us, including Allison and Benjamin, so we are all working more than usual to get matters in order. Other than the few days I took off work for our short vacation a couple of weeks ago where I could entrust everything to my brother and sister, I have never completely shut my office down. Knowing I'll be spending more time with my woman, where she'll be wearing hardly any clothing with the sun on her face, I'm once again...okay.

When we part ways to head into our own offices, I yearn for the days when she worked in mine. She'd sit there in that chair in front of my desk oblivious to the way I would observe her more than I would focus on my actual work at times. How she would chew on that bottom lip of hers and mouth the words when she was reading something would make me salivate, hypnotized by her moving lips. Then when she would uncross her legs just to cross them again, it was her legs that would distract me. I guess it is a good thing she has her own office now.

We've been at work for a couple hours when Jane comes into my office with a tear-soaked face. I'm on my feet in an instant taking powerful strides, my heart racing and I'm already assessing her to make sure she isn't physically hurt. "Darling, what's wrong? What happened?" I hold her face in my hands.

"My mom," she sniffles, "she's in the hospital. My father..." Her chin trembles and new tears form in her eyes.

"Let's go, baby."

She's tranquil on the outside as we make our way to the hospital through the city traffic. But I know her well enough to know how she blames herself on the inside. I should feel guilty as I subliminally persuaded her not to answer. I should. But the one to blame is her father; second is her mother herself.

As we make it to her room at the hospital, we stop outside of the door. "I'll be right here if you need me," I say thinking she would like some privacy.

She looks up at me pleading. "You're not coming in with me?"

"I didn't think you would want me to, darling."

"I do. I need you."

I squeeze her hand back in mine and feel the swell of pride in my chest expanding it. I enter the room with her but hang back. She claims she needs me, but I don't want her to feel like I'm at all intruding. She knows I'm here if she needs me.

Her mother looks as bad as I expected she would. There're welts and discoloration covering her face, and bruises in the shape of fingers along her arms.

"Mom," Jane says cautiously as she runs to her bedside.

"Jane," her mother smiles, as if this were a pleasant surprise visit.

I lean back against the wall with my hands in the pockets of my coat. Her mother glances over at me, her smile faltering, then plasters it back on for Jane.

"Mom," she says quietly with a cracked voice as she takes in all the marks on her mother. "I can't believe he did this. You better press charges this time."

"You really want your father to go to jail?" she asks aghast.

My fists clench in unison with Jane's that hang at her sides. "For beating you to a pulp?! Yes, I do. And so should you!"

"I agree that he needs some professional help and that I should've gotten him some a while ago—"

"He needs jailtime, Mom," Jane growls. "This is beyond needing professional help."

Her mother sighs. "Well, it doesn't matter anyways. Our neighbor called the police. So, it's not up to me." She at least has the decency to look somewhat ashamed of her current position.

"And what if they let him go? What then?" Her mother avoids eye contact and doesn't respond. "You'll let him back, won't you?"

"He's my husband, Jane. And your father."

"He's your abuser! And mine!" I stand up straight as my spine goes rigid. I'm ready to step in when Jane shakes her head and says, "You're pathetic." Her mom snaps her gaze up to Jane in shock, and I have to look down to hide the smirk on my face. "Either you press charges to make sure he gets jailtime and you leave him, or I'm done with you both. I mean it, Mom. You will never hear from me again and never see another penny from me. You'll be on your own."

The fuck? She was giving them money?!

"Jane, I can't leave him," she says, now crying.

"Then I am no longer a part of your life. If you ever decide to finally leave his sorry ass, then—and only then—can you contact me."

"Jane—"

"No." She puts her hand up and backs away. Her mother begins to cry harder, and I know Jane could possibly cave. I come up behind her to remind her that I'm still here. "Goodbye, Mom."

Jane swivels around with her chin trembling, and I give her mother a last look of disapproval before I escort Jane out. She's choking on her corked tears as I hold her protectively with one arm around her slender body. I know that if I say anything right now, the damn will break, so I wait until we're back in the concealment of the car.

"You did the right thing, darling," I say gently, and she shakes against me as she releases the pent-up tears. "I'm so proud of you, baby." I stroke her silky hair away from her pink-touched face soothingly.

"They were the only family I had. And now, I don't even have them anymore."

I restrain the forthcoming agitation with her sad words. My quick temper is still instinctual, and I have to remember when to be gentle with Jane. "Hey." I force her to look at me with my hand gripping her jaw. "You have me. I am your family. And you have my family as well. When we get married it will be official. You will be a Waldorf, so don't ever say you don't have any family. You understand me?"

She gives me a teary smile and nods her head. "Okay."

I'm still tense as we silently focus forward on the ride home. I'm withholding so much right now, I might combust.

"You're upset about the money," she murmurs quietly.

"We don't need to talk about that right now," I say tightly.

"It somehow lessened the guilt I carried from not answering her phone calls or coming to her aide when she begged me." I tilt my face down to hers. "But I'm done, Don. I swear I am. She's completely on her own."

"Okay." I press my mouth to hers.

FORTY-SEVEN

Jane

I'm sitting on pins and needles, high-strung with nerves.

I want to think Donavon will be excited, but I could be totally wrong and mortified in front of his whole family. I'd like to think I know Donavon like the back of my hand, but there are times where he does something completely unpredictable.

So, I called in some reinforcements from my future sisters-in-law. We're in Bora Bora staying in those bungalows over the crystal waters, and I told Don I was going to have some girl time with his sisters. Even though we had a few days here alone before the rest of his family joined us, he made a fuss about it.

Finally, they come knocking and I practically yank the both of them inside and slam the door shut. My feet begin pacing as I build the courage up to tell them. To rip the Band-Aid off and blurt it out.

"Whoa, what's going on?" Allison asks first.

"Yeah, are you okay?" Kenna adds.

I stop and face them, taking a deep breath in and letting it rush out. "I'm pregnant."

Both of their eyes pop wide and they swivel their heads to look at each other then back at me. Kenna is the first to squeal and start jumping up and down, and Allison is right behind her. I can't help but grin when they both throw their arms around me for a group hug. I giggle and fight them both off.

"Okay, okay!" I laugh some more as they continue their excitement.

"Are you sure?" Kenna asks.

"Did you already take a pregnancy test?" Allison asks.

"Does Donavon know?" Kenna asks.

"What about our parents, do they know yet?" Allison asks.

"One question at a time," I chuckle and sit down on the edge of the bed. "I took four pregnancy tests the day before we left, and no, no one else knows yet. I wanted Donavon to be the first to know, but I'm sort of freaking out about it."

"Why?" Kenna asks.

"Yeah, I'm sure he'll be ecstatic," Allison says, and I give her a dry look. "Okay, maybe not *ecstatic*, but he'll be happy."

"You think?"

"I mean, what are you guys using for a contraceptive?" Kenna boldly asks.

"Um," I say chuckling nervously. "I'm on birth control, but there was a little gap where I wasn't. After my accident."

"And Donavon knew that?" Allison presses.

My eyes widen as I vigorously nod my head. "Of course, he did! I told him right away when we made up and insisted on using condoms until I got back on the pill, but he..."

"He what?" they ask in unison.

"He refused," I mutter, sparing his sisters the intimate specifics. "I got back on the pill only two days after we got back together, but I know it still takes some time to begin working again." I sigh then find the courage to take a peek up at them and catch them giving each other a cheeky smirk. "What?"

"He was totally trying to get you pregnant," Allison says as Kenna nods her head next to her with a grin.

I roll my eyes. "No, he wasn't. We were both being too careless, and it happened. It wasn't intentional."

"Maybe not on your end," Kenna mutters and they both giggle. "But Donavon doesn't do anything on *accident*."

I give them a salty stare. "Come on, guys. Donavon would not try to purposely get me pregnant. Not without talking about it and definitely not this soon." They look at each other again then burst into laughter. After hearing my own words play back inside my head, I realize how right they are. "Oh, my God," I growl under my breath. "That bastard." *He wouldn't, would he? Holy hell, he totally would.* What that man wants, he gets.

"Oh, Jane," Allison coos and comes to sit next to me on the bed and Kenna kneels in front of me. Both of them putting a hand on me somewhere for comfort. "You honestly have nothing to worry about in telling Donavon news he's probably expecting."

Kenna grins brightly. "We're going to have a baby!"

I laugh and shake my head as they both gush over the life altering news. There's definitely the question of whether or not Donavon wanted to get me pregnant, but with the girls being so happy about this, I can't help but to be excited as well.

"Should I be upset about this? That he may have purposely been trying to get me pregnant?" I ask as they go to leave.

Kenna shrugs a should and Allison says, "It takes two to tango, baby."

I thank them and know that I don't need them to let Donavon know to come back. He's probably pacing close to the front of our bungalow. As if on cue, Don comes in.

I moved to our balcony and I'm sitting on the edge with my feet dangling over the water. Donavon comes to join me, and he takes my hand in his as we both stare out at the beautiful scenery before us. The crystal waters, and clear skies. The smell of the salt water comes in waves off the ocean.

"Something weighty has been on your mind," he says after a few blissful moments.

I swallow hard and look down at our conjoined hands, then I nod my head.

"Jane, please look at me when I'm talking to you," he says gently, but it's no less authoritative.

I face him and he begins cataloging every inch of my face to find out what's going on. Staring into his dark blues, I know right then and there, I have nothing to be nervous about. "I'm pregnant."

When he totally surpasses a state of shock and instantly grins, I know damn well it was his plan all along. "You are?"

I smile nodding my head. "Took a bunch of tests before we left, and ah—" I squeal when he easily scoops me up to place me in his lap. I don't dare comment on the fact that people can definitely see us.

He's now beaming, his whole face dazzled. One of his large hands slides up into the back of my hair as his other rests on the small of my back. "You're happy about this?" I murmur.

"I am, darling." He picks me up with him when he stands and takes us to bed.

Both of us grin as he lays me back and peels my bathing suit off. He shoves his swim trunks down and stares at my belly with hunger as if he can already see it growing. He crawls over me and places the sweetest kiss on the center of my stomach. Then he looks up at me in awe. "Thank you, darling."

I chuckle and run my fingers through his hair. "For what?"

"Everything."

He scoots back to eat my pussy, feasting like he does every day, yet never eating me the same twice.

Epilogue: Donavon

The woman has been making me wait two goddamn years since I proposed to her to marry me.

No more excuses though. She will become my wife today.

First excuse: She didn't want to get married while she was pregnant.

Second excuse: She claimed she wanted to lose the baby weight, which was nothing.

Third excuse: We were too busy, and she wanted to focus on finding us our new place.

A few months after Preston was born, we moved into the penthouse at Waldorf Luxury Hotels and Suites. Babies are small, but the older they get, the more our home is overrun. And come to find out, Jane is quite finicky when it comes to finding us our home. We've looked at close to one hundred places in and around the city. But I honestly think she enjoys living here where there is twenty-four-hour room service, valet, and an indoor pool and gym.

Consequently, I learned everything she does not like, and the few things she does. And I'm confident I have found what she possibly had no idea she was looking for. An old church that wasn't even on the market. Typically they cannot be sold to the public. Good thing I am not part of the public.

I'm having my father's construction company fully gut it and renovate it to her every need, and if she doesn't like it, then I'm at a loss, and we'll end up living here forever.

It's the Saturday before her birthday, and I informed her of the plan to meet with the family for dinner, then they'll all fight over who gets to take Preston for the night so Jane and I can have an evening to ourselves.

I walk into our closet to find her standing there in only a bra and panties. Her body still the sexiest thing. Her breasts were enormous when she breastfed, but now that that's over, her body has completely bounced back. But either way, I loved it through all the stages it went through. Pregnancy, post-pregnancy, the in between, then back. It was all beautiful. I couldn't see her any other way.

Sidling up behind her, I wrap my arms around her waist and bury my face in her latte-colored hair. "Darling," I murmur and move her hair off her neck, so I can press my lips to her skin.

"Hey, baby," she says, sagging in my embrace some. "I can't figure out what to wear."

I had anticipated this little dilemma. Hoped for it. "Why don't you wear that dress from Kenna? The one you wore two years ago."

"Yeah?"

"I think so," I mumble against her, sending chills down her one side. "I love that dress."

She grins as she hooks one arm around my neck. "How sentimental of you," she muses. "That's what I'll wear then."

That was easy.

I let her finish getting ready and go to check on our son. Preston is just over a year old now, and he has the sweetest demeanor. His eyes are a dark blue like mine, and so far his hair is blonde.

"Dada," he says from the floor where he's playing with his trucks.

"Yes, dada," I say as I sit down with him. Hearing him call me that never gets old. For Jane it does because it was his first word, and it took him a while to finally be able to say mama. But for months it was all dada.

He's our pride and joy, and Jane and I always disagree on who he looks more like. She swears he looks just like me, and all I can see is my Jane.

Parenthood came naturally for us both. She was a wreck when we rushed to the hospital after her water broke, afraid she would be no good at being a mother. But I had no doubt about her. She took to it instantly and has only done her best. She's amazing.

Jane emerges from our bedroom, and I feel exactly what she accused me of being. Sentimental. I think back to when I asked her to marry me in that dress and those red sole shoes I gifted to her, and now I can imagine her saying 'I do' in the same outfit.

I'm drawn to her as always and take her around the waist. "You look incredible."

She looks up at me, still starry-eyed, and I never want to lose that look from her again. "Thank you."

We head downstairs as a family, and make our way to the ballroom. I told her we'd meet the family at the bar before leaving, but we pass it, and she looks up at me in suspicion. "Donavon..." she warns light-heartedly, knowing I'm up to something.

With Preston in one arm, I squeeze her hand with my other, and we turn into the ballroom. Like a rerun of the past, everyone yells out, "Surprise!"

"Oh, my God!" Jane looks up at me in delight laughing. "I cannot believe you did this again."

I watch her as she takes in the place and realize the difference between this time and last. "Wait. Donavon?" She looks up at me stunned and I'm suddenly nervous she might hate this idea. But too bad. I have been a patient man. "Is this...?"

I have an arm around her now and I lean into her ear. "This is our wedding, darling. I'm not letting you stall any longer. I want you as my wife. Now and forever."

Preston reaches for her, and Jane takes him from me on instinct, her eyes still fixated on me. "You're serious? We're about to get married?"

I nod. "That is, if you still want to," I mutter.

"Donavon," she turns into me, her arm hanging on the back of my neck. "Putting off the wedding plans was never intentional. I swear to you. Of course, I want to marry you." She smiles with tears in her eyes. "Maybe I was afraid it was still too rushed for you."

"Darling," I pull her in closer as everyone continues to murmur around us, "I would have married you the same day that I asked you to if I had it my way. I've been a very patient man."

"You have."

"But I'm not waiting another day."

"I won't ask you to."

I bring my forehead to hers. "Marry me tonight," I rasp.

"Yes."

In front of our family and close friends, we stand up and say our vows, with our son smiling at us from the front row as he's being passed around from lap to lap. He's the first grandchild, so of course he's spoiled with all the love and attention. I know it makes Jane happy to give Preston the upbringing she never had.

Parenthood is difficult when running a billion-dollar company, especially when both parents can be workaholics, but we both agree on what is always most important. Our family of three.

And if I have it my way, it'll be a family of four by next year.

And I always get my way.

www.ingramcontent.com/pod-product-compliance
Lightning Source LLC
Chambersburg PA
CBHW022016310726
48972CB00006B/1674